Shut Out

A Bayard Hockey Novel

Kelly Jamieson

———

To all my readers—I love, love, love to write romances and I'm honored and appreciative every day that I get to share them with you. Thank you for buying and reading my books and telling me you love them—it means so much to me.

Chapter 1

Jacob

I DIDN'T DO IT.

I'm tired of saying it so I just think it—for about the millionth time since that fucked-up night went down three weeks ago. My insides are knotted so tightly I might puke. My shoulder and neck muscles are like boulders and my hands keep curling into fists. There's so much tension and adrenaline building up inside me I feel like I'm going to explode.

This is so fucking unfair.

"So I can't play in the playoffs?" I manage to choke out.

The general manager of my Western Hockey League team regards me with sad resignation from behind the desk in his tiny office. "No. I'm sorry, Jacob."

My throat feels like I've swallowed a hockey puck. I turn to my parents, who are with me for this meeting. I'm an adult at age nineteen, but this is some serious shit happening, and they flew here from Kamloops to help me deal with it, and to talk to Mr. Gagnon today.

"There were no charges laid against me," I remind him.

"We know that, Jacob. But you were involved that night and all three of you have been removed from the team."

I swallow again.

Hockey is my life. My passion. I've always known I'm going to play in the NHL one day. I don't consider myself The Next One or another Sidney

Crosby, but I have talent and I've worked my ass off. The playoffs are only a week away and I've been kicked off the team. The draft is coming up in a couple of months. This was supposed to be my year. The scouts from all the NHL teams have been at our games this year and I know the buzz is out there, and it's not *whether* I'll be drafted, but rather how high I'll go.

Now that's gone. I close my eyes against the sting behind my eyelids.

Jesus. I'm six foot three inches tall, nearly two hundred pounds. I have no problem dropping the gloves to fight if the situation merits it. I'm not going to fucking cry like a baby here in Mr. Gagnon's office.

But damn . . . if I can't play hockey . . . what do I have?

Nothing.

"Jacob," Dad says, leaning forward. "It's too late to fix things this year. But there might be a way to try next year."

I grit my teeth and open my eyes to focus on him.

The disappointment and strain on his face makes my insides hurt even more. I glance at Mom, whose face wears a similar expression.

I've never let my parents down before. Well, okay, they weren't happy the first time it snowed after I got my driver's license and I cracked up the car they'd bought me. But nobody'd been hurt and the car was insured, so they got over that. And they got over the first time I got drunk and came home and puked in my bed. But this . . . they aren't going to get over this, and it fucking kills me.

My parents have done so much for me to get this far. Sacrificed so much. They don't deserve to be paid back like this. I'm *such* an asshole.

"Next year?" I glance at Mr. Gagnon.

He shakes his head. "Not for the Warriors. But I've been helping your parents explore some options."

"Like what?"

"There's a college down in the States that's interested in you," Dad says. "Actually there are a few. But we've talked to the coach at Bayard College."

"I know him," Mr. Gagnon says. "We played for the Leafs together years ago."

College hockey down in the States? I frown.

I can't do school full-time while I'm playing major junior hockey, with all the travel and practices involved, but I've done a few university courses—some of them online, a few in the summer.

"It's not guaranteed that you can play with them," Mr. Gagnon says.

"The Canadian Hockey League includes some players who've signed professional contracts, so the NCAA considers it a professional league, which makes you ineligible for NCAA competition. But there are ways to have eligibility reinstated. The school has to start the process. They're interested enough in you that they're willing to do that, but like I said, we don't know for sure if it will be approved."

"They also have a strict policy about their school athletic programs," Dad says. "Athletes have to maintain certain grades and they have to stay out of trouble. But . . ." Dad hesitates. "Well, not to be crass, but they need funding and they need to win. Their NCAA hockey program is big there. You have talent and they're willing to take you on."

"Go to school?" My eyes widen at Dad. "Full-time? *And* play hockey?"

I'm not stupid, but I never planned on getting a university degree. My path to the NHL was clearly mapped out by playing in the Western Hockey League, getting drafted and possibly spending a year on a farm team—although I'm goddamn determined to give my first NHL training camp everything I have in an effort to prove I can play in the big league right away. I have a plan. Or at least, I *had* one.

"Yes. You have to keep at least a C average. Also, they have a Code of Conduct that you absolutely cannot violate. And you're going to have to participate in a new training program they have for freshmen and transfer students."

I scrunch my face up. "Which is . . . ?"

Dad glances at Mom. "It's a Sexual Assault Prevention and Awareness Program."

I draw in a long, slow breath as heat rises inside me again. I've already had this conversation with my parents and they insist they believe me, but once more I want to tell them, *I didn't do it.* I meet Dad's eyes. "You believe me, don't you?"

"Yes, son. We believe you."

My throat tightens up again. I'm not entirely sure if I buy that, but they've stood by me through this mess and I fucking love them so much for it I could weep.

"They're piloting this new program as part of their orientation." Dad stares at a paper in his hand and reads from it. " 'To promote healthy relationships, teach non-violence and equality and advance a respectful, consensual and safe environment for all members of Bayard College.' "

I nod, letting this all sink in. It sounds like some kind of sex offender rehab program. Jesus Christ. I cover my eyes with one hand. Can my humiliation get any more painful? But apparently every new student has to go through this training.

"Um, where is this college?" Maybe somewhere sweet like California or Florida . . . ?

"Upper New York State. Ridgedale. Not far across the border, actually." Great.

"More and more NHL teams are drafting NCAA players," Mr. Gagnon continues. "Last year's number one draft pick played NCAA and now plays for the Oilers."

I'm aware of this.

"If you play well and stay out of trouble, teams will be interested in you." Mr. Gagnon pauses. "This scandal will die down."

"Last year, guys who played for the Coyotes got suspended because of something like this." I meet Mr. Gagnon's eyes. "*They* didn't get kicked off the team. And two of them are in the NHL now."

Mr. Gagnon nods. "Yes. And I'm not gonna lie to you. There were a lot of people outraged they got off so easy. You know it's been in the news, the talk about rape culture in male sports. The police didn't find sufficient evidence in this case to press charges, but it's been a big of enough deal to hit national news, so we can't sweep it under the rug."

Hell yeah, I know it's been in the news.

"If you think this isn't hard for me, you're wrong," Mr. Gagnon adds, his shoulders drooping. "We supported your career, Jacob. You had—*have* a bright future."

Great. Not only have I disappointed my parents, I've let down the entire team.

"We had a chance at the league championship this year," he continues. "Maybe we could've even won the Memorial Cup. Without you . . . probably not gonna happen. There's been pressure from both sides, on the one hand to somehow make this go away so we can win . . . on the other hand . . ."

I get what he's saying. Loud and fucking clear. They're making an example out of Crash, Ace and me. Just fucking great.

American college hockey. I have no clue what I'd be getting into. A million fucking questions blast through my head. Where will I live? I won't know a soul there. I have a brain, but do I really have what it takes to pass a

4

bunch of college courses? I'll be playing for a whole new team and won't know the coach or any of the players either.

I rub my forehead. What fucking choice do I really have? I'll have hockey. And that's all that matters. "Okay." I swallow once more past that puck lodged in my throat. "If that's the only way I get to play hockey, then I guess that's what I have to do."

Chapter 2

Skylar

I HAVE GOALS FOR MYSELF, which I have typed up, printed out and pinned to the bulletin board above my desk in my room. Goal number one: Get straight As in every course. Goal number two: Get straight As in every course. Goal number three: Get straight As in every course. And of course, get into medical school at Harvard.

My freshman year last year at Bayard College sucked huge effing donkey balls. It was the worst year of my life, and I'm not being all drama queen when I say that. It started so promising, my two high school besties, Brendan and Ella and I in college together, on our own, free and ready to take on the world.

We were having fun, exploring our independence and freedom away from our parents, maybe making a few bad decisions like staying up way too late the night before a mid-term, or blowing the budget on a new pair of boots instead of food. But hey, everyone does that kind of stuff.

Then in our second semester, Brendan took his own life.

Yeah. Saying it was hard doesn't even mean anything. I was messed up. I somehow managed to pass three courses by the skin of my teeth, which isn't good enough. I flunked the other two. This was another big blow, because I'd let my parents down. All my life I've worked so hard to please them, and damn, it was hard to tell them I'd failed two courses and would have to take them over.

Thinking about Brendan still makes me ache. I'll never get over it, never forget him. I had to dig myself out of a deep black hole, but I understand more about grieving, and more about the demons Brendan was fighting, and I'm moving forward. I got some counseling through this great program we have at Bayard, SAPAP, which mainly helps people with sexual abuse but also helps with other crises and does a lot of outreach work on campus. That made me want to get involved with them, partly for selfish reasons because I needed something to get away from my thoughts but also to give back and help others.

And I still have Ella. She and Brendan and I were a trio our freshman year at Bayard, and now Ella and I are roommates in the off-campus house we share with two other girls. Yes, it's crowded and crazy sometimes, but I need to live as cheaply as possible.

Volunteering at SAPAP makes my schedule even crazier with my part-time job, the appointments I still have occasionally with Frances, and studying my ass off because I am going to *do* this. My parents probably don't believe I can, and they're helping foot the bill for my high-priced education, so I have to show them I can be as good as my sister, Elisha, who's now a medical resident in Boston.

Today I'm in the boardroom of the SAPAP offices in the South Quad Academic Complex for a meeting to brainstorm and plan out some of this year's events. It's mid-September and we've been back in class for a couple of weeks. Victoria Meyer, Director of SAPAP, is my idol. I worship her. I want to be her when I grow up.

"How was it presenting to the senate subcommittee round table?" Leah asks Victoria.

"Amazing." Victoria smiles. "I love sharing the things we're doing here and talking about what other campuses can be doing." She talks a bit more about that, then says, "Okay. Let's start with a recap from the various committees of what we accomplished last year. Skylar?"

My belly flutters, and I tuck some hair behind my ear. As coordinator of the Men's Activism Group, I have my summary typed up and open on my laptop. I'm new to this, and I want to do well. I hate being unprepared, so I spent a lot of time last night reviewing my files from last year and working on my summary.

"Last year we started the year off by promoting and participating in the No-Shave October for Consent Campaign. We created our first-ever promotional video that included everyone in the campaign, not only men who could grow beards. We reached over eight thousand people on Facebook and received over five thousand views on YouTube. During that month, we hosted an open mic night at a fraternity on campus and we ended the campaign with a flag football tournament oriented around sexual violence awareness, deconstructing rape myths and bystander intervention. We have over two hundred participants who signed the No-Shave pledge to practice consensual sex, which we consider very successful."

I pause and look around at everyone. Hopefully it doesn't sound like I'm taking credit for all this, because I wasn't even involved until second semester. I just want everyone to know what we accomplished. Victoria smiles encouragingly and I take another breath. "This year, obviously we want to exceed that number. Last spring, we developed and presented a new program called Frat Chat, for men in fraternities to give us feedback on the workshops and other programs, and to network with us for future planning. We got great feedback from them and hopefully will be able to incorporate that into our planning for this year."

I finish my update and listen to Leah and Grace present their summary of last year's accomplishments for the peer-led support group and the networking committee, respectively.

"Excellent work everyone." Victoria nods. "You're an amazing group. I'm so proud to work with you all."

This is one reason I love her. She always appreciates what we do and gives us positive feedback. And because even though the work we do is serious, she encourages us to have fun.

"Now let's talk about our ideas for the coming year."

I'm happy and excited to do that. I also prepared for this. "We actually started working on our No-Shave October planning at the end of last school year by looking at what merchandise we still have, scheduling the events we knew we wanted to repeat and booking venues. I have some ideas for other fundraisers, like a benefit concert and a pizza get-together. I'd like to set some concrete goals in terms of how much money we raise as well as how many new men volunteers we can recruit to the program and how many people we can get to sign affirmative consent pledges."

Victoria looks pleased at my ideas. "Thank you, Skylar."

The others put forward some ideas and we get into an energetic brainstorming session. I find myself volunteering for various tasks until Victoria says, "Skylar. I appreciate that you want to be involved, but do you think you're taking on a little too much for one person?"

I blink at her. Oh shit. I've done it again. I have this tendency to over-commit myself.

"I'm worried you won't have time for your studies. Or your job. Or maybe having fun once in a while."

I make a face. Having fun is a low priority for me. Especially since Brendan's death. I know there are lots of people at college who are here just to party. My housemates Brooklyn and Natalie have busy social lives. Apparently they passed their courses last year—barely—but neither of them have jobs. Ella's been going out with them more and more.

I've been kind of worried about her. She's been acting different ever since Brendan died. Which is totally understandable; we were both devastated by what happened. At first I didn't even notice what was going on, I was in such a fog of grief myself, but last weekend she came home super late —or super early in the morning, depending how you look at it—totally wasted, and spent the entire next day in bed recovering. And then went out and did it again the following night. That's when I realized she's been doing it every weekend. On top of that, she's been hooking up with random guys, sometimes staying out all night, sometimes bringing guys she doesn't even know back to the house, which makes me uncomfortable. I'm not judging her, but you do need to be careful.

I meet Victoria's gaze. "Don't worry." I flash a smile. "This is fun for me. I can handle the pizza fundraiser if someone else can tackle the benefit concert."

"I can do that," Grace says.

"And I'll do the research into getting best prices on T-shirts," Leah says.

"Okay, that would be great."

"Now let's talk about how the new training program is going," Victoria says.

The other thing I've volunteered to do is assist with the pilot program we're doing for all freshmen and transfer students, to educate them on healthy relationships, non-violence and equality, and affirmative consent. We developed this program last year and started rolling out the sessions when classes started. Next week is the third group to go through it, which I'll be doing along with Victoria, Grace and another volunteer, Chad.

We get an update on how things are going and some of the feedback we've received, which is mostly positive, then I pack up my laptop and drive my tiny little Chevy Cruze home. It's Friday afternoon, I'm done with classes, and now I have not only a lengthy list of tasks to do by our next meeting, but also reading for Human Physiology and Organic Chemistry. Fun times.

I walk into the house to the pounding beat of Pitbull. Natalie's amazing Bose speakers in the kitchen and living room are usually rocking with some kind of tunes, and truthfully, I love it. I love music, and my cheap little docking station for my phone doesn't have nearly the same quality of sound. Luckily I like almost any kind of music—Luke Bryan or Rhianna or Kanye, but I really like a lot of indie music, like Arcade Fire and Boy Kill Boy. Actually there are times I like to chill out to Enya. Brendan used to bug me about listening to music his grandma liked.

I sigh at the pang in my chest remembering Brendan and that he'll never tease me again about music.

"Hey, Skylar!" Ella calls to me from the kitchen. "We're making sangria. Gonna order pizza. You in?"

"Sure." Pizza sounds good, better than cooking, and we get it from a great place that's not expensive. We order our agreed-upon favorite—the Santorelli special with bacon, no anchovies.

"We're going to a party tonight," Ella continues. "You're coming, right?"

Of course she's going to a party. I swallow my first reaction, which is, *Hell no, I have no time to party.* I tip my head back and gaze at the ceiling. It's cracked, because this is an old rental house that nobody takes care of.

Victoria's comment about having fun sticks with me. I can say all I want that my idea of fun is different than others', that I have no time to party, and turn my nose up at that frivolity . . . but the truth? I'm a little envious of my housemates, who go out and have fun all the time. Not only do they party, they go for lunch, have coffee, even get mani/pedis together.

Sometimes I wonder if I'm really worried about Ella or . . . jealous. Or maybe both.

I'm not jealous of her being so hungover she can't get out of bed. I can't afford to waste a whole day like that. She knows how hard I have to work to earn half-decent grades, though, so I do get a little resentful that my best friend isn't staying home studying with me. Which is completely unreasonable, but there you have it. I'm not perfect, much as I try to be.

So right now I want to push aside that awful resentment and envy, and just go have fun.

"Okay," I say. "I'll come."

Chapter 3

Jacob

I HAVE to go to this big off-campus party tonight. I keep saying no to the party invites, but not only is it making me fucking lonely, the guys I live with think I'm some kind of pussy or stuck-up asshat. I've had the occasional beer, but I don't go out and get shitfaced or stoned like they do every weekend since school started. I like to have fun, but a drunken party is what got me here, living in a house with three other hockey players off campus at Bayard College, trying to keep my ass out of trouble. They don't know why I turn down invitations, in order to stay home and play Xbox. Or jerk off to Internet porn, which is sadly what my sex life has become. Or study.

Fuck me, I've never studied so much in my life.

But when you're sitting at home alone in a town where you know nobody, what the fuck else are you going to do? There's only so much porn you can watch before you become numb to it.

I can do this. I can go to a party, have a beer or two, maybe meet some new people and have a few laughs and leave sober and alone. If I don't, these guys are never going to accept me as their buddy and teammate.

The guys I live with are all Bayard Bears players—Ben Buckingham, known as Buck; Grady Rockwell, aka Rocket, and Hunter Campbell who is called Soupy for cheesy, obvious reasons. I'm known as Flash, partly because my last name is Flass, but also because people think I'm flashy on the ice. I say this in all modesty.

Rocket grabs a beer from the fridge and slams the door shut. As he slides onto a stool at the kitchen island, Buck glares at him. "Thanks, bud. You could've brought me one too."

"Nu-uh." Rocket shakes his head and lifts the bottle to his lips. "This is your level one infraction punishment. You have to get your own beer."

I eyeball them both. "Level one punishment? For what?"

"He hid beer." Rocket shakes his head in disapproval. "That's a level one infraction."

They have this stupid Bears Bro Code they keep referring to. "Someone please tell me these rules. I'm terrified I'm going to screw up and one morning I'll discover my eyebrows have been shaved off." I feel like an idiot, but then this whole year is apparently intended to make me feel like a big loser.

"We can't explain it." Buck shrugs and moves to the fridge, accepting his punishment. "It just is."

"I think you make shit up."

Buck and Rocket grin at each other and bump fists, which makes me feel . . . left out. But that's how I usually feel around here lately. I can't wait for our games to start so I can show these guys I do fit in.

I volunteer to be the designated driver, which gives me a plausible excuse for not drinking. Buck, Rocket and Soupy all go for this because it means none of them has to drive, it and has the added bonus of being one mark in the "good books" for me. They give me directions how to get to the house party and a while later we pull up in front of a huge Tudor-style house where a bunch of guys apparently live. It's a warm September evening, already dark, and there are people outside on the lawn, drinking and laughing. The music is audible even here and it blasts us in the face as we enter the house, the atmosphere warm and humid from the crush of bodies, the scent of beer mingling with the odor of marijuana.

Some chicks are dancing in the dining room, tossing their hair, arms in the air, asses shaking. The living room is packed with people yelling at one another over the music. We head to the kitchen so the guys can get drinks. I crack open a can of Coke Zero and lift it to my lips as I survey my surroundings.

People greet Soupy, Buck, and Rocket, mostly girls, who all flash me flirty smiles. I smile back. Damn. I don't think I've ever seen so many hot chicks in one place in my life. My resolve to avoid women is crumbling like a stale cracker.

"Hi," one of the girls says. "I'm Tiffany. I lost my phone number so can I have yours?"

I laugh uneasily. "Ha. Good one."

"Are you a hockey player too?"

"Yep. I'm Jacob."

"Are you a freshman? Because I don't remember you playing last year."

"I'm new to the school, but not a freshman." I have just enough semester hours for the college to consider me a sophomore. I don't have to declare a major yet, and I don't plan on being here long enough to actually graduate, so I can take courses that interest me, mostly science stuff.

"Where were you last year?" Tiffany asks.

"I was playing hockey in Canada."

Her eyes widen. "I knew you were Canadian! I could tell from your accent."

I chuckle. "I don't have an accent."

"Yes, you do! The way you said 'Canada' . . ." She repeats it with a nasally "n" sound that I'm pretty sure I didn't use, so I laugh again. "I like Canada. It's beautiful."

"You've been there?"

"I've been to Niagara Falls."

"Ah."

"And I looooove hockey."

"Me too." That, I can be honest about.

"When's your first game?"

"October third. An exhibition game against Queen's University." They're a Canadian team up in Kingston, not part of our league.

Someone is trying to squeeze through the crowd, and Tiffany moves closer, her boobs pressing into my arm. My southern region takes notice. Goddammit.

I shift away and the other girls all introduce themselves, and then a few guys who I don't know join us. They shake hands with me and I try to remember names. It's no problem that I don't know anyone there besides my housemates, as people seem eager to meet me, so there's that. The attention helps my slightly battered ego.

My eyes are drawn to a girl across the kitchen. She's sitting on the counter, her hands holding the edge as she leans forward to talk to a dude standing next to her. She's wearing frayed denim cutoffs that show a lot of leg, and a loose white lace top that falls off one shoulder. It's her hair I first notice because it's long, nearly down to her waist, blond and fantastically thick and wavy. I have a weakness for blondes and also for long hair, because of the very first girl I banged, who let me wrap her hair around my dick. To this day, I get a semi when I see long blond hair. There are a few girls with long blond hair at this party, but this chick's is sweet and as she moves I can see the underneath layer is pink, which amuses me. Plus she has an amazing smile, and the way she's leaning forward is giving the guy standing beside her a view of her cleavage. I don't blame him for looking, because holy fucking amazing.

She has a vibe about her that's both hot and sweet.

Tiffany is waiting for an answer to a question I haven't heard. "Sorry." I flash my best smile at her and wink. "I zoned out."

She follows my gaze across the room and her smile goes tight and kind of scary. "Uh-huh." She sips her beer. "I asked what position you play."

"Oh. I play left wing." I set my can on the counter and take a pretend slap shot.

"You probably score a lot."

Ha. I meet her gaze and smile and give her my wicked grin. "Yeah. I do."

Her smile relaxes and her eyes darken.

I could totally tap that. Damn.

I pick up what Buck and Soupy are talking about and interject a comment. My eyes stray back to Rapunzel across the kitchen. She's sitting straighter now, swinging the foot that's crossed over the other leg, wearing a flat, strappy sandal. The languid movement attracts my attention to her legs, which are also primo.

She lifts a red Solo cup to her mouth, and as she does, her eyes meet mine across the kitchen. You know how that happens, right? You look at someone just as they turn to look at you and your eyes meet? It can be weird and you jerk your eyes away and pretend you weren't caught. Or you can hold the look and smile.

That's what I do. I smile at her.

Her eyebrows climb and she holds my gaze too, in a little bit of a challenge. Then she gives me a slow smile back, her lips shiny and pink like her hair.

Then, in a move that kind of confounds me, she dips her head. Her hair falls over her face and she tucks it behind one ear. It's sort of shy and cute and at odds with the eye fuck and the sexy smile. She nods, apparently listening to the guy talking to her. Then she peeks back at me.

I'm still watching her.

My groin tightens.

Shiiiiiiiiit.

I haven't even been at this party for half an hour and I'm getting a hard-on for any girl who looks at me.

I need to hang out with guys.

I turn away and shoulder back into the conversation Buck and Soupy are having about which team is going to be our biggest competition this year.

Apparently it's Harvard.

"Glad you lowered yourself to hang with us tonight," Buck says to me.

They think I'm stuck-up because I won't party with them. Fantastic. I take the jab but keep my expression easy. "Hey, I can slum with the lowlifes once in a while."

Buck's lips twitch.

"So we know you're Canadian." Soupy squints at me. "But that doesn't mean you're a goddamn hockey god."

My annoyance level reaches the point where I can't stop myself from asking, "What the fuck? What's up with the trash talk? You guys hated my guts before I even got here."

They exchange glances. "Coach told us not to haze you. Apparently you're some hot shit NHL prospect they don't want to piss off."

I narrow my eyes at them. That's what they think? Ha. "Yeah," I say slowly. "That's not exactly it." I don't know these guys well enough to be sure I can trust them with the true story. On the one hand, they might actually be impressed in a sick sort of way. But if they start shooting off their mouths all over campus, I'm fucked. I don't want people to know my sorry shit.

This is fucking me up in all kinds of ways. Nothing's ever been this hard for me before. All my life, people have liked me. Guys like me because they want me to play on their team, no matter what sport. I'm good at pretty much all of them. Girls also like me. I've never totally gotten why jocks are so popular, but I don't question it too much. Once I was playing major junior

16

hockey and puck bunnies were coming on to me all the time, I just gave a high five to the gods above and went with it.

Now these guys I don't even know hate my fucking guts. I can't be my fun-loving, beer-guzzling, man-whoring self with them, so they're never gonna like me. Even my profs are giving me squinty-eyed looks. I'm not going to be getting any easy As because of who I am. It's pissing me off.

Not only that, I've never been so stressed in my life. I need to seriously learn some time-management skills. Between courses, workouts and practices, I barely have a minute to myself. Luckily I have no social life; otherwise, I'd never have time for studying.

And what *is* coming easy? Girls. Except once again I can't be my man-whoring self around them. What if I hook up with someone who gets a wild hair and decides she didn't really consent after all? Nobody will believe me a second time. If I think I'm fucked now, that would be the end of my life.

So I'm not going there. I can flirt a little but I can't touch.

Only they don't know that, so the flirtation continues.

"I've heard hockey players have good hands," a girl named Amy says in a breathy voice.

Tiffany, still hanging out near me, giggles. "I *know* they have good hands."

"We also have great stamina." I wink at her.

"But you gotta date a defenseman," Soupy smirks.

"Oh yeah?" Amy flutters her eyelashes at him. "Why?"

"We care about your back door and pay a lot of attention to it."

Jesus. Everyone bursts out laughing at the dirty joke, including the girls.

I'm not sure how much more of this I can take.

I decide to use the bathroom to get a break from the sexual references and frank come-ons. I make my way through the crowded kitchen and into the hall. "Bathroom?" I ask someone.

"There's one at the end of this hall and a bunch upstairs. Want me to show you?" she asks hopefully.

"That's okay, doll, I got it."

There's a group of chicks hanging outside the bathroom door on the main floor, so I take the stairs at a run, my long legs easily eating two steps at a time. The hall upstairs is surprisingly empty and quiet, although as I pass a bedroom door I hear obvious sex sounds. I roll my eyes, a feeling of déjà vu making my gut cramp.

I spot a closed door and test the knob to see if it's unlocked. It turns and I shove it open. Whoops.

The blonde Rapunzel I'd been making heavy eye contact with earlier is in there, buttoning her cutoff shorts. Her eyes widen and she yelps.

"Sorry!" I back out and slam the door shut.

I slump against the wall and close my eyes. Jesus. That could have been so much worse.

The door jerks open and she glares at me. "What the hell?"

"Sorry!" I hold my hands up. "Why the hell didn't you lock it?"

"I thought I did!"

I frown and step past her into the bathroom. I jiggle the doorknob then shrug. Yep, it's broken. "Hey, you wanna wait and stand guard for me outside?"

She rolls her eyes. "Seriously?"

I give her my best grin. "Hell yeah. I don't want anyone walking in on me."

And someone appears at the top of the stairs—Tiffany. Somehow I know she followed me up here. Her gaze moves between Rapunzel and me and she hesitates, one hand on the big newel post.

"I need to wash my hands," Rapunzel protests.

I grab her wrist, yank her into the bathroom and close the door.

"Hey!" she protests again. "What are you doing?"

"Wash up." I gesture at the sink. "Take your time."

"What?" She gapes at me.

Damn, she's pretty. White teeth, small nose, big eyes. Her mouth is a little wide but sexy.

"Go ahead and wash your hands." I move closer and she edges back, her eyelashes fluttering. "Oh hey, you don't need to be afraid of me." I lower my voice. "I think that girl followed me up here."

Rapunzel scowls. "Really? Because you're that irresistible?"

I give a cheeky grin. "Yeah."

"Ugh." She cranks the water on and squirts some hand soap from a container, then rubs her hands together. "That's some ego you have there."

"Is that what you were looking at earlier?" I fold my arms across my chest and lean against the wall. "My ego?"

Her eyes fly open wide. "Wow. It *is* huge."

"Yeah, that's what she said."

For a moment, she goes still, then her head bends and her hair falls over her face . . . but not before I see her lips twitch.

"Come on, Rapunzel, that was funny."

She lifts her head and, yeah, her lips are curved into a smile and her eyes are dancing. Her eyes are brown, a light golden brown. "Rapunzel?"

"Sorry, I don't know your name. But I noticed your hair earlier. It's gorgeous."

"Um, thank you." She hesitates. "I'm Skylar."

"Jacob." I extend my hand. "I'll shake your hand now that you've washed up."

She rolls her eyes, still smiling, hangs the towel back on the hook beside the sink and takes my hand. Hers is small and soft but her grip is firm. I like that.

We make eye contact again and my skin heats. "I like the pink." I release her hand and gesture at the under layers of her hair.

She runs her fingers through it. "Thanks. It's new for me."

"Can you see if Tiffany's still out there?" I jerk my chin at the door.

Her eyebrows pull together. "Are you avoiding her?"

One corner of my mouth lifts. "She was coming on pretty strong."

"Ah." Her top teeth drag over her bottom lip briefly. "It looked like a lot of girls down there were."

I smile. "You noticed that, huh?"

Color floods into her cheeks and, damn, it makes her even prettier. "How could I not? It was embarrassing for womankind."

I laugh. "Oh, come on."

"Those girls who stalk the hockey team, the football team, the basketball team . . ." Skylar shakes her head. "They're shameless."

"Sometimes, yep."

"Aaaargh. You're a pig."

"I'm a guy. I like girls." I shrug. "Also luckily I didn't really have to take a leak that bad or I'd be in pain by now."

She shakes her head, but her lips twitch again. "You *are* avoiding her."

"So that means I'm not a total pig, then."

When I meet her eyes, it's like there's a crackling energy snapping between us. Damn. I just jumped out of a frying pan and into a goddamn fire. I know she feels it too, because she stares back at me for long seconds before she reaches for the doorknob. She peers out into the hall through the crack of the barely open door, then glances at me over her shoulder. "There are three girls out there now."

"Jesus Christ."

"Come on, dude. They're not *all* after you."

I lay my hand on my heart. "Ouch."

Skylar laughs, a low warm laugh that makes my groin tighten. "You're impossible."

"Will you guard the door for me?"

"They're probably wondering what the hell we're doing in here."

"They're probably jealous of you."

"Oh my God!" She glares at me but when she sees my smile, she starts laughing. "Fine. I'll guard the door for you."

"Thanks, babe."

Chapter 4

Skylar

I STEP OUTSIDE the bathroom and close the door behind me. I lean against it and smile at the girls standing there. Tiffany, Amy and another girl I recognize but don't know her name. "Hey. Jacob's just finishing up. Be warned— the lock on the door doesn't work." I wrinkle my nose.

The waves of hostility coming off them are palpable despite their phony smiles.

Holy shit. He wasn't kidding. These chicks are seriously annoyed I was in that bathroom alone with him. Tiffany gives me an icy glare. She's never even noticed me before. She's definitely one of the women who goes to all the games and has probably slept with most of the players on the team. I've never seen Jacob around before—because God, I'd definitely remember that —so I assume he's new this year. For a freshman, he seems pretty cocky and confident.

He's good-looking, there's no doubt about that. His face has a sculpted bone structure with high cheekbones and a strong jaw with a hint of a cleft in it. His eyes are dark and intelligent, his nose a strong wedge, and his mouth . . . wow. The corners of his mouth seem to be perpetually deepened as if he's always amused. It's stunningly attractive. There's something about him . . . if my roommate Natalie were here, she'd probably say he has a strong aura. It's like a magnetic force field that surrounds him, throwing off a glow that makes everyone turn and look at him, not just girls but guys too.

21

His egotistical, bragging comments should be repulsive, but when I looked into his eyes and saw the twinkle there, the corners of his mouth lifting in that sexy way, I . . . melted. He clearly doesn't take himself seriously, and the glint in his eyes and almost self-deprecating smile make me suspect his bravado is more an act than real.

I hear water running and take a step forward just as the door opens behind me. Jacob emerges and, shockingly, slings an arm around my neck. "Hey. Let's find another drink, Rapunzel."

The glares I'm getting from the girls in the hallway could freeze lava. I don't really care; none of these girls are friends of mine. It's kind of funny, actually, because I'm no threat to them. I don't think I've ever been the recipient of envy like they are clearly feeling. It's kind of a little boost for my own ego, which is about one five-hundredth the size of Jacob's.

We pass the girls and start down the stairs. Halfway down I can't stop the chuckle that rises to my lips.

"Something funny?"

I turn to glance at him over my shoulder, ready to say something about how hilarious it is that the girls upstairs would actually think I'm some kind of rival, but my foot misses the next step and I pitch forward. My stomach leaps and my blood flashes hot as I give a squawk, anticipating the pain I'm about to feel. But Jacob reaches out and grabs me, stopping my headfirst tumble. "Hey there."

Pulled up against him, my back to his front, his arms around me, my heart thudding, I give an embarrassed laugh. But I can smell his aftershave—or cologne, I guess, since he's got a nice layer of stubble—and it's so freakin' sexy I inhale a big breath of it, then let it out. "Thanks," I say breathlessly. "Thought I was a goner there."

"You okay?"

"Oh yeah. Just red-faced."

"Let me see." He steadies me and turns me on the stairs, studying my face with intent eyes. "Yep. You're cute when you blush."

Yeah, that doesn't help. My cheeks grow hotter. Also other parts of me get hot. Melting hot.

This is really . . . weird.

I haven't felt this way for a while. It feels good, but scary.

I don't know why this beautiful guy is paying attention to me, flirting with me. I mean, I'm not a total troll. I've gone out with some guys at

Bayard, and I had a high school boyfriend. But this guy is way out of my league.

For some reason, this relaxes me. Nothing's ever going to come of it, so I might as well have fun. A sexy athlete telling me my hair is gorgeous and I'm cute when I blush? I laugh out loud, despite the lust curling deep inside me.

"That's funny?" He lifts an eyebrow.

"No. Never mind. Come on. I need a drink."

I start back down, this time paying attention to where my feet land.

Jacob follows me into the kitchen and I'm surprised when he hands me a hard lemonade from a big cooler but takes a Coke for himself.

"Designated driver." He lifts one shoulder. "Someone has to do it."

"That's very responsible of you."

He makes a face. "That's me. Mr. Responsible."

He's obviously being sarcastic, but I don't know him well enough to understand why. I'm curious, though. I lift the bottle to my lips and take a gulp of the cold, fizzy beverage. I don't usually drink fizzy drinks because they hurt my nose, but I need this. "You don't strike me as Mr. Responsible."

"No? How do I strike you?"

I study him. "Playboy. Lots of fun, but unreliable. Your whole life is one big party."

He blinks at me, his beautiful mouth going slack. "Whoa." A faint crease appears between his eyebrows. Then it smoothes and he smiles again, but it's a little forced. "You nailed it, babe." He gulps his Coke. "But my hockey coaches would disagree on the 'unreliable' part. I was captain of my team back in Canada, and every guy on the team knew he could count on me. I show up and give it everything I've got, every practice, every game."

The intensity in his voice and the blaze in his eyes when he says this are so different from his earlier laid-back attitude and swagger. I can't look away from his face, mesmerized. Intrigued. And totally convinced he's telling the truth.

"Team captain, huh?" I hide the fact that I'm impressed. "Captain Fun, no doubt."

He narrows his eyes at me. "Okay, I'll admit I like to have fun. But I'm very serious about hockey."

I pat his chest with my fingertips. Eeep. That might have been a mistake because he is *built*. But I keep my smile in place. "I believe you."

He shakes his head. "Jesus. You're fucking with me."

I laugh. "Maybe a little. You kinda deserve it, Captain Ego."

He rolls his eyes.

Somehow we have isolated ourselves in a back corner of the kitchen, near a door to a main floor laundry room. The party is rocking around us, his hockey friends having moved on to a rowdy game of beer pong in the dining room. I'm about five-seven, and Jacob towers above me, obviously well over six feet tall, and he bends his head and leans into me in a way that makes me feel . . . protected. Not intimidated, which is more how I've felt lately anytime I've been around guys. His body is amazing—wide shoulders, muscled chest and flat abs in a blue-and-beige plaid shirt loose over nicely distressed jeans. His attention is all focused on me and even though I've had less than two drinks, I feel like I'm drunk. Like the carbonation from the drink is fizzing through my veins.

"So, Rapunzel, what's your story? Are you a freshman?"

"Sophomore. You?"

"Yeah." He shrugs. "Sophomore. But I don't get the whole naming the years thing. We don't do that in Canada."

I laugh. "It depends on how many semester hours you have."

"Yeah. I had enough from some courses I took back in Saskatoon that they consider me a sophomore."

"How old are you?"

"I'll be twenty in November. You?"

Huh. "Nineteen. I'll turn twenty in May."

"What's your major?"

"Um. I think . . . biology."

"You don't sound too sure."

I nibble my bottom lip. "I want to be a doctor."

His eyes widen. "No shit. That's impressive."

"And probably ridiculous." I sigh and trace the top of my bottle with an index finger.

"Why ridiculous?"

"Pre-med is incredibly hard. And doesn't come super easily to me." I give him a crooked smile. "I'm taking a bunch of science classes and they're killing me."

"Then why do it?" He gazes at me with genuine curiosity. "If you take something you like, it should be easy."

I snort-laugh. "If you have brains, yeah."

"Clearly you have a brain, Rapunzel."

"I'm not a genius like my older sister." I glumly study my indigo-polished toenails. "She's now a resident in Boston. It's easy for her. Me, I have to work my ass off."

He blinks at me as if he doesn't understand that concept.

"Like you do at hockey," I prompt him. "Right?"

"Oh yeah. Right." He frowns. "Actually, hockey's pretty easy for me. I mean, I work at it, and I work out to stay in the best shape I can, but it's not like it's hard."

"Oh." I purse my lips. "What are you taking?"

"Some engineering courses. A math course. Physics."

"Physics? Seriously?"

"Yeah. Physics is cool and it actually applies to hockey. Like, skating. The friction of a skate blade with the ice. A skater propels himself forward by pushing off the ice with a force perpendicular to the skate blade. Then when he pushes off with his back leg, a perpendicular force is exerted on the skate by the ice. To push off the ice with greater forward force, and accelerate faster, he has to increase the angle, which increases the component of force in the direction of motion."

I stare at him.

"Uh, sorry." He swipes a hand over his face. "I forgot I'm not supposed to talk about shit like that at parties. It makes people's eyes glaze over."

"No, no. It's cool. You're not just a big dumb jock." I nudge him with my shoulder.

"Yeah, actually I am." He makes a face. "I never planned to go to college, other than some courses I took to fill time. I had to take things that were easy, otherwise all the time I spent on the road would make it impossible to keep up. Plus I'm kind of interested in building stuff."

"I'm sure you had all kinds of girls willing to loan you their notes. Help you study."

His lips curve into that sexy smile. "Well, yeah."

I shake my head, smiling back at him. "And physics is easy for you? Jesus."

He shrugs. "It's just the way my mind works. When it comes to writing papers, I suck. I can't spell for shit and my grammar is pathetic."

This cocky guy being smart *and* admitting a weakness makes him even more endearing. That buzz of attraction grows stronger, his magnetic pull more powerful.

"So just because your sister is a genius and is going to be a doctor doesn't mean you have to if you don't enjoy that stuff."

Ugh. I sigh. I know he's right, but I've spent my whole life trying to keep up with my older sister. Trying to prove to my parents I'm as good as she is. As smart. As talented. Except so far it's never really worked, so I have no idea why I think this is going to. And even if I actually do make it into med school, Elisha will probably end up being a neurosurgeon and I'll be a family practice doctor. "Well." I beam a smile. "Some things are worth working for, right? I mean, some of my classes are challenging, but that just means I have to work harder."

"Determination, eh?"

I can't help my grin. "Canadian, *eh?*"

He looks abashed. "The guys keep bugging me about that. I didn't realize how often I say it. That one slipped out."

"It's cute."

His eyes flicker, as if he's not sure I mean it or if I'm flirting with him because he's a hockey player.

Am I?

No. I don't care if he's a hockey player. He's cute and smart and funny and I'm enjoying talking to him. And I know it's not going anywhere, so I can be myself without worrying if I'm making a good impression or coming across as dorky and studious. Or if it's going to lead to something more than I can deal with.

He lifts a hand to shift some hair off my face with a gentle gesture and his gaze moves down over my hair. He likes it.

My breasts ache and my nipples tingle. Oh wow. When our eyes meet, I see the same kind of heat reflected in his.

I haven't felt this alive in months, and only with this arousal shimmering through me do I realize exactly how . . . anesthetized I've felt.

"You have a very sexy mouth." Oh my God. Did I really just say that?

"Thanks. I thought the same about you." And he touches my face, his thumb brushing over my lower lip.

Heat spirals up through me from my core and my gaze is locked to his. My lips part and I am aching for him to kiss me. I want to know if his sexy mouth tastes and feels as good as it looks.

This is so not like me, and I don't know what's getting into me. Maybe it's the heady feeling of knowing I'm with a guy every other girl at the party wants. Maybe it's the hard lemonade. Maybe it's relief at knowing I can actually feel this way again. My body is tingling and warm everywhere, especially between my legs and in the tips of my breasts. So I go up on my toes and touch my lips to his.

We're still staring at each other, but his eyelids grow heavy at my soft kiss. His eyes close briefly, and his hand goes to my hip and pulls me closer. Then our eyes meet again and fire consumes me. His lips quirk in that sexy way. "You just kissed me."

I blink. "Uh . . . yeah."

"Okay, then." And his eyes close as his mouth moves back to mine.

I'm helpless to resist. I'm longing for a deeper taste and I close my own eyes as our mouths meet.

Kissing is so lovely. And Jacob is an amazing kisser. His mouth is firm and warm, with just the right amount of pressure, and his tongue licks inside with confidence, not aggression. He's bold, but tender. His hands clasp my hips and pull my lower body flush against his, and I set my hands on his shoulders.

His bones are big, his muscles thick. I feel his arousal growing against my lower belly. He's turned on too.

I mean, it doesn't take much for guys to get hard. But still, it's a rush knowing that's for me.

My usual good judgment has disappeared as I fall into the kiss with everything I have. My fingers curl into his shirt, then I slip one hand around the back of his neck. I rub my fingertips over the short hair and soft skin at the nape of his neck and he groans into my mouth.

He lifts his mouth only long enough to tilt my chin to a different angle, then claims me again in another long, lush kiss. My heart is pounding, my blood rushing hot in my veins. I press my aching breasts against his chest and another rumble rises there.

Over and over our mouths meet and cling, part, then meet again. I lick his tongue, nip at his bottom lip. His erection is getting even bigger. I want to feel it, but dimly recall that we are in a kitchen with other people around.

We're not the only ones making out, I know that, and I heard that couple having sex in a bedroom upstairs. I want to be upstairs, in a bedroom, alone with Jacob, stretched out on a bed so we can twist ourselves together.

Thick, liquid heat converges low in my belly, forming an insistent throb behind my clit.

Finally, Jacob lifts his head and gives me a dazed, hot look. "Jesus, Rapunzel. What a mouth."

The tip of my tongue touches my top teeth. "Is that a compliment?"

"Hell yeah." He lifts a hand to cup my face, his thumb petting the corner of my mouth. I turn my head, open my lips and bite his thumb. His eyes darken and I suck his thumb into my mouth. It feels so good and I can tell we're both thinking of me sucking on other parts of him.

"Holy hell, you're sexy," he rasps out. He grinds his hips into mine and my belly does a flip of lust.

"So are you."

I've never in my life done this—I mean, I've had sex, but I've never been the one to come on to a guy like this, especially someone I just met. But I want to have sex with him. It's crazy because I don't even know him, but I'm so attracted to him and I'm so turned on, my panties are soaked right through to my shorts. The intense ache there is obliterating reason. And I shock myself as I whisper the words that spring to my lips. "Want to go upstairs?"

He gazes at me, his hand curled around the side of my neck, his beautiful mouth wet from our kisses, eyes heavy-lidded. His eyelashes lower to rest on his cheeks. He pulls in a harsh breath, then slowly lets it out. "I can't."

My body stiffens. Somehow, I never thought he would turn me down. He seemed as into the whole making out thing as I was, and his arousal is undeniable. But right, guys get turned on so easily. It's not me. It's just . . . a girl, pressing her boobs against him and throwing herself at him. It's a physiological response. Seriously, I just learned about that in Human Physiology.

I swallow and step back, and he releases me. His eyes are shadowed, his jaw tight. Mortification scorches me from the inside out until I swear I'm probably glowing red like a traffic light. I am such an idiot.

"Oops," I try to say in a light tone. "Sorry." I hold up my hands. "I obviously misread things there."

"Skylar . . ."

I scrunch my face into a smile. "Hey, no worries." I lift my chin toward the wide doors leading to the dining room. "You should see if your friends need any help in their beer pong tournament."

I whirl around and resist the urge to bolt right out of the house. Instead I saunter across the kitchen, plucking another bottle from the cooler, hoping I don't appear rejected and pathetic to everyone else in the kitchen. I head to the living room, seeking out Ella, Natalie and Brooklyn. There they are, dancing. That's what I need. I need to dance.

They welcome me with hip bumps and smiles, and as I move to the music I try to ignore the humiliation burning inside me.

Chapter 5

Jacob

I WALK into the South Quad Academic Complex for my first training session at SAPAP Monday evening. I've had two classes today and an intense workout and practice session and I have homework, so this is the last place I want to be. I'm still not sure what to expect from this training. I've read the info online about the pilot program. I get it. But it seems like overkill to me. Is something like this really necessary? Not all guys are asshole misogynists.

I'm pretty sure I can't even spell that word.

I love women. I respect women. I would never hurt a woman. Why the *fuck* am I here?

Right, right, everyone has to be here. I heave a sigh as I walk into the office that houses SAPAP, summoning my most charming smile. A girl standing at a printer glances up at me and smiles. "Hi. Can I help you?"

"I'm here for the new student training."

She's cute, with shiny brown hair and a nice rack.

"Oh, come on in, then, I'll show you where the training room is." She leads me down a hall and we enter a large, gray-carpeted room, tables and chairs arranged to face a projection screen at one end. It appears this room can be divided up into smaller meeting rooms, or with the partitions pushed back, opened into this huge space. There are already a bunch of people here and I spot one of my teammates, Dan Churchill, who's a freshman. I head his way. "Hey, Danny. How's it going?"

"Good." He gives me a friendly smile. As a rookie, he doesn't have the same animosity some of the other guys have for me.

More people are coming in, so we grab chairs at a table at the back of the room.

An older woman—and by "older" I mean about thirty—who is smokin' hot moves to the front of the room. "Okay, it's a little after eleven already, so let's get started. Welcome everyone. I'm Victoria Meyer, Director of SAPAP."

She makes eye contact with a bunch of people, even me, sitting as far at the back as possible.

"Our goals are to educate the Bayard College community about sexual assault, intimate-partner violence, sexual harassment and stalking, and to raise awareness and promote a non-violent campus community. We work with various campus organizations and community agencies on a number of different strategies. Last year, the college administration asked us to develop a program that would be part of the orientation for all freshman and transfer students at Bayard and we're very pleased to be offering it this year. Welcome to Bayard College and thank you for being a part of our pilot project. Your feedback will be valuable in helping us determine the effectiveness of the training and how we can improve it."

She continues. "Your training will take place for an hour each evening this week, concluding on Friday."

I cringe, although I knew this. My schedule's already crazy with classes, study groups, workouts, team meetings, and practices, and we haven't even started the hockey season yet.

"We'll be covering topics such as sexual assault." She pauses to make more eye contact and let the seriousness of these topics sink in. "Intimate-partner violence. Stalking, sexual harassment, rape culture, healthy relationships, and bystander intervention."

I shift in my seat and pick at a piece of cuticle that's loose on my thumb.

"After the training, if you're interested in being actively involved in the movement to end sexual and intimate-partner violence at Bayard College, and society in general, we have three student volunteer groups: the Men's Activism Program; our Networking, Publicity and Activism Program and a Peer Education Program. As well, there are a variety of opportunities to participate in some of the awareness events and fundraisers we work on throughout the year."

She smiles.

"Now I'll introduce you to your facilitators: Grace Smith, Skylar Lynwood, and Chad Bukoski."

My head whips around as two women and a dude join Victoria at the front of the room. My jaw drops. Rapunzel.

I barely hear Victoria introduce Grace, but then focus as she outlines Skylar's experience with SAPAP. Skylar smiles at everyone but when her gaze skims past mine and hesitates, and her smile falters, I know she already saw me there. So she had a few minutes to get her shit together, while my own shit is all over the goddamn place, totally messed up by seeing her there.

I've been trying to put her out of my head since Friday night, not totally successfully. Remembering the hurt look on her face when I turned down her so sweet and sexy invitation. Goddamn, I wanted to go upstairs with her, toss her onto a bed, kiss that hot mouth and bang her into next week. But hell, I've been at Bayard a few weeks, how could I abandon my plans that fast?

I haven't quite figured out how I'm going to go all year without sex. On the one hand, I think I've read that monk like abstinence can make you stronger. On the other hand, I'm pretty sure I'm going to end up in the hospital with blue balls as big as bowling balls. They're going to have to do some kind of emergency procedure to save me. Possibly involving a hot nurse, in a short, tight uniform.

And just like that the hot nurse morphs into Skylar. God, what is wrong with me?

Putting aside thoughts of sex, which intrude into my mind with disturbing frequency, the last couple of days Skylar featuring prominently in my porn fantasies, I again try to focus on what's happening.

"So as Victoria said," Skylar says with a sweet smile that I can tell wins over everyone in the room, "this is our first time presenting this training program. We want to make it not just relevant and informative, but interactive and fun."

She's well spoken, making the same eye contact Victoria had, at ease in front of people. I admire that. I have some experience with it too, talking to media after games, dealing with fans. For me it's easy, and for her . . . it seems easy as well. I smile.

I'm here because I have to be, and I seriously doubt it's going to be fun. But this is what I have to do if I want to play hockey and if I want my shot at being drafted into the NHL. As far as the awareness stuff goes, once I'm done with this training, I'm done. No way will I be volunteering on one of those committees. The team's schedule of workouts, team meetings, and practices is rigorous, not to mention our upcoming game schedule.

I'm here, as in, I'm present. I'll do what I have to do. But I can't do more than that.

"First a few housekeeping things." Skylar talks about where the bathrooms are, when breaks occur, how the facilitators are committed to starting and ending on time, ground rules about sharing and privacy, blah blah blah.

Then we break into smaller groups. Victoria directs Skylar to sit with my group, which clearly does not thrill her. But she smiles and asks us to all introduce ourselves. Ugh.

I give my best smile as I tell them my name and a little about myself. When I mention I play for the Bears, a bunch of freshmen girls sigh.

And Skylar's lips tighten. She gives me a glare before moving on to Danny, but hey, he gets the same reaction.

After we've all heard each other's names and a bit about each person, we return to the bigger group and move right into the first module—sexual assault.

Yeah, I'm sweating.

"This training will draw on the experience and viewpoints of the participants," Skylar says, having completed all the bullshit introductions. "It will be dynamic and interactive and result in skills that you'll be able to use in a variety of situations. One thing I want to mention is the use of pronouns. In most cases, gender-neutral plural pronouns such as 'they' and 'them' are used throughout this training to refer to victims. But because most victims of sexual assault are female, we do occasionally use female pronouns. In the module dealing with male sexual assault, we will of course address all victims/survivors as males."

My eyebrows lift. I guess I've never really thought about male sexual abuse victims. I rub my forehead and shift again in my chair.

With PowerPoint slides projecting onto the screen on the wall, Skylar, Grace and Chad take turns talking. "The definition from the U.S. Department of Justice is 'any type of sexual contact or behavior that occurs without the explicit consent of the recipient.' " Skylar surveys the room with unsettling gravity.

My armpits are prickling with sweat and my muscles are tight. I slouch into my chair.

The visual on the screen changes.

"Let's talk about victim versus survivor. It's difficult for anyone other than the individuals themselves to determine when the shift from victim to survivor occurs. Some people feel they are survivors from the moment they escape their assailant." Skylar pauses. "Or assailants."

I slump lower. Skylar flicks me a brief frown.

"They may prefer the term 'survivor' even in the emergency department, where others use the term 'survivor' for someone who's achieved progress in recovering from their experience."

It's hot in this room. Is it hot is this room? I glance at Danny, who's nodding and attentive. He's not sweating like I am.

About an hour later, we're done. We have homework—reading to do before our session tomorrow evening. Crap. Thankfully the training will be done before hockey season starts, because I already have enough homework.

I pick up my messenger bag and lift the strap over my head, my gaze going to Skylar. She's talking to a couple of other people but, as if she feels my gaze on her, like she did that night at the party, she meets my eyes.

Her gaze is cool. Hell, I don't blame her. I should apologize. But maybe that would make it worse. I can't really explain to her why I turned her down, but I want her to know that it wasn't her, it was me.

Fuck, that sounds lame.

The next day, I've sat through three classes by noon. I make my way across the Quad to the dining hall, hungry enough to eat my shoulder pads. Although we live off campus, my housemates and I have meal plans so we can eat on campus if we want. It's actually good because the dining hall has buffets with tons of choices and we all eat a lot. And none of us are great cooks.

But that's okay. Despite these guys still not totally accepting me, living with them is kind of cool. Last year I was billeted with a family who had a seventeen-year-old son who played hockey on my team. We ended up driving back and forth to the arena together. He was a good kid, and the family was awesome, but I have to say living on my own with a bunch of guys my age is a lot more fun. Or it could be.

I spot Buck, Rocket, and Soupy at a table and I stride over to them and drop my bag onto an empty chair. They look up. "Hey, Flash. What up?"

Their greeting is cordial but not warm. Tightness squeezes my chest. Everyone is supposed to like me.

"I'm starving," I answer. "Gonna load up. Be right back."

I fill a plate with chicken, pasta, salad, and a couple of rolls, plus add a piece of pie and a brownie for dessert to my tray. I have a sweet tooth. I'm supposed to avoid too much sugar, but it's not like I'll get fat. I have a hard time keeping weight on, in fact, with the way I'm built and how much I work out. When I was under two hundred pounds, I was scrawny by NHL standards so I worked hard over the summer and put on fourteen pounds—but that was muscle, not fat.

Back at the table, Soupy and Rocket are ragging Buck about his clothes. He's wearing a pair of narrow beige pants, argyle socks and a pink T-shirt.

"Do I look like a fucking girl?" he asks mildly in response to Soupy's comment about the shirt.

He does not. His shoulders are wider than mine and his dark beard stubble takes him about two hours to grow. If anyone can pull off a pink shirt without his masculinity being questioned, it's Buck. But what are friends for if not to bug you about your fashion choices.

"That shade of pink is good with your skin tone," I say helpfully.

Buck meets my eyes and I lift one eyebrow. His lips twitch. "Thanks," he drawls. "I thought so."

Not only is the shirt pink, it probably cost a hundred bucks. Buck likes nice shit, including expensive clothes.

"Wait till he wears one of his hats," Rocket says. "You'll want to walk a few paces behind him."

"Fuck you. My hats are cool."

"Uh-huh."

These guys all know one another and are comfortable enough to trash talk, and I try not to feel like an outsider as I eat my meal.

A girl passes by our table and shoots Soupy a disgusted scowl that none of us miss. She continues on and sits with some friends.

"Dude," Buck says in a low voice. "Isn't that the chick you left with Friday night?"

I was the designated driver, but only Rocket came home with me that night. Buck and Soupy both left with girls, which depressed the hell out of me since I actually turned down an offer, for fuck's sake.

"Yeah." Soupy drops his gaze to his empty plate.

"Apparently she's not too impressed with your mad sex skillz."

"Fuck off."

"Oooh." We all exchange glances. "It must be good. Come on, bro, tell us all."

Soupy rolls his eyes. "Okay, fine, I didn't get laid."

"Couldn't get it up?" Buck's eyebrows shoot up. "It was probably just whiskey dick—"

"That wasn't it." Soupy frowns and picks up his paper napkin. He sighs. "Fine, here's what went down. We went back to her dorm. I didn't have a condom, so she told me to go get one from this box her RA has on the wall outside his room. I grab one, jump into the sack with her, and things are going great. Then I get ready to glove up. I open up the package, and bam, powder everywhere."

We all frown.

"The whole bed smelled like chicken. I know, what the fuck? I turn on the light and discover it was a packet of soup mix from some goddamn ramen noodles." Soupy scowls. "Needless to say, that kinda killed the mood."

We all dissolve into laughter, falling back in our chairs. I'm picturing Soupy naked in bed covered with powdered chicken soup. My eyes actually tear up I'm laughing so hard.

"Oh, man, that is priceless." Rocket slaps Soupy's shoulder. "No wonder you didn't score."

"Most embarrassing night of my life," Soupy mumbles.

"You didn't realize it wasn't a condom?" Buck grins. "How could you not?"

"I was riding the buzz train, if you'll recall."

"Riding the buzz train to Pussytown," Buck adds.

Still chuckling, we pick up our stuff to go work out. I drive to the arena myself, though I offer the guys a ride, but they all came together in Buck's Mustang. The DeWitt Center is a huge gym and rink facility, state of the art, and pretty damn cool.

My new coach has impressed me so far. Coach Klausen is in his early forties and has a great track record. The guys told me there are rumors the NHL is interested in stealing him away from Bayard, but he's still here. He's tough but has a way of knowing exactly what each player needs from him. We had a one-on-one meeting last spring, before they'd even started the process of trying to get the rules bent so I could play NCAA hockey, and although he was serious, I felt like we clicked. That's important.

In the locker room I change into a pair of shorts and a T-shirt and make my way into the weight room.

I love lifting. It makes me feel strong. Plus, after sitting in classes all morning, I really need to burn off some energy. Sitting still for a few hours isn't easy for me and I'm ready to get physical.

I pair up with Buck and we alternate sets of clean and jerks, deadlifts, and various other tortures while the music of DJ Rapture blasts around us, accompanied by the clangs of dropped weights and grunts of effort.

Dripping sweat, I grab my towel and swipe my face, loving the heat in my muscles, which means I'm getting stronger.

"You pressed one-ninety," Buck notes as I pick up some dumbbells to do biceps curls. "Impressive."

Hey. A compliment. "Thanks." I shrug. "I worked really hard over the summer. Still aiming to bench-press my weight." Since I hadn't even been able to play in the playoffs, it was a long summer for me. I'd taken out my frustrations in the gym in the spring, then did a high-performance training camp in the summer. I'm in the best shape I've ever been in. My new strength and conditioning coach, Jaegar, who's across the gym watching Soupy lift, has given me a workout schedule that will build on it.

I'm determined I'm going to kick ass here this year.

"Ten reps at one-ninety is great."

Warmth spreads through my chest at Buck's approval.

As I lift the dumbbells, my mind goes back to Skylar. I'm going to be seeing a lot of her this week. That's not a bad thing—she's hot and I really like her. But it's uncomfortable after how things ended Friday night, and I don't know how to make it right.

The idea of being honest with her floats through my brain as my biceps burn with another rep. Nah. She'd hate me even more if she knew the truth about me.

Chapter 6

Skylar

I CAN'T BELIEVE Jacob ended up in one of my training groups. It's a pretty big freshman class this year, along with students transferring in, so we split everyone up into smaller groups.

Which means I'll be seeing him every evening this week. Screaming Jesus on a Ferris wheel.

When I saw him sitting at that table this evening, my heart leaped in my chest and my belly did a flip. Damn, he's gorgeous. And charming.

I was hyperaware of him all through that hour. I felt his gaze on me a lot. At times, I sensed his discomfort, which made me curious.

I walk into the house to find Ella, Nat, and Brooklyn sitting in the living room doing Limoncello shots, music blasting. They all have laptops open on their laps and are laughing like crazy about something.

"Whoa, guys, it's Monday night." I drop my purse on the coffee table and sink into an armchair. I kick off my shoes so I can wiggle my toes on the cool bare wood floor.

"So what?" Ella gives me a tipsy smile.

I'll admit that last year, my first year living away from home, I was quick to get a fake ID so I could go to bars and buy booze. I loved the freedom of cracking open a bottle of Moscato anytime I wanted without parental super-vision. We partied a lot our freshman year. I'm not turning all teetotaler, but Ella's drinking every night bothers me.

"You have class in the morning," I remind her.

"You sound like my mom."

Yeah. I hate sounding all parental. I don't want to nag her; I'm just worried about her. But my attempts to bring this up are always met with defiance and denial.

"Chill, Skylar," she adds. "At least I don't have FOGO."

I grit my teeth. While I think she goes out too much and is using alcohol and sex as unhealthy coping mechanisms, she has accused me of having "fear of going out," or FOGO, because of what happened with Brendan. Of course I deny that. I'm not *afraid* to go out. I just don't want to.

Really.

"Here." Nat hands me a shot glass full of yellow liquid.

After the day I've had, I accept it and toss it back. Does that make me a hypocrite? Very possibly, yes.

When Ella and I are alone moments later, I lean forward. "You sure you're okay, El?"

She frowns and blinks. "Of course I'm okay."

I tuck some hair behind my ear, not sure what to say. "You seem different . . . since Brendan died."

Her lips push out and she nods slowly. "I'm still sad. I still miss him. But I'm okay. Really."

I nod, though I'm not completely convinced. "I'm still sad too."

There's a distance between us that never used to be there and I hate it.

Nat and Brooklyn return with a bowl of chips. "Hey, Skylar. We were talking before you got home about having a party here this weekend."

"Here?" Inwardly, I cringe. There's no avoiding a party held in my own house. But I'm one out of four, so voting against the idea probably isn't going to work. I gave in and went to that party last weekend, and look how that turned out.

"Yeah! It'll be fun. I'm going to put it on Facebook now."

"Do you think that's a good idea?" I heard about a party that was posted on Facebook, people kept sharing it, and like two hundred people turned up and totally trashed the place.

Nat pulls her laptop close and starts tapping on the keyboard. "Don't worry, it'll be fine."

In the morning I force myself to pay attention in my Physics class and Organic Chem lab. Then I rush home to change into my uniform for an afternoon shift at the Taste of Heaven Diner. Now that I'm done with my counseling appointments, it makes my schedule a little easier to manage.

My uniform is cheesy but kind of fun to wear—a tight pink dress with a flared skirt and puffed sleeves, and a black apron. I guess it's supposed to be sort of fifties-retro. I also wear white ankle socks and tennis shoes.

It's Tuesday afternoon, so it's not super busy at the diner. I'm nearly done my shift and keeping myself occupied by refilling ketchup bottles when a bunch of guys storm the place. I mean, they just walk in, but it feels like a storm, because they're big and loud.

Hockey players. They're instantly recognizable, some of them wearing sweatpants or athletic shorts and Bears hoodies. I can't stop myself from scanning the bunch as they pile into a big booth, and yeppers, there's Jacob.

I nibble briefly on my bottom lip and glance at my co-worker Taisha. I consider asking her to take care of their table even though it's in my section, but she's busy with another big group, in her own section. With a sigh, I start toward my table.

"Hi, guys." I smile brightly. "Welcome to Taste of Heaven. Can I start you off with something to drink?"

"I'd like to taste your heaven." One of the guys gives me an up-and-down inspection.

I'm used to smart-ass customers so I'm not really fazed by this, but I am startled when Jacob lunges across the table and grips the guy's hoodie in a fist. "Dude," he snarls. "That was inappropriate."

Silence descends around us. My body goes on alert while thoughts speed through my brain, like . . . *Wow, we've barely even started our training and Jacob's already got harassment down*, and *he's really pissed*, and *Dear Lord, please don't let a fight break out.*

"What the fuck, man?" The guy knocks Jacob's arm away. "She your girlfriend?"

Jacob subsides back into his seat.

My gaze snaps back and forth between him and his teammate and I'm happy to see the dude he grabbed looks a little shamefaced. He glances at Jacob, then at me, and mutters, "Meant it as a compliment."

One corner of my mouth lifts. I believe him. "You think I haven't heard that line before?" I shake my head. "Come on, at least be original."

"I didn't know you work here, Skylar," Jacob says.

"Yeppers, I do. Drinks?" I remind them, still smiling.

"Chocolate milk, please," Jacob says.

I take their beverage orders and turn toward the kitchen to fill them. I guess none of Jacob's friends recognizes me as the girl he was making out with in the kitchen Friday night. Probably just as well. I still don't know what came over me that night.

Okay, yes, I do know. Jacob came over me.

Even seeing him now has my girl parts warming up. So this is going to be a challenge, running into him on campus, and seeing him every evening in the training. I'm not sure what to do about it. His vehement defense of me confuses me after he rejected my lust-drunk offer to take our make-out session to a bed.

I'm so distracted I overflow his glass of chocolate milk all over the counter. "Shit!"

"What the hell, Skylar?" Edrick, one of the cooks, calls out.

"Sorry, sorry." I hastily mop it up. I pour chocolate milk into a clean glass and add it to my tray. Damn.

It's kind of cute that he drinks chocolate milk, like a little boy, and yet he's all man, so big and muscled. I suck in a breath, square my shoulders, and hoist my tray to go serve them.

I'm prepared for knowing smirks or something like that, imagining Jacob has told them how he knows me. But there's nothing, only polite smiles as I set their drinks in front of them.

I start to turn away, but Jacob says, "Hey, Skylar."

I turn. "Are you ready to order?"

"Um, yeah, but I was going to introduce you. These are my housemates—Ben, Grady, and Hunter."

"Hi, guys. Nice to meet you. So you all live off campus somewhere?"

"Yeah. Oak Street."

I nod. That's only two streets over from where I live, the neighborhood full of big old houses that mostly house college students since it's so close to campus. So, great—we're neighbors.

The guys give me their orders and back to the kitchen I go, stopping on my way as another customer flags me down to request coffee refills. "You bet!"

A few more people come in and sit in my section, and I have to hustle, which is good, as it doesn't let me be obsessed with Jacob. Waitressing is hard but this is a good place to work, near campus and home, and it closes at ten so I don't ever have to work super late.

In a bit of a lull, I pour myself a glass of lemonade and lean against the long counter for a minute.

"Hey."

I turn to see Jacob. Greeeeaaat. "Hi."

Compared to his cocky assurance the other night, he now seems hesitant, hands in the pockets of his jeans, rocking back and forth on his feet, forehead wrinkled. His Bears sweatshirt hangs from his broad shoulders, the hood making him look super cute.

No. I refuse to succumb to his charm again. He's an asshat. I keep my expression distant and wait for him to speak.

"I was surprised to see you at SAPAP last night," he says.

"Yeah, I was surprised to see you too. Although I guess I should have known there was a chance you'd be in my group, since you're a new student here."

"Uh. Look. I feel like I should apologize or something."

My eyebrows rise. "Apologize? For what?"

"Uh . . . shit. There's no good way to handle this, is there?"

"Nope. If you're apologizing for leading me on and then rejecting me, that's just insulting and humiliating all over again. If you're apologizing for not being interested, ditto. If you're apologizing for how you handled things . . . nope, still not good." I shake my head. "Look, forget it, okay? I have."

"No, you haven't. You keep giving me looks that could slice me open."

"Phhht. You're imagining it." I wave a hand. "You're not that important, hockey boy."

Now his eyes narrow and his gorgeous lips tighten. "Fine. It's forgotten." He lifts his chin, and my eyes catch on that adorable cleft in the middle of it, almost like a fingerprint. It makes me want to touch my own fingertip to it . . . as I lean in and . . .

Heat rises inside me and as our eyes meet again, those sparks that flared up the first night shimmer around us. Damn.

Friday night I was so attracted to him, and I was so surprised and happy to be feeling that way about a boy, I let it override my good sense. I'm not doing that again.

I step back abruptly and knock over a sugar container on the counter. It rolls and crashes to the black-and-white tiled floor. Everyone in the place turns to look.

Heat washes up into my face. Jacob moves to pick up the container, which didn't break but the lid came off it and there's sugar all over the floor.

"I better clean that up." I take the container from him and rush away to find a broom.

He's back in the booth with his friends when I return. One of the busboys offers to sweep up the sugar, which is good, as I have customers to look after. The hockey guys have finished their meals and I need to clear their table and get them their checks. But I'm all hot and flustered, and this isn't how I want to be around a guy who rejected me, which annoys me even more.

Then, moments later when I turn to observe their table to see how they're doing, there are literally five girls crowded around them. All of them have perfect wavy hair, tight jeans, and shiny lips, and they're giggling and fluttering their eyelashes at the hockey players. I roll my eyes at them.

Finally I give them their checks and they leave. When I start clearing their table, I find a couple of dollar tips and then as I remove Jacob's plate, I find a twenty.

What. The. Fuck.

I stare at it. Rage builds in my chest, a hot pressure. My head whips around, but they're gone.

I scoop it up and shove it into my apron along with the other bills. I finish my shift on fire, whirling, serving, clearing, and cleaning, ready to stomp into that training session and stuff the twenty-dollar bill into Jacob's mouth with my fist.

After going home to change out of my uniform, I get to the training room early enough to quickly review our materials. Soon people are entering and my nerves heighten as I check out each arrival to see if it's Jacob.

When he walks in, his presence is like flicking a switch—everyone turns to look at him, and the air in the room becomes vibrant.

"Is that coffee?" His eyes brighten as he spots the cardboard boxes that Luda's Deli uses for take-out coffees, and the smile he flashes as he strides across the room is brilliant.

"Here, let me pour you one." One of the freshman girls jumps toward the box and grabs a cup.

I resist the eye roll.

"Hey, thanks." His eyes crinkle up all attractively when he directs his smile at her. He takes the cup and turns his attention to me. His smile fades. "Hey, Skylar."

"Hi." I pull the twenty-dollar bill out of my pocket and edge closer to him. I shove it into his front pocket.

His eyes go wide and I realize how close I am to his groin. Now I know he dresses left, and by pushing the bill into his left pocket I am within inches of touching his junk.

I jerk my hand away and stammer, "That's the tip you left me. I don't know what you were thinking, but that was ridiculous."

He blinks slowly at me. "I was thinking you deserved a tip for putting up with our assholish comments to you."

My mouth falls open. "You weren't assholes. You think I haven't heard worse lines than that? And your friend Hunter actually looked ashamed of himself, so I think he doesn't quite qualify as an asshole."

Our eyes meet. Once again, heat burns through me from his gaze, a feeling of being trapped, caught in a web of warmth that pulls me to him.

"Okay, it was a bit over the top," he admits. "But I don't know why you're so pissed about it."

I gaze back at him for a long moment. Finally I admit, "Neither do I."

"You hate me." He makes a face. "That's why. I get it." His mouth tightens and his voice takes on a bitter edge. "I guess I deserve it. Like I deserve all of this." He slashes a hand out, then turns and walks away to find a seat.

I stare after him. What does that mean? His shoulders are tense, his spine stiff . . . and still, I can admire his ass as he walks away. Unlike some guys who have a serious case of lack o' ass, he has an amazing butt.

I whirl around. Here I am trying to educate people about sexual harassment, and I'm objectifying him based on his ass. More hypocrisy. What is happening to me?

I take a few deep breaths and go over my training materials again. Soon I'm facing the group.

"Let's review our learning objectives for this module. By the end of it, you all will be able to correctly answer at least two questions about the incidence and prevalence of sexual assault, identify at least one factor contributing to the underreporting of sexual assault, and list at least two myths and two facts about rape and sexual assault."

I focus on delivering the training. By the end of the hour I sense the energy in the room dipping. We need to do something to get people more involved.

I studiously ignore Jacob as he leaves the room along with the others, then turn to Grace and Chad. "I think we need to do something different for the next session."

"Like what?"

"Well, for the myths and facts part, I'm thinking about handing out sticky notes for people to write their ideas on. Then they can bring them up and put them on the flip chart."

Chad nods. "Sure. We can try that." But Grace makes a face.

"I think we need to be a bit more interactive," I explain. "A few folks looked like they were falling asleep tonight. Plus, I feel like some people . . ." Okay, specifically the men in the group. ". . . aren't totally comfortable speaking up about these things. That way it will be anonymous."

"Okay, sure, then."

Grace still didn't seem impressed with my suggestion so I'm a little nervous the next day, but I leap into it. I ask everyone to close their manuals and I hand out sticky notes. "Take a few minutes and write down ideas about either a myth or a fact about sexual assault on these sticky notes. When you're done, come on up and put your notes on either the 'myth' side or the 'fact' side." I've already drawn the schematic.

When that's done, we break into smaller groups and I start reading out the answers people have put on the chart, asking everyone to comment on whether the note is in the right place. Gradually, everyone opens up and we have some pretty interesting discussions about some of the things people have posted. Then I bring up a few that weren't mentioned and we talk about whether rape can occur in same-sex relationships, and if men can be raped.

"Why do you think there's a myth that men can't be raped?" I scan the room, now that we're back in the large group, avoiding Jacob's eyes.

However, it's him who speaks up. "Biology," he says dryly.

I nod, and wait for other responses.

"I think there's a belief that sex is something that men do *to* women," one woman says slowly.

"Yes, exactly."

"There's a belief that men *always* want sex," someone else says.

After a few minutes, I share a true story I learned last year, not using names, about a guy who got drunk at a party. This isn't part of the usual training, but it was really impactful to me and I think it makes a point. The guy's girlfriend had left the party, but he didn't want to and kept assuring her he was fine. He passed out on a couch, and one of the hostesses offered to let him use her bedroom. While he was there, a girl climbed into bed with him and tried to convince him to have sex. "He was barely conscious, and she took advantage of him even though he tried to tell her he had a girlfriend and he didn't want to do it." I pause. "What do you think his friends said the next day when he told them about it?"

There's silence for a minute, then one guy says, "They probably thought he was lucky."

I nod. "Yeah, when he tried to tell his friends the next day, they were all astonished. They made comments like, 'Lucky you, bro, give us the deets' and 'I bet she didn't hold you down, you dog.' They didn't believe that a woman could have made him do something he didn't want to. Some of them implied that he must have wanted it to happen. Imagine if the gender was reversed."

Everyone is gazing at me raptly. Yeah, using this real-life story is effective.

"Because of societal pressures like that, men are less likely to report rape, but the effects on a man can be exactly the same."

We wrap things up for the day. Everyone rises. Jacob stands too and stretches his big, muscled body. Our eyes meet and I see something on his face I don't know how to interpret. His face is tight, his shoulders tensed and hunched. Then he turns away, pulling his cellphone out of his pocket, and I peer down at the empty coffee cup in my hand as he leaves.

Chapter 7

Jacob

I DON'T KNOW how I'm making it through the prevention and awareness sessions, but I am. Not only is the subject matter horrendous, I have hard time sitting still for very long. Even an hour class has me fidgeting in my seat.

The only thing keeping me going? Skylar.

She's fucking astounding.

Talking about shit like this can't be fun for anyone—it's not supposed to be, I guess. It's supposed to be serious and educational. And yet she makes it interesting and relevant too. By the end of the third session, the group is talking out things way more openly than they were at the start.

I resist getting drawn into discussions because I really don't want to be there. On the other hand, it would be disrespectful to Skylar to sit scowling and silent, and I find I can't do that to her.

I hardly know this girl, but damn, she's got me torqued up.

As I arrive on Thursday, I find myself surrounded by three freshmen girls, who start complimenting my biceps, asking me how much I work out, and when does the hockey season start. I look up to see Skylar frowning at us, but she turns away immediately. A few minutes later, she's trying to get everyone's attention to start the session and the three girls reluctantly move to their seats. I meet Skylar's eyes and give a little shrug, but she coolly ignores me.

Today we're talking about consent.

"We define consent as voluntary, positive agreement between the participants to engage in specific sexual activity." Skylar's eyes avoid mine as she talks, clearly remembering back to our make-out session and me turning down her invitation. Shit.

"Do you all think that verbal consent in an absolute requirement for consensual sexual activity?"

People consider that.

"There are other ways to show you consent," one woman offers.

"Yes, there are."

"Talking about it beforehand kind of kills the mood," Danny says.

There are murmurs of agreement from everyone.

"That can be true too," Skylar agrees. "And it can feel awkward. But talking about what you want and need, and what your limits are, is important if you're going to be that intimate with someone, and it really is the basis for a positive experience."

I have to admire how she can talk so openly about stuff like this and not seem embarrassed or uncomfortable. She makes it less uncomfortable for everyone else too.

Almost everyone else. I find myself shifting in my seat a few times.

"So verbal consent isn't absolutely required, but it is the best way to make sure consent is clear and unambiguous. And the absence of a 'no' should never be understood to mean consent is given. Now, what about alcohol and drugs?" Skylar looks around. "Someone who's incapacitated by drugs or alcohol isn't capable of giving valid consent. Drugs and alcohol can definitely impair judgment about whether consent has been asked for and given."

The question is burning inside me. I lift my hand and ask it. "What if someone is asking for sex? Is that consent?"

Skylar gives me a level look although her cheeks go as pink as her hair. "Is that someone sober or intoxicated?"

"Um . . . I guess that makes a difference."

"Possibly." She takes my question seriously, though. "Asking for sex when one's judgment isn't impaired certainly indicates consent. But when under the influence of drugs or alcohol, asking for sex could be a serious lapse in judgment. Depending on the situation. Also, a person can change his or her mind."

5

I try not to frown. That wasn't what I wanted to hear.

We move on to talking about bystander intervention.

"Bystander intervention is a social science model that predicts that most people are unlikely to help others in certain situations." Skylar makes eye contact again. "I don't know how many of you have ever witnessed something that you're not comfortable with and wondered if you should do something. One time I saw a mother give her young child a smack on the butt, right on the street while we were waiting for a bus. I felt so uncomfortable and so conflicted. I hated seeing her hit that boy. But is it my business how she disciplines her child? The child wasn't seriously hurt, but he was crying and upset. What if she did worse to him at home?" She looks around. "Anyone else ever experience that?"

Well, that opens floodgates. Everyone has a story, some good, some scary.

"Research has shown that one major reason bystanders fail to intervene is that the situation is too ambiguous, and like me seeing the mother spank her child, the bystander is worried about misjudging the situation and being embarrassed by intervening. Sometimes they think the victim is in some way responsible for the situation and is getting what they deserve. Like, I may have thought that child was acting out and needed to be reprimanded. So what we're going to learn today are the skills we need to be able to make that decision and intervene effectively when it's needed."

I like talking about skills. Skills are something concrete and relatable. We talk about hockey skills all the time, so I can get into this.

"Here on campus, there are many situations where we might encounter a situation when it would be good to step in. There may be situations you see someone abusing alcohol. Maybe a hazing situation. Maybe a friend who you suspect has an eating disorder. Or, yeah, possibly sexual assault."

She outlines a model called Step In, with four specific steps that are actually pretty cool and could be helpful.

Whoa. I'm really getting into this. What is even happening to me?

Then we're doing role-playing—which is kind of cheesy, but whatever. I've never been worried about making a fool of myself, so I throw myself into my role. There's lots of laughing and yet people are taking it seriously and really trying.

This makes me feel good for Skylar. What she's doing is amazing . . . and successful. Hell, she even sucked me in—Mr. Bad Attitude.

I'm both aware of her and protective of her. If anyone said or did anything not cool to her, you can bet I wouldn't be standing by, I'd damn well be intervening, punching their lights out.

Yeah, punching isn't one of the actual strategies, but I'm not afraid to throw down when it's needed.

Huh. I don't think I've ever felt protective of a girl before.

Skylar relates the bystander intervention back to consent and checking in to make sure that someone really is consenting. "It's about respecting yourself and others," she finishes.

We end our last session on Friday evening with a review pop quiz that is actually hilarious, with some multiple-choice answers that are over the top, and Skylar and Grace summarize the training. Then we're given information on the various groups within SAPAP we could volunteer for if we choose.

Back home, I wearily toss my messenger bag onto the floor in my room and throw myself down on the bed. But I can only lie there for a minute, energy burning through my veins. I need to go for a run.

I jump up and change into track pants and a T-shirt, then lace up my Nikes. In the kitchen I pause to grab a bottle of water from the fridge. "Whoa, what's with all the beer?"

"For the party tomorrow night," Buck answers from his seat at the kitchen table, where he's got a textbook cracked open.

"What party?"

"You said you were coming." He narrows his eyes at me.

"Bullshit."

"Yeah, you did, we talked about it this morning."

"Christ, that was before I had coffee. You know I don't function before caffeine."

"A house party. You gotta come."

"Why do you care about my social life?" Then I sigh. "You want me to drive again."

"Nah, man. That's against the code."

Oh yeah. The mysterious Bears Bro Code.

"You drove last time, that means we owe you one," he continues. "But not this time. It's only a few blocks from here. We can walk."

"Oh." Well, if it's only a few blocks, I can go for a while and slide out without anyone noticing. "Okay. I'm taking a run. Be back in an hour."

"All right. We're ordering pizza."

"Sounds good."

I fill my lungs with fresh fall air as my feet pound down the pavement. I've been using my runs to learn my way around campus and town. Running is a good way to work my body, but also to empty my head. Today, I find myself thinking about some of the things we talked about in the training. But that's not what I want to think about, so instead I think about hockey and do some visualization about how our first game will go.

I'm still trying to find my place on this team. Coach seems like a good guy. When he sat down with me, he was up front about my past and that I'm being held to a high standard. But he was also enthusiastic about my hockey ability. I've enjoyed our practices so far. He's tough and makes us work our asses off, but I already feel like I've learned a few things from him.

Back home, dripping sweat, I jump into the shower. Lately, showers are time for a little yank and spank, and I lean against the wall as my soaped-up hand slides on my dick. Oh yeah . . . that feels so damn good . . . Dammit, who am I imagining? Skylar.

Why couldn't I have just been a jerk and taken her up on her offer to go upstairs that night? She offered. She was as turned on as I was, and I don't think I'm being an asshole when I say I know that. Neither of us was drunk, it could've been so good . . . even though we'd just met.

Pleasure pours through my body as my orgasm explodes, my body shuddering. The water washes away the evidence and I stand beneath the scalding hot shower for a long moment to catch my breath.

I sigh as I towel off. Naked, I walk from the bathroom to my room.

"Oh hey. Nice."

The female voice stops me in my tracks.

I stare in horror at the girl who's emerged from Rocket's room. I lower the sweaty clothes clutched in my hands to cover my groin. "Sorry! Didn't know anyone was here."

She smiles. "Don't apologize. That was totally my pleasure." She waves a hand up and down toward me as I back into my room.

Damn.

I'm so used to walking around naked—in the dressing room and here—I never even thought there could be someone other than one of the guys around. Well, at least she liked what she saw.

In my room, I discover I've run out of clean clothes.

"What the fuck," I grumble as I shake out a T-shirt I pull from the hamper. I know this is gross, but what else can I do? I step into a pair of black sweats and head downstairs. No females are in sight, only Buck and Soupy opening the pizza boxes, which were just delivered.

"Who do I owe for the pizza?" I grab a plate.

"Me," Buck says. "Ten bucks. Thanks, man."

I'm starving after my run and could eat a large meat lovers' pizza all on my own. "Who was the girl up in Rocket's room? I just flashed her."

"Ha-ha-ha." Buck grins. "That gives new meaning to your nickname, Flash."

Soupy cracks up too. "Seriously?"

I grin. "Didn't know she was here."

"That's the girl he left the party with last Friday." Buck gives Soupy a smirk. "Some people got lucky that night. And by 'some' I mean not you."

"Yeah, yeah, shots received, dickhead."

Buck now frowns at me. "Dude. That shirt is nasty."

I sigh. "I know. I need to do laundry."

"Get on that."

I hate to admit it, but I do, anyway. "I'm not exactly sure how."

They gape at me. "What?"

I shrug. "I missed Laundry 101 when I was traveling and playing hockey. My billet family did my laundry for me."

"Jesus." Buck sighs. "Okay, tomorrow morning, you and me. Laundry lessons. It's pathetic, but I'll help you out."

"Sounds like a fun Saturday."

"No shit." He starts going on about separating lights from darks, the use of stain remover, and hot water versus cold.

"Jesus. I guess when you spend as much as you do on clothes, you have to learn to look after them."

"True that." Buck grins. "You don't wanna ruin a hundred-dollar pair of jeans, that's for sure."

"So what are you guys up to tonight?"

"Poker and cigars night. Barks and Jimmy are coming over."

"Cigars? Barf."

Buck laughs. "Yeah, I kinda agree. But it's a tradition." He pauses.

I don't want an invitation to join them. I need to study, and cigars disgust me. Yet . . .

"You wanna join us?" he says.

"Sure."

I try to sound casual, but I mentally smack myself at my excitement of maybe finally fitting in.

Chapter 8

Jacob

SATURDAY NIGHT, we've just finished our first game of the year, the exhibition game at home against Queens. I've been waiting for this for weeks now—no, *months*, actually, a chance to get on the ice and shoot the puck and play a real hockey game, goddammit.

In the dressing room after the game, I feel the difference. It's subtle but there's a shift in attitude toward me. I'm included in the trash talk and high fives. The guys are all in a great mood from the win, which hopefully sets the tone for the season just starting, and I think they know that I was part of that.

But only a part. Hockey is a funny sport because there can be individual stars—but they don't win games by themselves. There's no getting away from the fact that it's a team sport. I can't score goals unless someone feeds me the puck. Well, I can, but what I'm trying to say is a win comes from the whole team playing together and never from just one player.

Even though I know I have talent, the hockey community teaches us to value teamwork, team success and team rewards. A talented quarterback can be in the spotlight, but a hockey player is nothing without his team.

The only guy who still seems hostile is Black Jack—Jack Jones, who's been a pain in my ass since I arrived here. Our very first practice on the ice he slammed me into the boards with bone-breaking force. I had to hit him back to maintain respect, but that seemed to piss him off even more. Honestly, he's kind of an asshole. He's a senior, so he's been playing on the team for a few years, and I have total respect for the veteran players and try not to overstep my newbie boundaries, but he's not that great of a player and I'm starting to think he's a little bitter about that. Three players on our team have already been drafted into the NHL, but not him. Plus, he's selfish with the puck and some of his hits are bordering on dirty. But I ignore him because the others seem to be more accepting of me.

Adrenaline is still buzzing through my veins from the game and my muscles feel pleasantly tired. I'm gonna have a huge goddamn bruise on my calf from that shot I blocked—what the fuck was I thinking? This was only an exhibition game, there was no need for heroics. But I'm desperate to show everyone I belong here. And maybe I also need to show *myself* I belong here and restore a little of my damaged self-worth.

With hockey. It's who I am. I love it and it felt fan-fucking-tastic to have a stick in my hands and my blades scraping the ice. I love watching plays develop around me, knowing intuitively how to respond, where to go so the puck is on my stick. I love spotting a lane and that moment when I shoot the puck and then wait and watch the twine bulge. The crowd cheers and it's such a fucking rush. It's addictive.

Buck and I first go back to our place to change, because we're not going to that party in our game day suits. Especially Buck, who's wearing some god-awful shiny silver suit that makes me want to cover my eyes. He seems to think he looks all that in it.

I quickly pull on a pair of jeans, a white T-shirt and a gray V-neck sweater, all clean thanks to Buck's laundry lessons this morning. I have to admit he knows what he's doing when it comes to laundry. He's wearing designer jeans and a crazy plaid shirt.

As we walk to the party, I ask, "So who invited us to this? Whose place is it?"

"Natalie. She invited Barks, but told him to invite whoever he wants, and he invited us." Barks is Adam Barker, one of our D-men.

We enter the house and it's the usual party scene, music playing from a sick sound system, the living room packed. I accept a beer someone hands me and Buck and I clink our bottles together in a celebratory toast.

"It's only the first game," he says.

"We made some mistakes," I add. "But we can work on those things."

"Yeah."

Buck plays center and Coach put him and me on a line together for a while tonight, although he was switching things up and who knows what the regular lines will be, but I liked playing with him. I felt like we worked well together and with more time we might have some great chemistry.

"Hi, guys!" A girl with long dark hair greets us with tipsy enthusiasm. "Come on in! I'm Natalie!"

"Hey, Natalie. We're friends of Barks. Er, Adam."

"Ooh, you play for the Bears, don't you?"

"Yep. Is Adam here?"

"In the kitchen." She waves a hand.

Okay, this party is edging into crazy land. "What the fuck is happening?" I mutter to Buck, gesturing. On one side of the living room, four guys have their shirts off.

He frowns. "Those guys are football players."

"We're having a hottest abs contest," Natalie cheerfully tells us. "Excuse me, I'm one of the judges."

"I give him eight out of ten," a girl calls. A cheer erupts from some other onlookers.

"Eight," Buck scoffs. "As if. Now, the guy on the end . . . he's ripped."

I pause to objectively assess the dude's abdominal musculature and nod in agreement. "Yeah. I'd go up against him, though."

"Keep your shirt on, Flash. Your soft, doughy abdomen won't win you shit."

I crack up. Soft and doughy. Bahahaha. "Speak for yourself, my beer belly buddy."

He snorts.

We find the kitchen of the house, which is actually a similar layout to ours. Barks is there and he's surrounded by girls. Sweet. He greets us and we join them. The girls are all pretty. Introductions are made.

"Why do you all call each other such funny names?" a girl named Angela asks.

I shrug. "Guess it's a hockey tradition."

"I love hockey."

Yeah, I've heard that a time or six hundred. I'm experienced enough to know that often it's not true. In the past, I've never really cared to differentiate between loving hockey and loving hockey players, because hey, female attention is goddamn nice. But since I've been at Bayard, I get this feeling of being . . . prey. Which is pretty weird, because I'm usually the one . . . er, preying.

"So what *does* make a blow job great?"

That catches our attention. We all turn to the girl who asked the question and exchange glances.

"Wet," Buck interjects. "It has to be very wet. Too dry is painful."

"But not sloppy wet," Soupy adds. "That's gross."

I decide to contribute, against my better judgment. "The most important thing? The girl's gotta enjoy it. Nothing hotter than a girl who loves giving head."

A chorus of male agreement greets my words. "Oh, hell yeah. It's a total turnoff if she looks like she's being tortured by doing it."

"Also, no teeth," Rocket says.

"What?" The girl who asked the question looks confused. "No teeth? I thought guys like teeth."

We all share a horrified look while silence falls.

"No," Buck says decisively. "No teeth."

"Oh my God." The girl closes her eyes.

"Well, I don't mind a little bit of teeth," Rocket clarifies. "You know . . . maybe just a gentle scrape . . ."

"No wonder he told me to stop going down on him." The girl shakes her head. I'm not sure who she's talking about, but . . . *ouch*. "Why didn't he tell me?"

We exchange glances again. "You know," Soupy says, shifting closer to her, "maybe you just need some lessons . . ."

They move away from the group. My eyes go wide and meet Buck's and we bust out laughing.

I try to mingle and talk to other people. I meet Colt, the quarterback of the Bayard Blazers, the football team. He wasn't one of the guys in the abs contest. I've heard there's a rivalry between hockey and football at Bayard, but this guy seems nice enough. He has a couple of babes hanging around him laughing at everything he says and fluttering their eyelashes, but then another girl comes up and slides her arms around his waist, pressing her front to his side.

"Hey, this is my girlfriend, Addy," Colt introduces us. "Addy, this is Jacob Flass. He plays for the Bears."

I smile at her while the other girls turn their disappointed attention to me. Great. Now I'm second choice. Wait, I don't want to be *any* choice. I want them to leave me alone. Colt and I were having a great discussion about NCAA sports.

I'm trying to make an escape but somehow I end up with Angela again, who seems to be stalking me. The irony of this is not lost on me, that usually I'd be in heaven with all these college girls coming on to me, but now I've committed to not being that guy anymore. Somehow I hadn't anticipated this.

If only I had a girlfriend.

Whoa. What is even happening to me, thinking things like that?

It's because I just saw Colt with his girl, and how that made other girls back off. But it's crazy thinking. I have no time or desire for a girlfriend. I need to keep my nose clean, keep my marks up, and show everyone I belong here and on this hockey team, especially NHL scouts.

Which means now is a good time to sneak out and head home.

Before I can make my getaway, Tiffany, who I met last weekend, appears next to me with a huge smile. "Hey, Jacob! Congrats on the win tonight! I was at the game!"

She hangs on to my arm and presses her boobs against me, fluttering her eyelashes.

I don't want to be rude, but I'm not interested. Last Friday I got Skylar to help me out. What am I gonna have to do to get rid of her tonight?

Then I look up and goddamn if I don't see Skylar moving toward me, carrying a glass of some bright red drink. She takes in Tiffany hanging on my arm and her eyebrows rise. Shit. But I smile at her as she moves a few steps closer.

"Hey, you," I call out to her. I disengage myself from Tiffany and close the distance between Skylar and me, suddenly struck with inspiration. I slide an arm around her waist and lean down to kiss her temple. She goes stiff and wide-eyed against me.

Hey, this worked for Colt earlier.

"Work with me," I mutter near Skylar's ear.

I turn to Tiffany and the girls who'd been talking to Jimmy and Soupy. Oh fuck. What if they know Skylar? But they're regarding her with expressions that indicate they don't. Their expressions *do* indicate confusion. Or maybe annoyance.

58

"So glad you're here, baby." I give her a squeeze. "This is Tiffany. Tiffany, this is my girlfriend, Skylar."

Skylar chokes as Tiffany nods and gives her a tight smile, then wanders off.

We're alone. In a crowd of people, mind you.

Skylar gives me a shove on the chest, but I band my arm tighter around her. She doesn't fight back too hard because she's holding that shittastic bright red drink. "Please." I bend my head. "Just go with it for a few minutes. Save me."

"Save you? Are you kidding me?" She leans back to glare up at me. "Oh, right, I forgot you're so irresistible that girls don't leave you alone."

"I can't help it." A defensive tone edges my voice. "I don't encourage them."

Wide-eyed, she stares at me and then starts laughing. "Jacob, *everything* you do encourages girls."

I'm not sure what's she's implying. Is she calling me a man whore? Because I probably deserved that name at one time. But not now.

"Seriously." I keep my voice low. "You could really help me out here. Can we go somewhere and talk about this?"

"Are you for real? You rejected me. Remember?"

"Aaargh." I close my eyes. I don't know how to get out of this fucked-up situation. All I know is if I let her go, she'll disappear. I glance around. A few people have noticed us, but mostly the drunken party continues around us. I meet Skylar's eyes again. "Please. I'm not trying to be an ass. I know you think my ego is huge, but I really don't want all this attention. I'm trying . . ." I hesitate, knowing she's going to laugh her ass off at this. "I'm trying to stay away from girls this year. I need to do well at school. And especially hockey. I need to stay out of trouble."

She eyes me, a little crease appearing between her eyebrows. "Girls are trouble?"

I let out a long breath. "Girls are awesome. But yeah, sometimes they can be trouble." I study her face, sensing that she's actually listening. "Colt Severn has a girlfriend."

She huffs out a laugh. "Colt Severn, the quarterback of the football team?"

I nod.

"Ooookay. Is this a competition?"

"No! I mean, he has a girlfriend and that keeps other girls away from him."

"Ha. You'd be surprised how it really doesn't."

"Okay, I guess there are some chicks who don't care, but come on, that's pretty cynical."

She wrinkles up her nose and it's so damn cute. "You're right. Sometimes I am cynical."

"Anyway, I figure if they think I have a girlfriend, they'll leave me alone."

One corner of her mouth lifts as she contemplates this. "Hmmm."

"Just pretend to be my girlfriend. For tonight."

She gives a delicate snort-laugh. "Oh sure. And how do I explain that to my friends?"

"I'm sure we can figure out a way." I pause. "I know you hate me, but I'm really not a bad guy. That night you asked me to go upstairs . . . I wanted to. So damn much." I close my eyes and swallow a groan. In fact, my body is responding to having her so close to me again, remembering the sweet taste of her mouth and the feel of her tongue against mine.

Ah shit. The guy downstairs is stirring.

I continue. "Like I said, I'm trying not to get involved with girls this year. That was why I turned you down."

To my shock, she bursts out laughing. "You expect me to believe you're going to be abstinent all year?"

I bite my lip. "No, because I'm not sure I can do it either. Just being honest."

Her smile softens and amusement dances in her amber eyes. "You're serious, aren't you?"

"As serious as a breakaway on an empty net."

She laughs again. "So what do I get out of this deal?" Then she smacks my shoulder. "And you better not offer to pay me! That was so insulting."

"Okay, okay. No money. Um . . ." My mind searches. "Okay, how about this. Pretend to be my girlfriend and I'll get all the hockey guys to come to your big pizza fundraiser and sign those affirmative consent pledges."

"Hmm." Her eyes narrow at me. I know the fundraiser is important to her, from when she was talking about it before one of the training classes. "Really? You'd do that?"

"Sure." I'm not actually sure if I can deliver on this, but I'll definitely try. "I'll even help with the fundraiser. What do you need me to do?"

She blinks. "Uh. We need prize donations for the silent auction. People to serve pizza and sell silent auction tickets, and help us set up."

"I can do that." Christ, I have enough on my plate, I don't know why I'm saying this. Okay, I do know.

"All that and just for one night I have to pretend to be your girlfriend?"

"Hmm, you're right. I think you should pretend to be my girlfriend for . . ." I get stuck on this. I have no idea how long I'll need her. "The rest of the school year."

She chokes again. "What?"

"Ah hell." I frown. "If guys think you have a boyfriend, nobody's going to ask you out." My spirits plummet. This has to be a major "con" for her in this plan. "You probably don't want that."

She shakes her head. "I'm not interested in dating."

"Why not?"

She drops her gaze to my chest and sighs. "Well, like you, I'm trying to do well this year. Last year, I, uh, failed two courses."

"Shut the fuck up. No way."

"Way." She nods, still not looking at me. "Something happened and I was kind of messed up. I told you how hard I have to work to just pass my courses, never mind get marks like my sister did. My parents were so disappointed in me. I can't let that happen again. Plus with my part-time job and my volunteer work . . . I don't have time for a boyfriend."

"Perfect! You have time for a fake boyfriend."

She lifts her chin and our eyes meet. "I don't know. How much time is this fake boyfriend going to require?"

"Ha. Minimal. We just need to be seen together once in a while. You know . . . lunch. Studying together. Maybe the odd time we could go to a party together. The guys get on my ass if I spend too many weekends studying."

"As do my friends."

She appears to be actually considering this genius yet somewhat insane idea.

Chapter 9

Skylar

AM I actually thinking about agreeing to his ridiculous suggestion?

Getting all the hockey players involved in the fundraiser would be a major, major coup. And not only would Victoria be impressed with me, we really would be able to reach more people, because although it pains me to admit it, if the hockey guys are there, a lot of other people will want to come. It would be fantastic.

Yeah, guys won't ask me out if they think I have a boyfriend. But they aren't beating my door down for dates anyway, so it's not much of a loss, and I'm really not interested. Or, I *thought* I wasn't interested, until Jacob somehow got my girl parts all revved up. Plus, maybe it would also keep Ella, Nat, and Brooklyn off my case about partying if I have study dates with a hot guy.

Me with a hot guy.

Faking it, mind you. Totally faking it.

I eye Jacob. My body is tingling everywhere, with him holding me against all his muscles. He's strong and warm, and that face . . . He thinks girls are all over him because he's a hockey player, but the truth is, they'd be all over him if he were the Zamboni driver. That cleft chin, the high cheekbones, that smile. I'm melting and this is all fake.

Okay, not *all* fake. There was a busload of chemistry between us that night, and we were exploring it. I was ready to throw good judgment under the wheels of that bus to go upstairs with him and . . . yeah, I probably would have had sex with him if we'd done that.

I swallow. I haven't had sex since . . . well, quite a while. I'm nervous about it, honestly. But Jacob made me totally forget that. Now I'm supposed to hang out with him and pretend to be his girlfriend? I'm somewhat concerned about my ability to be that good an actor. Because that chemistry is still smoking between us.

The warm sincerity in his eyes now tugs at something inside me. He really wants to avoid girls so he can do well at school? My heart goes all wobbly. Holy duck fuck, if he asked me to strip naked and get up on the coffee table and dance, I'd consider it right now.

"Fine." I toss my hair back. "As long as it's mutually agreeable. Either of us can end this at any time."

"Deal."

His smile makes my heart leap in my chest and my girl parts squeeze. And judging from the bulge behind his fly, he feels the same.

"Um, I'm just gonna say it . . . this deal doesn't include sex, does it?"

His grin goes wicked. "Only if it's mutually agreeable."

"Oh, you're good." I arch an eyebrow. "That would be taking a fake relationship a little too far, don't you think?"

"Okay, honestly, I wasn't thinking about sex. Christ." He closes his eyes. "I can't believe I just said that. I'm pretty much *always* thinking about sex."

I laugh. "At least you're honest."

"I am. I *am* an honest guy."

His earnest words have my heart fluttering wildly again.

"So no sex," he adds, but he looks like he's in pain. This doesn't help my aching pussy. It also weirdly reassures me that he didn't reject me last weekend because I'm a total loser. "And I'll deny it if anyone asks if we are, and defend your virtue."

"That's really not necessary," I say dryly. "Not that our fake sex life is anyone's business, but I'm not a virgin."

"Hey, here's an idea. We can just take things slow, right?" His smile makes my nipples harden.

I smile back, somehow totally hooked by his charm.

"What are you drinking, anyway?" He glances down at my glass.

"Kool-Aid."

"What?"

"Cherry Kool-Aid. Want some?"

"Uh, no. I haven't drunk Kool-Aid since I was about ten. Is there vodka in there?"

"Nope." I smile. "Just Kool-Aid."

"Okay."

"It's good. I'm trying to stay sober tonight so I don't try to proposition the first hot guy who talks to me." I make a face. "Unlike last weekend."

"Are you sure you aren't interested in a boyfriend?"

"Yes, I know that wasn't exactly in line with my plan to not be distracted from studying. I was a little, uh . . ."

He smirks.

"Don't let your already oversized ego get so big you can't get through the door."

He laughs and releases me, finally, but I only move a little apart from him so I can take a sip of my drink. "Did you come with your friends again?"

"Nope. I live here."

"Shit. Really? This is your place?"

"Yeah. Natalie's one of my roommates. She and Brooklyn and Ella all wanted to have this party. Me, not so much. Another reason for staying sober —to make sure things don't get out of hand." I bite my lip. "Actually, it might be too late for that."

"Nah."

I turn and survey the room. It's packed with bodies, the music is loud, people are yelling, but so far things seem benign. There's a couple making out in an armchair and—

A crash of breaking glass in the kitchen has us both going on alert. Our eyes meet.

"I better go check that out." I scurry toward the kitchen. I find a girl and two guys laughing hysterically as they try to clean up a broken glass.

"Oh shit, I cut myself!" The girl holds up her hand, dripping blood.

"Aw fuck, don't show me that, I can't stand the sssss—" And one of the dudes passes out, sprawled on the tile floor.

"Shit," Jacob mutters behind me.

He rushes over and lifts the guy's shoulders. "Skylar, help her." He nods at the girl who is still laughing and dripping blood.

I grab some paper towels and wrap her hand in them. "Come to the bathroom with me so I can see how bad it is. We'll find you a bandage."

The unconscious guy and bleeding girl have put a damper on the hilarity and others are quietly cleaning up the mess. I leave them to it with a quick, concerned glance at Jacob and the other guy. Luckily he was crouched on the floor when he passed out. Jacob's trying to get him to come to, his head shoved between his knees. I'm worried about how much the guy has had to drink.

"I'm Skylar," I tell the girl, leading her upstairs. "And you're . . . ?"

"Uma."

"Okay, Uma, let's see that cut." She sits on the toilet and I unwrap her hand. My stomach clenches, anticipating the worst, like a severed finger or something, but it's only a small cut. I clean it up and wrap a Band-Aid snugly around it. "There you go."

"Thanks." She wiggles her finger. "Sorry about the glass. I guess it wasn't really that funny."

"Well, a broken glass isn't a big deal. A severed finger on the other hand . . . Luckily you're okay."

"I'm good. I better go check on Kyle."

"Is he your boyfriend?"

"Nah, just a friend. He's pretty squeamish."

Kyle is fine, now seated on a kitchen chair, drinking a glass of water, a little pale. The floor has been cleaned up. "Jesus," Kyle says on seeing Uma. "You okay?"

"I'm good. You?" Uma sits on his lap. Just friends? Oooookay.

I meet Jacob's eyes, draw in a long slow breath and let it out. Wow. Suddenly I think I need to sit down.

"C'mere." He reaches for me and pulls me into a hug, resting his chin on top of my head. "Okay?"

"Yeah. Scared me a bit." It feels good to be held like this when I'm a little shaky.

"No shit. Could've been way worse."

"I wish there weren't so many people here."

"Yeah." He pauses. "You want more Kool-Aid?"

"Sure."

With my glass full, he leads me to a chair in the dining room. "Sit here for a minute. I'll be right back."

I sip my drink and watch him wind through the bodies. His size means people move out of his way. He pauses near his friends that I met at the diner the other night and says something to them, then gives one guy a clap on the back. They all nod.

I watch him do the same thing with a different guy, who Natalie introduced me to earlier, another Bears player. Then Jacob returns to me.

"What are you doing?" I tip my head way back to squint at him.

"Just mentioned to the guys to keep any eye on things. Anything starts getting out of hand, we'll take care of it."

I give him a slow blink. "You guys are our party cops?"

He grins and tweaks my chin. "Yeah. That's it."

"Is that what hockey players do?"

He shrugs. "Nah. It just helps when you're bigger than most people."

Something in my chest goes soft and warm. "Thank you."

"See? Told you I'm a good guy."

I'm not completely convinced yet, but I have to admit Jacob is winning me over.

He drops to a crouch next to me. "So hey, I wanted to tell you . . . you were amazing in that training."

My mouth falls open. "What do you mean?"

"You're really good at it. You got everyone involved, even when nobody was saying much at the start. Kept the energy up. It seemed like you were really reading everyone."

I don't even know what to say. My mouth closes. Then opens again. Finally I come up with, "Thank you."

"Plus you're knowledgeable and you obviously care a lot about what you're teaching."

I nod. "Yeah." I take a quick sip of my drink. "It's important. SAPAP helped me last year through a tough time and I like the feeling of helping others."

He frowns. "You . . . ?"

My insides tighten up. "My friend Brendan took his own life. I went for some counseling there."

"Oh." His frown changes. "I'm sorry."

I drop my gaze. "Yeah. It was tough. It still is."

"That's what happened? You said last year something happened and you were messed up."

"Yes."

He curls his fingers around one of my hands. I can tell my hand is icy, mostly from holding the cold glass of Kool-Aid, because his is so warm. And strong. His thumb rubs over the back of my hand. "That really sucks."

I nod. "But I'm okay." I lift my head to give him a smile. "It sucked gorilla butt, but we're getting through it."

He chokes on a laugh, but his eyes are warm on me. "I have no doubt."

There's a minor skirmish in the living room and I hear a guy saying loudly, "Yeah, yeah, chill, man. Sorry."

Jacob and I turn that way, then look back at each other. My lips quirk. "Your boys are stepping up."

He grins. "Damn straight. Come on. Let's go join the party."

He pulls me out of the chair and we walk hand in hand into the living room.

Weird.

It's not long before Ella corners me alone. "What's up with you and the hockey player?"

"You mean Jacob?"

She scrunches her face. "No, I mean Wayne Gretzky."

I laugh. "We're, um, kind of seeing each other."

"Since when?"

I tell her about meeting him that night at the party at Sigma house, and then him being in the training sessions, not really lying but omitting some details so it sounds plausible.

"He's hot, Skylar."

"I know." Truth.

She squeezes my arm. "Wow. Good for you."

Excitement wriggles inside me, which is stupid because Jacob and I are only pretending. But the reality is, it is kind of exciting being around him.

Since it's my job, I keep an eye on other girls to make sure nobody's bugging him, and for the most part, this does seem to be working. When we meet up again, we stand close together and I can feel the looks from other females at the party.

"You should come to our game Friday night," Jacob says.

I purse my lips. "Hmmm. I don't really care for hockey that much."

"What?" Eyes wide, he slaps a hand to his chest as if he's been stabbed. "You did not just say that."

I grin. "Sorry, I did."

"I can't even . . ." He shakes his head, but his lips are quirked. "But still, as my girlfriend you should be there to support me."

"Yeah, I don't know. I'm down with playing the girlfriend role when we're out together, but at a game?" I shake my head. "Besides, I could get a lot of studying done Friday night."

His shoulders slump.

"You really want me to come?"

"Well, sure. I saw you in action, doing that training. You should see me in *my* element."

"Your element. You're probably really good, aren't you?"

"Come and find out."

"I'll see." I'm actually tempted to do this, curious about him and his hockey skills. It's true I've never been a hockey fan—but then, I'm not into football or basketball either. I've never really gotten that whole jock appeal thing. I mean, I get that the guys are athletes and therefore in great shape, but what's so attractive about guys running around tackling each other or smashing each other into the boards?

Okay, I totally get the jock appeal.

I'm sitting in the stands at the DeWitt Center on Friday night with Ella, who agreed to come with me to the game as long as we go out after. I've blown off an entire evening of studying for this, and right now I don't even care.

I'm vibrating with adrenaline and arousal. The testosterone is up to the rafters of the arena, all those big bodies out there flying around at crazy speeds, flinging the puck at the net, hurtling themselves without any regard for personal safety to slam another player into the boards. They're fearless skating into the corners for the puck, knowing there's an opponent right behind them who's going to slam them hard. If that were me, I'd leave the puck there and run— er, skate—the other way. Or pass the puck to someone else as fast as I could.

It's only a game, but I see determination, courage, sacrifice, and loyalty out there on the ice. Some of the players are clearly better than others—and yeah, Jacob is one of those. In fact, he stands out with his speed and puck handling, drawing all eyes whenever he's on the ice. He makes it look so easy and yet I know it's not. But despite his obvious talent, he's no diva. He hits as much as he gets hit. He passes the puck to others and doesn't hog it. He threw himself in front of the puck to block a shot, sacrificing his body. He scores two goals, but he also gets two assists. He goes after one of the other team's players when that guy laid a hit on one of the Bears that had the whole crowd booing and yelling. I'm not exactly sure what the difference is between a clean hit and a dirty hit, but apparently everyone else here knows, and they're pretty upset about that hit and also by the fact that it didn't result in a penalty. They cheer when Jacob checks the guy at center ice the next time they're both on the ice together, laying him flat out.

As Jacob skates away from that, adjusting his helmet, I experience a fluttery sensation low in my belly. "Whoa," I breathe to Ella. "I think I just had an orgasm."

She giggles and leans her shoulder into mine.

"I should hate this," I say. "It's violent and brutal. I feel guilty for being turned on by it."

"Uh-oh. Did you just become a puck bunny?"

"No! Well, maybe."

"No, no, I don't think you meet the definition."

I slide her an amused look. "There's a definition?"

"Yeah. A puck bunny is only interested in hockey players because they're hockey players. Since you started seeing Jacob before you ever saw him play hockey, and you don't even like hockey, that's not the case."

"Truth." I nod. "Plus the term 'puck bunny' is a little demeaning and slut-shamey."

"Whatever, Skylar."

I'm a little overwhelmed by the Bayard Pep Band playing songs that people are shouting along to. There are all kinds of taunting cheers the crowd is yelling at the refs and at the other team. And there are a lot of mysterious names being shouted out at various points when the band plays that confuse me. I have to say, the fans here are really, really into this game. It's kind of cool.

My gaze follows Jacob down the ice. He gets the puck at the other team's blue line. There's a Princeton guy right behind him and two flanking him, trying to get the puck away from him. I don't know how he does it, but he stick handles around all three of them, skates in on the net, shoots, and scores. The crowd goes nuts.

"Wow." I shoot Ella a sideways glance as we stand, clapping. I lean over closer so she can hear me over the roar. "He wasn't lying when he said he's good."

"He said that?" She smiles. "Cocky much?"

"Oh yeah, he's cocky. But it appears he has good reason to be."

I watch him skate by the bench and bump gloves with the other players to celebrate his goal. "That's so cute."

He leaves the ice and scootches down the bench to make room for others. He's sweating and panting and holy duck fuck, my pussy is throbbing. He grabs a towel and cleans off the inside of his visor with fast, practiced movements, then focuses on the play as they drop the puck at center ice. He and the other guys all yell as one of the Bears gets the puck, beats the Princeton defensemen and races toward the Princeton net alone.

"Breakaway!" someone yells behind me, and everyone is shouting, "Go, go, go!"

When he shoots and misses, there's a huge collective groan. Weirdly, I'm more interested in watching Jacob on the bench than the player who could have scored. Jacob sits back at the missed shot and slams a hand onto the top of the boards.

Now I wish Jacob *was* my real boyfriend because, holy hotness, I want to jump him and ride him like a mechanical bull.

Chapter 10

Jacob

WHEN BUCK and I arrive at the party after the game, I immediately spot Skylar from across the room as she looks around with a hesitant smile, searching out . . . me, maybe? Or maybe anyone she knows. She tucks a strand of hair behind her ear in a gesture becoming familiar, one that makes my chest feel weird. I head toward her.

I noticed her in the stands at the game. I was focused on the game, but knowing she was there made every goal and assist that much sweeter. I wanted to impress her, because so far she's been decidedly unimpressed with me. I'm not used to that.

Our eyes meet and her smile widens. It doesn't feel like we're acting. When I reach her, I slide my hand around the back of her neck and kiss her forehead. "Hey, you're here."

"We just got here." She gestures to Ella behind her.

"Hi, Jacob." Ella smiles at me.

"Hey, Ella. Come on in. Let's get you ladies a drink."

"We brought Moscato." Ella holds up a bottle.

I lead the way to the kitchen, where there's a bar set up on an island. I open one of their bottles and pour generous portions into red cups. "Sorry, there doesn't appear to be fancy wine glasses here."

"No worries." Skylar takes a cup and gives me a smile.

I introduce Ella to Buck, and both of them to some of the other guys. Soupy and Rocket arrive and a bunch more people.

"So?" I peer into Skylar's eyes. "Did you enjoy the game?"

She sinks her white teeth into her bottom lip and nods. "Um, yeah. More than I expected."

Why does she look guilty?

"Yeah? Good."

"It's super fast," she adds. "And . . . violent."

I laugh. "It's physical, yeah. But there weren't even any fights tonight."

She eyes me as she sips her wine. "Do you fight?"

I shrug. "I don't look for fights, but there are times you just have to drop the gloves. But here, you get ejected from the game if you fight."

She gives a tiny shudder.

I nudge her with my body. "You're worried about me, right?"

She rolls her eyes, but her lips tick up at the corners. "Sure."

"I got two goals."

I instantly feel like a dummy for saying that. Like I'm fishing for compliments.

But she beams at me, eyes glowing. "I know! It was so exciting. And two assists." She hesitates. "Not that your ego needs any boosting, but you're really good, Jacob."

My chest tightens, but I keep my expression easy, a little cocky. "Yeah, I am."

She swats my chest, but she's laughing. I catch her hand and slide my fingers between hers.

"It felt great," I say honestly. "I love playing hockey."

"I can see that."

Our eyes meet and we share a moment of . . . something. She understands. This is my passion.

Skylar seems kind of buzzed and she hasn't even finished one drink. She's almost vibrating and tense, and her eyes are hot.

Okay, wait . . . she's turned on.

My dick takes notice of this. My dick *always* takes notice of Skylar but knowing she's hot for me because of watching me play hockey is even more arousing. The eye contact shifts as Skylar's gaze drops to my mouth. Blood rushes south. I want to kiss her so badly, it's like I'm starving. Heat builds around us. "Whoa, baby," I murmur, reaching to stroke some hair back off her face. "Keep looking at me like that I might have to get you alone and screw you silly."

She inhales sharply and her lips part even more.

"Do you want that, baby?" I pet her hair more. I love how silky it is. And how long.

"Okay, yes," she whispers. "But sex wasn't part of the deal. And we're supposed to take it slow."

"Maybe we could just make out for a while and see how it goes."

She chokes on a little laugh, which is good because I was trying to be funny. Sort of.

Okay, I do want to make out with her. A lot.

"How're you feeling, baby?" I shift closer so our bodies are touching. "Are you aching?"

Her eyes go dark gold and her lashes droop. She swallows. "Oh God. Yes."

"Me too."

What am I doing? Damn, she gets me all hot and twisted up inside. Why is that? I have puck bunnies coming on to me all the time. Yeah, they like it that I play hockey. I like it that they like that. But for some reason, *Skylar* liking it is a whole different hockey game.

Lust punches through my stomach, heat rushing through me.

"For Chrissake, would you two get a room?"

Buck's amused voice cuts through the fog of lust surrounding us. I exchange a wry glance with Skylar, whose cheeks go adorably bright pink, then shoot Buck a scowl. He's grinning.

"*Great* idea," I say.

"We're putting on a good act," Skylar whispers in my ear.

I laugh at that and slide my arm around her waist to pull her up against me. She feels slight and delicate, and I like that because I want to protect her. "Baby." I nuzzle her ear. "This is no act."

"Okay, true." She tilts her head and gives me a sleepy-eyed look. "We're physically attracted to each other. But we're not really a couple."

"Sure." I'm good with that. "Wanna go find a room?"

"Um." She presses her lips briefly together. "Yes. But no."

"Damn."

This is funny, considering that I turned down *her* offer to find a room and now she's turning me down. Only I'm not laughing.

"I can't stay late. I have to work tomorrow."

"Again, damn." I sigh. She's right. I recognize that voice in my ear—it's reason. Dammit.

I need to listen to that voice. I need to stay out of trouble this year. Having Skylar as my fake girlfriend is supposed to help me do that.

It's working. No other girls are throwing themselves at me or even flirting with me, although a couple have given me interested looks. But why do I feel like Skylar could be a whole lot of some other kind of trouble?

I give her long eye contact that makes my dick even harder, then turn. With my arm still around her waist, we move back into the crowd to mingle. It's not a huge party, but obviously people here are hockey fans who were at the game and who're eager to congratulate us on the win. Some guys want to dissect the play and discuss possible lines and how we could do better. I love talking hockey, so this is fun for me. Skylar's listening and seems engaged, but I wonder how much fun it is for her. She's doing a great girlfriend imitation, though.

Skylar and I separate as she starts talking to some girls about a course they were in together, but a while later she's back. "I'm going to find Ella and head home," she says, rising on tiptoe to speak into my ear.

I pull out my cellphone to check the time. "I guess it is getting late."

But after looking around, we can't find Ella. Skylar bites her lip and casts a glance up the stairs.

"You think she's up there?"

"Probably. Let me text her." She quickly sends a message.

"You think she'll answer you?"

"She better. We never leave each other at a party unless we know the other's safe."

I nod, impressed. "That's smart."

Skylar's phone pings and she peers at it. "She says she's fine and she's going home with Eric."

"All right. Did she drive here?"

Skylar shakes her head. "No. We took the bus."

"Okay, then, I'll take you home."

"You're okay to drive?"

"Yeah." Again, I'm on my best behavior because if I got caught driving drunk, I'd be out on my ass. "Let's go."

I find Buck talking to Jimmy and give them both slaps on the shoulder as

I tell them I'm taking Skylar home. Leaving this early would get me some snarky comments normally, but since I'm leaving with a girl, I get smirks of approval.

Skylar is quiet on the drive to her place. This makes me nervous. I've been with lots of girls, and there've been a few I dated more than once, but I've never had a real girlfriend, so I'm not that great at knowing what's going through a woman's head. Skylar's not really my girlfriend, so I'm not sure why it matters to me, but I like her.

So since I've always found it best in hockey and in life to just go for it, I say, "You're quiet. Everything okay?"

She gives a quick nod. "Oh yeah. Sorry. I'm . . . I've been a little concerned about Ella lately."

"Why's that, baby?"

"She's been acting different since our friend died. I mean, I'm not all judgy and prissy. It's fine to drink and hook up with guys. Yet every time I try to talk to her, it comes across as me nagging her like a mom, or being a big prude." She rolls her eyes. "So I've backed off, but she gets drunk every weekend and she's been hooking up with a lot of different guys."

"Huh." My fingers tighten on the steering wheel. "You know, that sounds like normal college stuff."

"Yeah, I know. That's why I've backed off. It might be just me overreacting. But I have this feeling that even though she says she's okay, she's not."

"Ah." I like it that she cares about her friend, but I don't like it that she's worried. "You know her better than I do. If you have a feeling, you're probably right."

She turns to me, her face shadowy in the dark car. "Thank you. Thank you for saying that."

Did I do something right? I don't even know. I nod.

I park in front of Skylar's house and walk her to the door. The house is dark so I wait until she unlocks the front door and steps inside to turn on the hall light.

I want to kiss her.

She's not my real girlfriend, so I don't have to end this "date" with a kiss . . . but I want to. Every time I think about kissing her and how sweet her mouth was and how soft her body was pressed up against me, it turns into me either fighting off a woody or wanking off. "So about that making out . . ."

She gives a soft laugh that relieves me. "Come in."

Kelly Jamieson

I follow her inside and close the door behind us, my blood racing hot and straight to my dick. We walk into the living room, where she turns on another light, a big floor lamp in the corner. I sit on the couch and lift my chin.

She's so pretty. I watch her walk toward me, her jeans hugging her hips and thighs, the hem of a sheer top fluttering beneath the thin sweater she has on over it. Her long hair shines gold in the light. She sits beside me by first setting one knee on the couch cushion, then tucking that leg beneath her, and she rests her arm on the back of the couch so she's facing me.

I shift so I'm facing her too. "Are your roommates all out?"

"Yes." She traces an index finger down my chest. "I don't know if making out is such a good idea."

"Yeah." I think I know where she's coming from. "But we both want to do it."

"Yes."

I lean in and touch my mouth to hers in a soft kiss. Her breathing hitches and her eyelids droop. I draw back and wait, studying her. Pink washes into her smooth skin and her soft lips are parted.

"Kiss me," she whispers.

There we go. I reach for her and pull her closer, tilting my head and finding her mouth with mine. She makes a low noise that sounds like relief or pleasure or maybe both, and that's exactly how I feel too.

With one hand on her hip, I tangle the other into her hair. Tingles work down the back of my neck and my spine, centering in my balls. Need for her burns over my skin. I use my grip on her hair to gently adjust the angle of her head and I feast on her soft mouth, licking inside, biting at her lips.

She opens to me, so sweet and lush, her body melts against me, and I know I'm in big trouble. One of her hands slides into my hair and pulls my head to her, even though we can't get any closer. Our mouths are fused together. Her other hand is on my back, pressing, like she's afraid I'm going to get away, and holy hell that makes me so hot. My dick is throbbing.

She makes a soft sound full of desire and I'm dizzy with lust for her. She tastes sweet, her tongue is small but strong against mine. I suck on her top lip, then her bottom lip, gliding my hand up her side, letting my thumb brush against the outer curve of her breast.

I keep kissing her and kissing her, sliding my tongue around hers, sucking on it. Then our mouths part and we both gasp for air. My heart is

76

thudding so hard I can hear it in my ears, my chest rising and falling with rapid respirations.

"Wow, Jacob." She rubs up and down my back, over my sweater. "You're such a good kisser."

I focus on her mouth, my vision a little blurry. Her lips are puffy and wet, and Jesus, my dick leaps. Lust is rampaging through me, shorting out my brain and making me stupid. All I can think is how much I want her.

"You are too," I manage to utter before going back in for more kisses. "Want your mouth again. Give me your mouth."

I get my arm around her slender torso and maneuver her beneath me so we're lying on the couch now, me half on top of her, my thigh between her legs. Her hair is spread out all around her head, so gorgeous. I kiss her lips, then run my open mouth along her jaw, suck gently on the skin beneath her ear, then lick it.

A moan leaks from her lips and her hips lift against my thigh. I meet her there because I know she needs that pressure. It's making me nuts. "Want to make you feel good, baby. So good."

She makes an unintelligible sound and runs her hands up and down my back and over my shoulders. Then she finds skin. Her hands slip under my sweater and T-shirt and clutch my bare back.

"Damn, baby. I love how hot you are for me."

"I am." She seeks my mouth with hers again, sounding almost like she's surprised. "I am hot for you."

Nobody's home. We can do whatever we want. That stupid voice of reason is speaking in my head again, though, reminding me that I'm supposed to be avoiding situations like this.

But I don't want to stop.

Chapter 11

Skylar

"Chemistry," I gasp. "If Organic Chem was this fun, I'd be a scientist for sure."

Jacob leans his forehead on mine, both of us panting. My body is hot and pulsing everywhere, but especially between my legs, where I'm aching with ferocious need.

"Hell yeah, we've got chemistry. But I don't think it's something you can put together in a lab." He brushes his mouth over mine again. "There's no formula for this. This is fucking magic."

My heart trips at that. I inhale a long, shaky breath and swallow.

I set a hand flat on his chest to hold him away from me, much as I want him to keep kissing me, to move his big body right over top of me and press me down into the couch cushions. The weight and heat of his body delights me and I crave more of it. And yet . . . "We need to slow down."

He closes his eyes and looks pained. "Okay."

Tension vibrates in him, his hot skin damp beneath his clothes, the enormous bulge behind his fly pressing into me. I know how hard this is for him, and it's hard for me too. This feeling . . . it's what makes people lose their minds and do stupid things. I don't want to be stupid. But damn, it's impossible to resist,

The weird thing is, I want to have sex. I want it so bad. This is the first time since . . . I squeeze my eyes shut, blocking out the memory. I never thought I'd want to have sex again, but Jacob has made me want it, so much I'm desperate and shaky and aching for it.

This is a good thing.

I go still, as that thought enters my head and circles around. This is a very good thing. It's good to feel like this again, to want this so much. So why am I hesitating?

"I'm sorry," I pant. "I'm just . . . this is . . . oh God." I'm terrified of how much I'm feeling when I haven't felt anything like this for nearly a year.

"It's okay." He strokes my hair off my face in a tender gesture that makes me want to jump him. "It's okay, Skylar. You know what? I want to make you feel good, but there are lots of ways we can do that."

My skin burns, heat sliding up into my face. I'm intrigued. "Oh yeah?"

"*Oh* yeah." He lifts one eyebrow. Screaming Jesus, he's sexy.

"What did you have in mind?"

His tongue drags across his bottom lip and his eyes are dark and heavy-lidded. "I have a confession."

I blink. "What?"

"The night after I met you at that party and we made out . . . I went home and jacked off."

My chest tightens and my belly warms. I smile at him, and caress the nape of his neck with my fingertips. "Well, then, I'll confess too . . . I did the same."

"Shit." He gazes at me. Then he gives his head a small shake. "Whoa. Just imagining that almost made me come in my jeans." The corners of his mouth deepen in that sexy smile of his. "Actually, I've done it more than just that night, thinking about you." He touches my hair again. "I can get you off. With my fingers. Or with my mouth."

"Oh."

"Or we can watch each other do it."

My head feels suddenly very light and spinny. "That is so hot."

"I know. Christ." A groan rumbles up from his throat. "I have a condom. But if you want to take things slow, we can do something else." His face sobers. "You're in charge here, Skylar."

My heart turns over in my chest. I can't breathe and my gaze is locked on him. My bottom lip trembles and I have to close my eyes. My breath comes in shallow bursts as I try to deal with the emotions swamping me.

"Hey. You okay?"

I nod and swallow through a tight throat. "Yes." Then I open my eyes and meet his once more. He has no idea how important what he just said is to me. "I am."

"Okay, then. Gonna get you out of your clothes. I'm gonna touch you everywhere and get you really hot."

"I'm already hot."

His lips quirk again. "Hotter. Because that'll make it even better. Then you're going to touch yourself and I'm going to watch."

"Will you . . ." I have to swallow again. "Will you touch yourself too?"

"If you want." He holds my gaze steadily. "I'm dying and I need to come so bad. But I can wait."

"God, now." I let out a groan. I want him to feel good too. "Please. You do it too. We can . . ." Air sticks in my throat. "We can watch each other."

He sucks briefly on his bottom lip and casts a look at the front door. "Here?"

It's risky, but I'm pretty sure my housemates won't be home for a long while. "Yes."

He leans down and presses a hard kiss to my mouth. Heat is racing through my veins and pooling low in my belly. With tender care, he sits me up and pulls my tops over my head. He leaves my bra on while he peels my jeans off me, which is a bit of a struggle because they're tight. The blaze in his eyes as he studies me makes my face heat even more but his words reassure me.

"Damn, you're beautiful." He runs a finger from the bow on my bra between my breasts down my abdomen to the bow at the top of my panties. "Sweet and sexy." He bends his head and kisses my chest between my breasts, pausing to inhale as if he's breathing me in.

My body goes liquid and every nerve ending jumps.

He slips his hands beneath me to find the clasp of my bra. Then it's gone too, and he makes a choked noise that sounds like awe. Pleasure pours through me and my nipples tighten.

"So beautiful." With almost worshipful touches, he cups my aching breasts in his hands. This makes me melt even more, sweetness drizzling down through me. My breasts swell against his palms and he gently squeezes them, then once more lowers his head to nuzzle, kiss and then, dear sweet Jesus, he takes a nipple into his mouth and tugs.

Sensation shoots to my core, my hips lift off the couch and I give a soft cry. My head goes back and my eyes close as he sucks and licks and pets me there, but I want to see him and when I drag my eyes open and lift my head to watch, heat flames around me. He's so beautiful, his eyes closed, his long lashes resting on those high, sculpted cheekbones, his mouth closed around my nipple. His tongue licks over my sensitive flesh and he lays a string of small kisses across to my other nipple, where he closes his lips around it and sucks again.

I was hot for him before, but now I'm burning up, the ache behind my clit sharpening into exquisite need. I try to grind up against him and he lifts his head and gives me a wicked smile.

"You wanna come now, gorgeous?"

"Oh God, yes!"

He presses a kiss right between my breasts. "Knew I could make you even hotter."

"You cocky ass."

His smile is sin and sex, and then he licks his way down my abdomen until he's kneeling between my spread thighs. He hooks his fingers into my panties and slides them down my legs.

I'm burning up, sensation sizzling across my flesh as he regards me in this intimate position. I keep my thighs pressed primly together but still he studies the triangle of light brown hair where they join. Then he rises up onto his knees, reaches for the hem of his sweater and lifts it up and over his head.

He's wearing two layers and they're both gone, tossed to the floor. My mouth falls open and I drink in the sight of his naked chest.

"Sweet Jesus on a Ferris wheel," I whisper, which makes him choke on a laugh.

"What?" XX

I shake my head, staring at his body. This shouldn't be a surprise to me— I can see how fit he is even with his clothes on, and he's a high-level athlete, but having this ripped, naked body right there in front of me stuns me.

I reach out to touch, exploring with my eyes and my fingertips and palms —the ridges of muscle, the hot satiny skin, the small nipples. "Wow."

His eyes darken and his sexy smile returns. "That sounds positive."

"Oh yeah."

He has to move off me to get rid of his jeans. He stands and takes his time with the button fly and then lowers them, almost like he's doing a strip-tease and deliberately tormenting me. It takes a lot of confidence to do that and he clearly has that in spades. When he's standing naked, I have to force myself to look at his cock.

My throat squeezes yet again. My skin burns everywhere but even though I'm embarrassed and self-conscious and nervous, I want to see him. He's so beautiful.

He grasps himself in one hand a gives a stroke. Wow. He's not only big—um, almost scarily big—his cock is gorgeous too, with a beautifully shaped head and a prominent ridge down the underside. His balls are big and full, the hair surrounding his package thick and dark and masculine.

Now I want to touch him and taste him and I'm kind of regretting his decision that we'll just watch each other. I swipe my tongue over my bottom lip.

He notices that and he grins. "Baby. You like what you see?"

"Again, you're a cocky ass." I smile. "But yes. I do."

He—apparently clearer-minded than I am, or maybe he's more experienced at this—grabs a couple of tissues from a nearby box and settles into the arm at the other end of the couch.

I don't know if I can stand it. It's so erotic watching him—naked, one foot planted into the couch, the other on the floor, thighs widespread. I think my heart is stopping. His thighs are massive . . . and hairy . . . and between them . . . I can't even breathe. I have never done anything like this.

My gaze tracks up from his junk, over those ripped abs and pecs, to his thickly muscled shoulders and then his face. His smile is slight but hot as he studies me too. "Open your legs, beautiful."

Another tight swallow. My tongue comes out again to wet my lips and I slowly part my thighs. My hand slips between them helplessly. I need to touch myself so bad.

Jacob's hand is stroking up and down over his shaft in slow, firm movements. Heat coils tight and low inside me. First I press my hand over my pussy, pulsing against my palm. Then I let my fingers slip deeper and they find wet. So much wet.

This is super hot, but God, I want to touch him. My fingers tingle with the need to feel the soft skin of his inner thighs, to weigh the fullness of his balls and measure the girth of his cock.

"That's it." He gives himself another pull, but watches me with hooded eyes. "Touch yourself. Are you wet, baby?"

"So wet." I dip deeper with my middle finger then circle it over my clit. "You made me so wet."

"Good. Because you made me this hard."

I bite my lip, watching him, mesmerized. I'm so close, this is going to be over like a firecracker. I don't want it to be over that fast, so I stop.

Jacob reaches down with his other hand to cup his balls.

I moan. "That's so hot."

"Fuck yeah. Look at that pretty pussy, all pink and wet."

Oh my God, I'm dying here.

"Next time I'm going to taste you," he promises, his voice low and gruff. "I'm going to lick you until you come."

I make another strangled-sounding noise and resume my self-pleasuring.

"And then I want to fuck that sweet, hot little pussy."

I whimper.

"Do you want my cock inside you, gorgeous girl?"

I can't even speak. He's both embarrassing me and turning me on. I've never been with a guy like him, who's talking through this and making this whole make-out/masturbation session so scorching hot I'm not sure I'll survive it.

"Tell me," he goes on. "Do you want me inside you?"

My cried out "Yes" is strangled by my orgasm as the tension coiling inside me spirals up so fast and hard, sensation explodes inside me and shimmers out to my fingertips and toes.

"Oh yeah, that's beautiful." He grunts and the couch is moving as his hand jerks faster on his shaft. I'm limp and languid but I want to see him come too, so I roll my head and force open my eyes. His head is back, his jaw tight as he jacks himself. His hand moves fast, up and over the head then down again and then he lets out a long groan. His hand slows and semen lands on his ridged belly in one long pulse after another. With a last slow movement, he squeezes his cock and then releases it. It's still big and beautiful.

Jacob opens his eyes and meets mine. Sparks arc between us. My eyes are glued to his magnificence.

"I can't believe we did that," I whisper.

His lips lift into a lazy smile. "I believe it." He glances ruefully at the mess on his stomach and grabs the tissues to clean himself up. He stands and looks around for somewhere to deposit them.

I wave a hand. "Bathroom's over there."

He walks naked across the room and disappears briefly, completely unself-conscious. While he's gone, I reach for my panties and pull them on, and I have my bra in my hands when he returns. He bends to scoop up his jeans, muscles in his thighs flexing, steps into boxers and then the jeans, then sits beside me on the couch, bare-chested. "You are so sexy."

A feel a blush heat my cheeks and he grins and touches his fingers to my face.

"And sweet," he adds. "You're blushing."

He helps me put my bra on. I sit forward and he sweeps my hair forward over my shoulder so he can fasten it. Then he brushes a kiss over my bare shoulder.

My heart is doing weird things, skipping beats and fluttering.

With impressive strength he lifts me onto his lap. I set one hand on his shoulder as he continues to play with my hair, which I love. "I guess I should go so we can both get some sleep," he says with a lack of enthusiasm that pleases me and strangely reassures me. "You have to get up early."

"Yeah."

"What are you doing tomorrow night?"

"I really need to get some reading done." I assume he's going to another party.

"Me too. Spending every evening in your training kicked my homework ass. So . . . we can do that together."

"Really?"

His hand slides down through my hair, making my skin tingle everywhere. "Yeah, why not?"

"I assume you go out and party all the time. Tomorrow's Saturday night."

He doesn't respond right away, just plays with my hair. "I don't actually go out that much. The guys were bugging me because I don't hang out with them and I felt I needed to."

My gaze skims over his face. "Why?"

"They think I'm a stuck-up douche or something." He shrugs. "They kinda hate me."

His words shock me. "They do not."

One corner of his mouth lifts. "Okay. We just don't know each other that well yet."

"You didn't know any of them before you came here?"

"Nope. The team arranged the housing situation for me so I had somewhere to live. Anyway, like I said, I've been trying to stay out of trouble, so I haven't been going out much. I've been studying lots to keep my marks up. I have to have a C average to stay on the team. And I *have* to stay on the team."

I know hockey's important to him, but the fierceness in his voice strikes me. "I understand."

"We can talk tomorrow. Figure out where we should go."

"Okay, yeah."

He gives me a soft kiss. We both pause and our eyes meet again, and then we're kissing, deeper, mouths open, tongues sliding. My blood heats all over again and then Jacob stands, lifting me to my feet. His grin is crooked as I open my eyes.

"We better not get carried away."

I sigh my reluctant agreement and we find our clothes and dress. I see him to the door and he gives me a chaste kiss on the cheek. "See you tomorrow, gorgeous."

When he's gone, I look around, blinking, kind of lost and dazed, then float across the room to turn off the lamp before climbing the stairs to my room.

I get ready for bed and then, between the cool sheets, I curl up on my side.

My body is still humming from the orgasm and my mind is spinning. I'm amazed by what just happened. It was both innocent and sexy. Risky but safe. It felt amazing and I'm not sure whether I'm relieved or still turned on or . . . I don't even know what I feel.

Other than I feel good.

Jacob. He confuses me and makes me curious. He's big and strong and yet gentle and considerate of me, not pushy and macho. He's confident and cocky, and yet I keep getting glimpses of a vulnerability that looks like fear. Why's he so afraid of failing? Despite his bravado, I think he's a decent guy. He told me I was in charge, and that almost brings tears to my eyes as I think about it.

I want to get to know Jacob Flass so much better.

Chapter 12

Jacob

I CALL Skylar the next day, later in the afternoon when I know she's off work. "Guess what I did today."

"What?"

"I told the guys about your goal of getting affirmative consent pledges signed and mentioned the pizza fundraiser."

"Really?"

She sounds like she doubted I would really do that. I frown. "Really. Did you think I wouldn't?"

After a short pause, she says, "I wasn't sure. But are they really going to come?"

"Honestly? I'm not sure about all of them." My jaw clenches thinking about Black Jack's reaction to the suggestion. But he's an asshat. "We'll see. I'll do my best. We have a deal and I never back out of a deal." I pause. "Unless *you* want to?"

She doesn't answer right away. My gut clenches at the thought that she's regretting what we did last night and she doesn't want to go through with this anymore. "No," she says, her voice neutral. "We made a deal."

I speak in a low voice. "Are you sorry about what we did?" I hesitate. "Did I read things wrong? Did you not consent to that?"

She laughs softly. "Oh, I consented. Jacob, you . . . you were perfect last night."

Huh. My chest expands. "Of course I was." Then I smile. "Although, I could have been better."

I hear her chuckle.

But I'm not as confident as I try to make out. I'm full of self-doubts and memories about the night that nearly flushed my hockey career down the toilet. "So tonight."

"Mmm, yeah?"

"I think we should go to the library."

"Okay."

I'm suggesting this because I know if I take her back to my place, we'll have to go to my room to get any peace and quiet, and I also know what that could lead to. I have no idea what's happening at her place, but regardless, the library seems safest.

"Sure. If you still want to do that."

I grimace and rub the back of my neck. "Not that I want to, but I need to."

"I can meet you there . . . around seven?"

I want more than that, but I nod. "Sounds good. See you at seven."

At home I make myself a sandwich in the kitchen, using the last of the turkey. I add a little mayo, some tomatoes, a bunch of lettuce then, what the hell, I layer some sliced dill pickles in there. I take a big bite and chew. Huh. Not bad.

Buck enters the kitchen. I survey his dark jeans and pristine white shirt. He's a laundry master. "Going out tonight?"

"Yeah." He makes a face. "Got a date."

"Shut the fuck up. Seriously?"

He flips me off for sounding so shocked. I grin.

"Where are *you* going?"

"Library."

"What the fuck? On a Saturday night? Are you sure the library's even open?"

I am, because I already went online to check since I wasn't sure before. "Yeah. I'm meeting Skylar there."

"Ah."

This makes my plans acceptable. I have to grin. This is working great. Win goddamn win.

She's sitting on the big stone steps of the library in the near-dusk when I arrive there, her blond and pink hair waving down over her shoulders. Her skinny jeans, black Converse and black Bayard hoodie make her look about twelve years old. But I know she's not. I've seen every inch of her sexy body and she is all woman, and hot as hell.

Christ. I can't be thinking things like that.

I walk toward her and she looks up. Her golden eyes and wide smile beam at me, and she pushes up to stand, lifting her bag.

"Hey."

"Hey, you."

We walk in together and find a table in the not surprisingly empty reading room. It's quiet and it makes my skin itch. I'm way more comfortable on the ice with guys yelling as we practice drills or play a game. I'm buzzing with restless energy. How the hell am I going to sit here for a few hours and actually read something? And retain it?

We get our books out from our bookbags. Skylar retrieves a hot pink highlighter and a sticky note, which she smoothes out and studies.

"What's that?"

"My to-do list."

Huh.

"I like lists," she adds. "They keep me focused."

"Sure."

She bends her head to her textbook, highlighter in hand. I stare at her, mesmerized by her hair yet again, my mind drifting into fantasies . . . damn.

I shake my head and open my own textbook. I read the words. Nothing sinks in.

Someone who's under the influence of drugs or alcohol can't consent. Her judgment is impaired.

Christ. I'm remembering stuff from the training. I've been thinking about it a lot, actually. I shake my head and try to focus.

"Are you okay?"

I look up at Skylar's whispered question. "Yeah. Why?"

"You seem . . . antsy."

I grimace. Damn. "I'm okay."

She eyes me, but nods and bends her head again.

I remember the discussion about rape culture. *Situations where sexual assault, rape and general violence are ignored, trivialized, normalized or made into jokes.*

I'm reliving that night. Now I've heard the four steps of the Step In program, I'm thinking of what I could have done differently. Shitdamnfuck.

Skylar's head snaps up and her eyes lock on me in a frown. "Now what?"

"What?" I gaze back in confusion.

"Why are you swearing? Is there something you don't understand?"

Hell, I cursed out loud. I close my eyes. "No. It's Mechanics of Solids. I understand it fine."

"Well, good, because I sure can't help you. In fact, I'm having a hard time with this."

"What?"

"Quantum mechanics."

"Ah, that's easy."

She gives a delicate snort. "For Einstein, maybe."

"Ha. I'm no Einstein, but maybe I can explain."

I read over what she's studying, and paraphrase it for her, finishing with, "So, to change the color of a radiating body, you have to change its temperature."

She peers at me with a crease between her eyes.

"Increasing the temperature of a body allows it to emit more energy overall, and means that a larger proportion of the energy is toward the violet end of the spectrum." I lift an eyebrow at her. "Red hot, baby."

She laughs. "Okay, yeah, I get it." She tilts her head. "Thank you, Jacob."

"You're welcome. I'm not just a pretty face, you know."

"Or a hot body."

I frown.

"I mean, you do have a pretty face and a hot body," she hastens to assure me. "Well, not pretty." Her cheeks turn pink. "Never mind. Thank you. I still think this is the stupidest subject on the planet."

"Anytime, gorgeous." I squint at her. "But why are you doing something you hate?"

"I told you before. I have to get into med school."

I don't get it. I mean, I get having a goal and being dedicated to it. *Totally* get that. But it has to be something you love. "I don't think this is making you happy."

She sighs. "How can physics ever make someone happy?"

"Well, when I shoot the puck into the boards and I know the angle it's going to come off and where it's going to be and—"

She holds up a hand. "Okay, it makes you happy. It gives me a headache."

I gaze at her sadly. "Really?"

She has a furrow between her eyebrows and her lips are tight. I don't like this look on her. She gives a short nod. "Sometimes it seems so impossible." She bites her lip. "I know I'm not the smartest person in the world, but it shouldn't be this hard."

"Fuck that." Oops. I glance around as heads lift. I lower my voice. "You are so smart."

"No, I'm not. I mean, I'm not stupid. I just have to work at it."

Dismay makes my insides tighten. "No. It shouldn't be that hard."

Her eyes flash and her lips tighten even more. "Sometimes things are hard, Jacob. Sometimes you have to work for what you want."

I feel like I've been smacked. She doesn't know how hard I've worked for what I want. But for me, it doesn't feel like work—because I love it. It's what I want to do more than anything. So yeah, I don't totally get where she's coming from. "I guess I see it differently." I try not to sound stiff.

She sighs again. "I know. You're a hockey player. Your passion is a *game*. But med school is serious."

Now I frown. "Hockey is serious too."

She laughs. "It's not quite the same."

Fuck this. I think she's awesome, but right now I'm getting pissed off. I wasn't in the best of moods when we arrived. I've been processing the stuff I heard during that orientation training, trying to make sense of it, especially in the context of the shit that happened to me. And now I'm being insulted?

"Okay." I flip my book shut. I'm getting fuck all done here, anyway. "Glad to know your opinion." I glance around. "A few people saw us here together, so that's good. People know we're together. Probably no need to see each other until next weekend."

Her eyes widen and her lower lip parts from the top one.

"If I'm going out somewhere, I'll let you know. It'll be good to have a fake girlfriend to keep the puck bunnies away. Thanks, babe."

I shove my things into my messenger bag. I round the table, bend down to give her cheek a kiss for the benefit of anyone watching us, then stride out of the library.

Chapter 13

Skylar

AFTER JACOB LEAVES, I have to fight back tears. I'm not sure why. He was angry. I didn't mean to insult him or his sport. But he doesn't get why I need to do this. Why I make my head hurt trying to understand physics. And chemistry. Why I have to work my ass off to keep up with my sister.

He thinks life should be easy. Well, it's not.

Maybe for him everything is easy. He has loads of talent. One day he'll be a superstar professional athlete making millions of dollars. It's not fucking fair that physics is easy for him too. One guy shouldn't get that much luck.

I stare blindly at my textbook. Dammit, I need to concentrate. I can't let myself be distracted again this year. Last year it was Brendan. I can't let Jacob destroy another school year.

A small voice inside reminds me that Jacob isn't doing anything to destroy my school year; it's me who's in control of that. I have to be strong enough and disciplined enough not to be distracted by him.

I can do it.

I stay at the library until it closes at ten. Then I go home. Ella has gone to visit her parents because tonight is their twenty-fifth wedding anniversary party. Natalie and Brooklyn are out. The house is empty. Just like it was last night when Jacob brought me home and when we had that hot non-sex on the couch.

I ignore the living room and walk into the kitchen. I open the fridge. I don't know what I'm looking for. I'm not really hungry or thirsty. Okay, I'm looking for comfort food. I close the door and open the freezer. Pretty barren. Just as well.

I mix up a jug of strawberry Kool-Aid and pour myself a glass. Then I remember Jacob teasing me about drinking Kool-Aid.

Ugh. *Stop thinking about him!*

You'd think we were really dating and had broken up or something, I feel so down. I'll see him again, if he needs my fake girlfriend services. That thought doesn't really cheer me up. Maybe he's so mad he'll decide he doesn't *want* my fake girlfriend services anymore.

Whatever.

I'm not doing a good job of dealing with whatever I'm feeling. Going to bed and getting a good night's sleep is probably a smart idea. So that's what I do.

I have an early shift at the diner Sunday morning, which is good because I'm running low on spending money and I could use some tips. It's busy today and I bring in a pretty good haul, plus being busy keeps me from thinking about Jacob.

This would be a good day to cook something healthy for dinner, so during my break I go to my Pinterest app on my phone and search through recipes. I find a healthy and easy one for braised balsamic chicken, and I write the ingredients on a list. I love lists.

I stop at a grocery store on my way home. In front of the balsamic vinegar selections on the shelf, I pause. Holy crap, this stuff is expensive. I vacillate over brands. Couldn't I use red wine vinegar? It's probably the same, and way cheaper. I grab a bottle and add it to the cart.

At home, I set about preparing the meal. Nat and Brooklyn are in the living room with their laptops, supposedly doing homework but mostly talking and laughing. Ella arrives back just as I'm covering the chicken to simmer. Now I need to cook the pasta.

"Hey," I call out. "How was your weekend?"

I haven't even seen her since the party after the hockey game. She disappeared with Eric, then left to go home Saturday while I was at work.

She drops her backpack and wanders into the kitchen. "It was okay. What are you doing?"

"I made dinner for us. Braised balsamic chicken."

"Huh. Cool. I'm kind of hungry."

"Was your parents' party nice?"

She shrugs. "Sure." Then she makes a face. "Brendan's parents were there."

"Oh." I pause with a box of pasta in my hands. "How are they doing?"

"They're . . . I don't know. They said they're doing okay, but I think his mom is a bit of a mess."

"Shit." It was hard for us to lose our friend; I can't imagine how his parents feel and what they're going through. It's been nine months so it must be getting easier. Or maybe it never does.

"Yeah."

We chat more about the party as I cook, then I ask, "So who's this Eric guy?"

"Just a guy."

"Are you going to see him again?"

"Nah." She doesn't meet my eyes. Random hookups are all she does lately. She doesn't seem interested in actually dating or getting to know a guy. I try to tell myself that's totally fine. Guys do it all the time. There's nothing wrong with a girl doing it. "How about you? You left with Jacob?"

I sigh. That seems like a lifetime ago. "Yeah." I haven't told her about our deal. In fact, I haven't told her much, because it seems we hardly see each other and we don't talk like we used to. That night at the game, she thought I was there because I really like him.

I *do* really like him.

"So what's up with him?" she asks. "You two are seeing each other?"

"Yeah. Sort of." I give the pasta in the boiling water a stir. "Last night we went to the library to study."

"Oooh, fun times."

I know she's teasing, but it kind of bugs me. Or maybe I'm overly sensitive. "Whatever. Anyway, we kind of had a disagreement, and I haven't talked to him since."

"Oh." She pauses. "Are you upset?"

She does sound like she cares, like my old Ella, and my heart squeezes. "A little."

"What happened?"

Since she's prompting me, I spill it all. "I think I insulted him," I finish. "I feel bad."

"So call him and apologize."

I nod slowly. That would be the right thing to do. Yesterday I'd been trying to convince myself that because I hadn't intended to hurt him, he was the one who'd overreacted. But hearing Ella say this makes me realize I probably do owe him an apology. Even if it doesn't make things better, I should still do that. "You're right. I will after dinner."

I serve up the pasta and chicken and all four of us sit down at the kitchen table to eat. The first bite of chicken is . . . interesting.

"Your aura is very brown tonight," Natalie tells Ella, a wrinkle between her eyebrows.

Ella's eyebrows lift and I smile at my plate. "Oh yeah? What does that mean?"

"It means you're confused. Or . . . discouraged."

Ella shrugs. "Well, I was home with my parents, which is often confusing."

We all laugh. I think Natalie's talk about auras is kind of funny. I'm skeptical, but she told me my blue aura meant I was an excellent communicator, a very good organizer and I could motivate and inspire others. I'd like to believe that.

"Hmm," Nat says. "This chicken is . . . very tangy."

I wrinkle my nose at my plate. "It definitely is."

We keep eating. It's . . . not great. "It's the vinegar," I decide. "Balsamic vinegar was so expensive, I used something else."

Nat and Brooklyn aren't my best friends like Ella is, but just then, I love them as they valiantly keep eating, and then thank me for cooking.

"That chicken was atrocious," I say as we do the dishes.

"Yeah, it was." Nat meets my eyes and we burst out laughing. "But you tried. Live and learn, right? We should do this every Sunday night. We could take turns cooking."

"I like that idea."

We agree that Natalie will go next week, then Brooklyn, then Ella. Hopefully their meals will be better than mine.

Up in my room, first I go online and reread the recipe I just made. Damn. I could've added a little sugar to the vinegar, instead of using balsamic vinegar. I sigh. Ah well.

Then I pick up my cellphone and pull up Jacob's number. Should I text or call? Probably an apology should be delivered via phone call, if not in person. So I call him.

I get his voicemail. *You've got the Flash. Leave a message.*

I roll my eyes. The Flash. "Hi, Flash. It's me, Rapunzel. I . . ." I pull a quick breath in and out. "I just called to say I'm sorry." Crap, I think that's the name of some old song. "I think I inadvertently insulted you last night. I didn't mean to. You're a talented hockey player and I'm sure you've worked super hard to get where you are. I wasn't demeaning your . . . your sport. Or career. I was frustrated." I pause. "That's all. So anyway . . . yeah. Bye."

I end the call and drop my phone on my bed. Okay. There. Done. I can feel better now.

Except I don't.

I spend the evening with Intro to Research Methods (psychology) and by ten o'clock I'm in bed. Wide awake.

My phone warbles.

It's a weird sound because I get so few actual phone calls. I blink into the darkness then toss back the covers and scramble out of bed. I dash over to the dresser, where my phone is plugged in.

The screen tells me it's Jacob.

My hands tremble a little as I quickly tap the screen to answer. "Hello."

"Rapunzel."

I huff out a laugh. "Yeah."

"I got your message."

"Okay, good."

"Thanks for that. And I'm sorry too."

I press my lips together, my heart beating fast.

"I was a dick," he says quietly. "I was in a bad mood. I wasn't listening to you."

I unplug the phone and take the three steps to my bed to sink down onto the edge. "Why were you in a bad mood?"

"Long story." He pauses. "D'you think your hair has magical healing properties?"

I choke. "What?"

"Like in the movie *Tangled.*"

"You've seen *Tangled*?" Then I shake my head. "Are you drunk?"

He gives a low laugh that slides into my ear. "Maybe a little."

"Jacob."

"Sunday's our day off. I did laundry. With only minimal supervision."

A smile tugs at my lips. "Good for you."

"It's an important skill. Sadly, I never really learned it."

"Who was supervising?"

"Buck. He's pretty good at it. I guess you have to be when you spend as much on clothes as he does. His jeans cost a hundred bucks."

"Holy crap."

"Yeah. So you have to separate the whites from the darks."

My smile broadens. "Yes. Yes, you do."

"And not everything goes in the dyer."

"Why are we talking about laundry?"

"Hey, it's a significant accomplishment."

"Okay, true."

There's a silence that stretches out and isn't weird. Finally, Jacob says, "I'll see you Wednesday."

At the fundraiser planning meeting. "Right."

"You forgive me for being a dick?"

"Yes. If you forgive me for being a bitch."

"You're not a bitch. You're Rapunzel. And I love your hair."

"Thank you." My heart swells up.

"Night, gorgeous."

"Good night, Flash."

I plug my phone back in and climb into bed. And now I can go to sleep.

I know the minute Jacob enters the meeting room on Wednesday afternoon. The air changes, becomes energized. He rushes in as if he's running late, commanding attention with just his presence and an easy smile. But he focuses on me. "Hi, Skylar."

"Hi."

His hair's a little damp, as if he just got out of the shower, and his high cheekbones wear a healthy flush.

I introduce Jacob to the others and we get to work planning the pizza fundraiser. After the meeting ends, Jacob hangs back while everyone else leaves. I shut down my laptop, then slide it into the padded case. Then we're alone.

"Thanks for helping with the fundraiser."

"No problem. My schedule's crazy but I'll fit it in."

He stands near me and I can smell his body wash, the spicy fragrance familiar to me. I want to press my nose against the side of the neck and breathe in the scent of his skin.

"I have a night class at seven," he says. "Want to get something to eat with me?"

"Do you need a fake girlfriend for that?"

One corner of his mouth deepens. "Yeah."

I look at him through my eyelashes, my head tilted.

"I was pissed," he says quietly.

"I insulted you. I know hockey is serious."

"It bugged me that you think I'm just fooling around playing a game."

I eye him. "Does it matter what I think of you?"

He's silent.

"I mean, I'm only your fake girlfriend."

He nods, still quiet. "Right."

"Well. Let's go. I'm hungry."

"Skylar?"

"Yeah?"

"It matters."

Warmth fills my chest.

We walk across the Quad to the dining hall. It's busy there but we find an empty table and dump our stuff. Then we take turns going through the buffet line. I get a chicken breast, which is thankfully much better than the ones I made the other night, some veggies and a salad. Jacob comes back with a plate loaded with spaghetti and meatballs, a salad, a bun and three desserts.

"Tell me more about hockey."

He stabs a meatball with his fork. "Like what?"

"Tell me how you got started. Tell me why you love it."

"Well, I started skating when I was two."

"Holy crap."

"And playing hockey when I was four. It was fun. I was obsessed with it. I used to play hockey in the dining room, much to my mom's dismay."

"Somehow I'm picturing her not able to stay angry at you."

He laughs. "Yeah, maybe so. I was a cute kid."

I shake my head, smiling.

"They moved all the furniture out and turned it into a rink for me."

My mouth drops open. "Seriously?"

"Yeah. The walls and baseboards got pretty beat up over the years."

"So your parents obviously supported you playing hockey."

"Sure. But they actually encouraged me to play a lot of sports. Baseball and soccer in the summer. And golf."

"What was your favorite hockey team?"

"Well, when I was little it was the Kamloops Blazers." He grins. "I thought those guys were amazing. They seemed like big men to me, when I was six. But they're just teenagers."

"Did you play for that team when you got older?"

"No, I ended up getting drafted by Saskatoon. When I was older, the Vancouver Canucks were my favorite team."

I listen and I can see the passion on his face and I'm struck by how down to earth his story is.

"And obviously you want to be a professional hockey player."

"Yeah." He drops his gaze to the plate in front of him. "I do."

"Is playing here the way to get that? How does that happen?" I shake my head. "I probably sound like an idiot. I don't know anything about professional sports."

"All the NHL teams have scouts. They travel around watching junior hockey in Canada, NCAA hockey here. They travel to Europe to scout players there. They report back to their teams about players who look good. Then I enter the draft. That's held every year in June."

"Do you have to enter the draft? Or they pick you?"

"You enter. Players who are eighteen by September fifteenth and not older than twenty by December thirty-first are eligible." I remember him telling me he's going to be twenty soon. Shadows darken his eyes and he looks away briefly. "But you have to be scouted, obviously, to get chosen in the draft."

"Wow. That sounds stressful."

"Yeah. It's exciting, but it would be a nightmare to sit there hoping to get drafted and not hearing your name, round after round."

"Realistically . . ." I hesitate to ask. "You'll get drafted?"

He meets my eyes. I wait for some kind of cocky comeback, but instead I see vulnerability. His shoulders hunch, then relax. "Realistically, yeah. I should get drafted."

I feel like he's not telling me something, but for some reason I don't want to push. I get the sense this is something so important to him that he's terrified he won't achieve it. And yet again, I don't know why, because he's obviously a talented player. Not that I'm as good a judge as an NHL scout, since I just went to my first ever hockey game last week.

He picks up his phone and glances at it. "I better go. I have a class."

"You're taking a night class?"

"Yeah. Wednesday nights. Fitting all my courses into the day is tough, since we practice four days a week and sometimes travel on Fridays."

I walk out with him. "When's your first away game?"

"Not for a few weeks. Our season starts out mostly at home."

"Cool."

We pause on the sidewalk. It's dark now, and the air has chilled, the crisp autumn nip scented with turning foliage. I shift from one foot to the other and peer at the sidewalk. I feel like we should kiss, but that might be weird. I'm his fake girlfriend, but we just sat and talked non-stop for over an hour. And the other day we engaged in a little mutual masturbation.

Our eyes meet. My skin heats and tingles everywhere.

"Thanks for listening to me blabber on about hockey."

"You don't have to thank me. I wanted to know more about it."
About you.

"We have another game on Friday night. It's the first game of the regular season. Will you come again?"

I want to. "I'll see if I can find someone to come with me." Ella will probably agree. Maybe I should see if Natalie and Brooklyn want to come too.

"Okay." He leans down and kisses my cheek, which is sweet and hot. My girl parts squeeze, wanting more.

I watch him walk away, his long legs taking big strides, moving with perfect athletic male grace, his shoulders wide and strong. So I guess we just had our first fight in our fake relationship, and we didn't even get to have make-up sex.

Maybe that would happen this weekend. I remember how turned on I got watching him play hockey. If that happens again, I don't know if I'll be able to stop myself from jumping him.

Chapter 14

Jacob

BEFORE EVERY GAME, I get nervous.

Last summer, there were two NHL players at the camp I went to and I talked to them about it. They said they still get nervous before every game too. So I guess it'll never go away.

There was a sports psychologist at the camp too. We talked about pre-game jitters and why we have them, one reason possibly being because during an actual game we have an audience, and also possibly because we have such high expectations of success. We learned about self-talk and how the things we're thinking can ramp up the tension even more. Like, if we're doubting ourselves or afraid of failing. He told us to accept the nervous energy rather than fight it, because it's normal, and we learned strategies to deal with it, like making sure to arrive early for a game so there's lots of time to get ready, and doing some visualization. During the game, the trick is to focus on the present and what's happening right then, not on the mistake you just made and not on the outcome of the game. Only that moment.

Right now, I have the puck on my stick behind our own net. I look up the ice. Way up the ice. Buck is 120 feet away just outside the other blue line, but it's a clear passing lane. I slam the puck toward him from behind the net and he catches the long pass perfectly, already moving, and crosses the blue line all alone. One of the Bulldogs is trying to catch him, but he can't and Buck pops the puck into the net over the goalie's left shoulder.

Fuck yeah!

The crowd roars, Buck's hands go in the air and he and Franco hug. I grin as I join them in the celebration.

That makes the score two nothing late in the third period, and I've assisted on both goals.

I sit on the bench, still smiling, and Buck pats my helmet. I pick up a water bottle and squirt some into my mouth, then spit it out.

The puck drops at center ice and I watch Jimmy win the face-off, then lose the puck to the Bulldogs. They get a chance on net that Alfie stops, but the rebound comes out. Fear bolts through me and there's a scramble for the loose puck, but Jimmy gets it and the play moves to the other end. Then we're changing and I'm back out there. I glance at the clock as I barrel over the boards and join the play. Barks has the puck behind our net to give us time to change lines. He passes it to Franco, and he passes it to me and we start off up the ice toward the Bulldogs' net. I get some speed, the puck on my stick, aware of Buck and Franco with me as this becomes a three on two. I thread through the two Bulldogs D-men, assessing the shooting lane, assessing the angles. There's no lane, I'm too far now to shoot the puck, but Franco is right there, in front of the net, so I throw it to him. He catches it and buries the puck in the net behind the goalie. The red light goes on, the horn blares and the crowd cheers as Franco skates at me and throws his arms around me.

"Yeah!" he yells. "Nice pass!"

We skate by the bench and bump gloves with the other guys. Only a minute left in the game and I think it's safe to say we've got this one. We watch Jimmy kill time with the puck as the clock runs down and then the horn sounds to end the game. We all pile over the boards and skate down to Alfie, our goalie, to congratulate him on the win. Not only a win, a shutout.

It's our third game of the season and we've won them all.

In the dressing room, music is pumping, and the mood is jubilant. Coach actually cracks a smile. I pull off my jersey and shoulder pads in front of my cubby.

"How do you find those plays, man?" Franco asks me, shaking his head.

I shrug.

"You two were skating circles around their D all night," Buck says. "Fucking A."

It's hard to describe the feeling inside me, the relief and joy and satisfaction that mingles. This team is good. The Bulldogs were good too. Notwithstanding the score, they tested us. I was worried about what it was going to be like playing college hockey, afraid it wouldn't be a challenge for me, but it is, and it's a challenge I'm up for.

I let out a long breath as I walk naked to the shower, still buzzing with victory, and in more ways than one. Because not only do I have to win against the other team, I have to win over my teammates.

I think it's happening.

After I shower and dress, I grab my phone to text Skylar, who was at the game. She's come to all my home games. A bunch of the guys are going to Curly's, a bar off campus. I hesitate about joining them. They tell me I don't need ID because they serve hockey players there without asking for ID, but I'm not sure if Skylar will want to come. I want to celebrate, but I don't want to get in trouble.

Sure we'll come.

She and Ella were at the game together. That's cool.

We arrange to meet at the bar, since I want to go home and change. Bayard upholds the tradition of dressing in suits on game day, but we don't want to go out after in suits. Before I can get out of the arena, though, I have to talk to a guy who writes a blog for the campus website, and a couple of reporters from the local newspaper about my three assists.

As usual, I talk about the team and how playing with these guys makes it easy, and we're just going to get better.

Finally, I walk into Curly's and Skylar's already there, sitting with Ella at a table near the bar, along with Rocket and Soupy. I grab another chair and join them, sliding in close to Skylar. She smiles at me—a wide, bright smile. Apparently she feels as good as I do. I like that.

"Hi, babe." I lay my arm along the back of her chair

"Hi. Congratulations."

"Thanks."

"Three assists."

"Yep."

Our eyes meet and it's a heated connection.

A waitress approaches and I order a beer. I notice Skylar's drinking some kind of pink cocktail. I lean in closer and ask in a low voice, "You get carded?"

"Yep. I have ID."

"Huh."

She winks at me.

I nuzzle her hair. She smells delicious. "I don't want to stay long. Okay with you?"

"Sure."

The buzz inside me feels like arousal and I'm getting that vibe from Skylar again too.

We hang out for a while. The bar gets busier and noisier. I finish my beer and as I set the empty bottle on the table, I glance at Skylar. "You ready to go?"

"Sure." She turns to find Ella, who's standing talking to a couple of the other guys. "Let me go tell Ella we're leaving."

I rise and slap Rocket and Soupy on the shoulders. "Later, guys."

Skylar returns and I set my hand on the small of her back as we walk out. "I parked around the corner," I tell her.

I breathe in the cool, crisp night air, with its faint scent of smoke.

"I think I'm starting to like hockey," Skylar shares.

I laugh and hook my arm around her neck. "It was only a matter of time."

I drive to her place, hoping like hell she's going to invite me in. Which makes no sense at all, because she's done her fake girlfriend duty for the night. She's been doing her fake girlfriend duty for a few weeks now, and the truth is, it doesn't feel very fake anymore.

When I pull up in front of her house, she looks at me. "Would you like to come in?"

I don't even hesitate. "Yeah."

We walk into the living room. I take off my jacket and lay it over the back of a chair, then sprawl on the couch.

"Would you like another beer? I think we have some."

I push out my lips. "Got any Kool-Aid?"

She smiles. "Yeah. Grape."

"I'll have some of that."

She bites her lip and rushes off to get it. I pick up the remote and turn on the TV. Maybe we can watch a movie. And make out.

She brings back two glasses and curls up beside me. "Looking for something to watch?"

"Maybe a movie?"

"Sure. What do you like?" She shoots me a glance. "Action? Comedy? Porn?"
I choke on my Kool-Aid.
She laughs. "Kidding. Sort of."
"You don't watch porn."
She frowns. "Why would you say that?"
"You're too sweet and innocent."
She snorts. "Right."
I eye her. "You really watch porn?"
"Sure. Why not?"
"Uh . . ."
She grins. "You have to find the right stuff. There's female friendly porn that's really sexy."
Mind. Blown.
"And I'm not that innocent. If I was, you really debauched me that night, right here on this couch."
Since then, we've been spending time together but we've been trying to keep our hands off each other. It's fucking killing me. "Debauched? Did you really just use that word?"
"What's wrong with that word?" She gets a teasing glint in her beautiful eyes. "You know what it means, right?'"
"I know what it means. I can't spell it, but I know what it means." She laughs again. I like making her laugh. "Did I debauch you?"
"No." She leans over and rubs her nose against mine. "I think I already told you, I'm not a virgin."
"Right."
"This might sound weird . . . or maybe not . . . maybe you've heard this a hundred times . . . but watching you play hockey turns me on."
My eyes fly open wide. "Seriously?"
"Yeah."
That chemistry is sizzling between us again, making my dick thicken and my blood run hot.
"Well, that works out pretty well, then, eh?"
Her lips quirk. "How so, eh?"
I shake my head but I'm smiling. "It works out well because after a game, I love to fuck."
Her eyes go heavy-lidded. "That does work out well."

Shut Out

I slide a hand around the back of her neck and pull her closer. Our noses touch and our eyes meet. Then I tilt my head, close my eyes and open my mouth on hers.

She's warm and sweet like grape Kool-Aid as my tongue slides into her mouth. She makes a hungry little noise and shifts closer to me, one hand on my shoulder. Heat pulses in my veins and my balls.

My hand plays in her hair, dragging down the silky waves, tangling in it and tugging. She whimpers little sounds of pleasure into my mouth and I bring her body closer still so we're pressed together. Then she climbs onto me, straddling my lap, our mouths still joined. She cups my jaw and rubs her tits across my chest. Heat zaps straight to my dick.

Making little pleasure noises, she bites my bottom lip softly, then licks it, then kisses me again. My hands cup her ass in her tight jeans, bringing her right against my aching dick.

"Jesus, baby," I gasp, pushing my hips up against her. "You are so fucking hot."

"I am." She kisses my chin. "I'm hot for you, Flash."

Fuck, I love that.

"You're not a flash in bed, though, are you?" She drags her tongue along my jaw. "Like, over fast?"

I groan. "I'd like to say no, but fuck, I might not even make it to a bed. Feel this." I press up into her again. "See what you do to me."

"Mmm. I like it."

"Let's take this upstairs."

"Yeah."

I stand, still holding her ass. She weighs like a buck twenty or something, and I'm trying to bench-press my own weight so she's nothing. She holds on to me with her arms and legs, and I climb the stairs.

"Impressive strength, hockey boy."

I smile. "This is easy. You're a feather."

"Ah." She kisses my cheek. "Compliments like that'll get you lucky."

"Good to know. Which is your room?"

"Second on the left."

We pass by another bedroom, the door open, the room dark, and a bathroom, then I push into her room. I carry her to the bed and lower her feet to the floor, then reach over to the lamp on the table beside the bed. It's a

105

funky-shaped lamp with a tripodlike base and I can't fucking figure out how to turn it on.

With a soft laugh, Skylar turns and flicks a switch.

"Thank you." I roll my eyes at myself, reaching for her hips. I pull her ass back against me and move her hair aside so I can kiss the back of her neck. Her body vibrates and I close my eyes and breathe in her scent. It reminds me of apples and vanilla and flowers, totally feminine and warm. "I love how you smell."

"Thank you. I've thought the same about you."

"That's a good thing, eh?"

Crap, every time I say that now I'm aware of it. Ah well. But I sense her amusement.

"Yeah, I'd say it's a good thing. If I thought you stunk, this wouldn't be nearly as much fun."

"You should smell me right after a game. There's nothing worse than the stench of sweaty hockey equipment."

"Hmm. I appreciate you showering, then."

I pull her hoodie up and over her head to find that she's wearing a cotton tank top beneath it. Fantastic. I open my mouth on her bare shoulder and gently suck. Her hair gathered up in one hand, I lick my way back to her neck. Her head tilts to give me access and she shivers as I pull her soft skin into my mouth. So soft. So sweet.

Her hand comes up to the back of my head, fingers sliding in my hair. I slip one hand over her hip, up over her flat stomach and then I cup a breast. Her softness fills my hand and I gently squeeze, my dick throbbing even more. Her tits are perfect, the perfect size, the perfect shape, and I can't wait to taste. Her pointy nipples are poking right through her thin bra and the cotton tank top. My fingertips tug the low neckline of the top down, along with the cup of her bra, and I look over her shoulder at pink perfection. A groan climbs in my chest.

I tug her nipple between my fingers and she makes more soft arousal sounds that I love. I kiss the side of her neck, fondle her tit again, squeezing softly, then plucking at the nipple. I can't wait any longer—I have to taste. So I pull her tank top up and over her head, unfasten her bra and toss it aside, then turn her in front of me so I can lean down and suck on her.

Excitement pounds through me, heat racing through my veins. I draw the tight nub between my lips and pull on it. Her fingers are still in my hair and she's trembling so hard I'm afraid she's going to fall. So I lift her onto the bed and join her. She supports herself with her hands planted into the mattress behind her, her back arched to give me full access to those beauties. But first I kiss her mouth, our tongues sliding together in a long, hot kiss.

Then I'm there, devouring those breasts, licking, nuzzling, sucking with greedy pulls. Electric need burns over my skin. My dick is on fire.

"You taste amazing," I pant. "And you feel amazing. Your tits are fucking perfection."

She huffs out a little laugh, but she's aroused too, her eyes drowsy, her lips parted and wet.

I slip one hand down between her thighs and cup her there, through her jeans. Damp heat meets my palm and I give a firm press to her mound, which makes her moan again. I love making her feel good.

She moves her arms and lies down flat, but still with her back arched, so I know her tits want more attention and I'm happy to oblige. I could live forever like this, I think, with my face buried between her breasts and my hand buried between her thighs. I rub her a little as I tug her nipples with my lips and her noises become more urgent.

"You're so fucking hot." I nip at her again. "I need to bury my cock in this hot, wet pussy."

She moans again.

I flick open the button of her jeans and then work the zipper down, which isn't easy with one hand, but her jeans are very low rise and the zipper is short and it's easy to push them lower on her hips so I can get my hand inside. She feels so small and delicate, so warm and wet, pulsing against my palm. More heat washes down through my body.

"Goddamn." I slide my other hand around behind her neck and hold her there as I feast on her mouth again, long openmouthed kisses. "So wet for me, baby. You need to be fucked."

"Yes." She whimpers again. "Yes, I do."

I move beside her, laying hot kisses between her breasts, down her belly and then above her panties. I ease her jeans down over her legs along with her bright striped socks, and when her legs are bare, I cup one foot and kiss the top of it, then kiss her calf. I look up at her face as I do so and her eyes are fastened on mine, hot and glowing. I hold her gaze as I kiss my way up to the inside of her knee.

Then I move up beside her again to kiss her mouth while my hand slips inside her panties, a tiny little hot pink thong held together with two strings. I kiss her over and over as I finger her pussy, so hot and slick, and she's whimpering and gasping into my mouth. I lower my head to her sweet nipples again to tug on them with lips and teeth until she's writhing, her hips lifting against my hand, her plump folds dripping.

I want to taste more of her.

I deliberately pull my hand out from her panties and lift it to my mouth, watching her face as she watches me suck her girl juices off my own fingers.

"Oh my God," she breathes.

"Mmm. You taste so sweet, baby. I want to put my mouth on that hot pussy. Okay?"

Her nod is barely there—but it's there.

I shift to kneel above her. I kiss her again, her mouth, her cheek, her neck . . . her nipple, her belly. I lick from her navel down to the edge of her panties. Then I look up at her and reach for her hands and pull her so she's sitting. I curve my hands around the back of her neck, my thumbs caressing her jaw as I look into her eyes, nose to nose. Our lips touch. Our eyes close as I kiss her again, then she lies back down. I bend her legs and lift them straight up and, holy Christ, her pussy is so pretty. Plump and pink and smooth.

With her knees at her chest, she holds on to one calf and I lean down to taste.

Fucking heaven.

I lick and nibble, slip a finger inside her tight passage, close my lips over her clit. She shudders and groans, and I smile. I lap up her taste, delicate and tangy and feminine. Then I move my head to kiss the inside of her thigh while I rub my fingertips over her clit.

Her soft, breathy sounds quicken. I glance up at her face. A flush climbs from her chest up her throat and into her face, and her lips part. "Jacob. Oh my God. Please."

"Yeah. You want to come, beautiful girl?"

"Oh yeah . . ."

I move my mouth back to her clit and tease it with my tongue. Beautiful.

She cups her own breasts, then lifts her hands over her head, eyes closed, as I lick her to an amazing orgasm, her body quivering, her clit swelling against my tongue.

Damn, I need to get my clothes off and get inside her. I drag the condom out of my jeans pocket where I'd stuck it earlier—so hopefully—and then roll off the bed to strip. Skylar turns her head and watches me through hazy eyes, her lips quirked in a half smile.

I move over her when I'm naked. "Don't want this to be awkward, baby . . . but you're consenting . . . right?"

She smiles, and it's so luminous and beautiful it steals my breath. "Yes. I'm saying yes. In fact, I'm begging you. Please, Jacob . . . fuck me."

Chapter 15

Skylar

MY BODY IS BURNING and trembling. The ache between my legs is unrelenting. I watch Jacob take his clothes off. He's so amazing. His body is muscled and hard and perfect, his chest smooth, his abdomen ridged. As his jeans loosen and lower on his lean hips, the V muscles that make me drool are revealed.

I've seen him before, but it still mesmerizes me. He drops his jeans and peels off socks, standing in a pair of Batman boxer shorts. I want to tease him about those, but I'm burning up.

Then the boxers are off too, and his thick erection is in his hand as he climbs back onto the bed. He parts my thighs and kneels there and that's when he asks me.

My chest swells with gratitude that he's taking the time to say that, even though I just want him to do it. Now.

"Please, Jacob . . . fuck me."

I can't believe I'm asking for this, but I want it so bad. I want *him* so bad.

He nods and reaches for the condom package he tossed onto the bed a moment ago. I watch him roll it on, excitement making my breathing shallow. I want to touch him there. I want to touch him everywhere. I want him to kiss me again and fill me up.

He's big and strong, shoulders wide, hips narrow as he kneels between my thighs. He smoothes his hands down the insides of my legs, studying me with a look of awe on his face that undoes me. I reach for him, gripping his big thighs as he fists his cock and runs the head up and down through my folds. A little whimper escapes me. I'm still so sensitive there from the stupendous orgasm he just gave me.

"You ready, baby?" He lifts his gaze to my face and I try to smile and nod.

He pushes inside me and, oh God, he's big. I feel a sharp pinch but then it eases as he pulls out again. When he pushes back in, it's better. "Gonna go slow," he promises me, watching where we're joined. "You're tight, baby. So fucking tight." He groans like he's in pain. "But hot and wet."

I tilt my hips to take him deeper. "Yes. That's it. Feels so good, Jacob."

He nods. "Yeah."

He's all the way in now and he goes still, pressed against me, filling me with exquisite pressure. He props himself above me on straight arms and stares into my eyes. "Just . . . need . . . a minute." Perspiration dots his forehead and upper lip, and his high cheekbones are flushed. I love that he's so aroused . . . for me. I caress his strong thighs, studying his body, every muscle defined, even his jaw. So beautiful.

"Do it," I urge him, tilting my pelvis even more. "Please."

"Aw yeah." He holds my legs and starts to move, sliding in and out of me. Every stroke leaves a glow of light and heat that spreads through my body. Sensations wind up inside me, tighter and tighter. I want to watch him but my eyes are so heavy and I need to come again so badly . . .

I slip my hand down to find my clit. Jacob groans and I rub in small circles . . . my God, with him inside me touching nerve endings so deep and sensitive, it's almost more than I can bear. Hot sweetness throbs through me, building up, and up.

Jacob asks, "Are you coming again, baby?" But before he even gets the words out, my body is contracting hard, flames licking over me, bright and blazing and beautiful. I can't stop the cries that spill from my lips as the ecstasy goes on and on.

"Holy hell, I can feel you coming on my dick. That's hot . . . oh Christ."

As my arm falls limply to my side, he stretches out over me and buries his face in the side of my neck. I grab his big biceps and hold on, then his shoulders, one hand going to his head, the other to his muscular ass. He rocks against me, fucking me hard, his breathing harsh in my ear. Then he comes, and our heads turn so our mouths meet and cling together, kissing and kissing as he pulses inside me over and over.

His weight is warm and wonderful on me. My heart is pattering in a crazy rhythm. I hold on to him. I never want to let go.

Wow.

Tears sting the corners of my eyes. It was so beautiful and amazing and better than I ever would have imagined, except a while back I couldn't even imagine having sex again, and gratitude and relief mingle with overwhelming sexual satisfaction. My arms tighten even more on him as I try to stop the tears from falling because, hell, I don't want him to think I'm sad. Because I'm not.

Eventually he rolls to his side, bringing me with him, still joined. He strokes hair off my face and my damp eyes flutter open. "Skylar." He touches his lips to mine. "That was amazing."

"I thought so too." I try to sound casual but we both chuckle.

He pets my shoulder, my arm, my hip, studying my face, which is almost unbearably intimate. This is crazy.

He makes a quick trip to the bathroom to get rid of the condom, riskily naked. He doesn't seem to be bothered by the idea and I guess he's used to walking around naked in front of other people. I picture the dressing room at one of his games, all those hot, muscled guys naked, strolling around, showering together . . . my pussy gives a happy little quiver and I feel my cheeks heat.

"Why are you all red?" Jacob slides back into bed with me. "Is that your post-orgasm flush?"

"Um, sure."

I'm not sure how he'd take my little fantasy if I shared it with him. Maybe I'll save that for later . . . maybe.

He snuggles me in against him, which is more wonderful, pulling the covers up over us.

"That went kinda fast," he murmurs in my ear. "Damn, baby, you get me so wound up."

"Me too." I give a little wriggle against him, still feeling that buzz of arousal, and he groans. "Maybe we can do it again."

He laughs softly. "Damn right we will. I just need a few minutes."

I love how he keeps running his hand through my hair. The tug on my scalp makes sensation slide down my spine. "Mmm." I'm a little drowsy too.

I wake up plastered against Jacob's hot body. I think we both drifted off to sleep but now he gently rolls me to my back, his mouth on my cheek, my jaw, my throat. The lamp is still on and I surface from deep languor to revel in the sensation of Jacob's mouth and hands on me, the scent of his skin, the soft pleasure noises he makes as he tastes me.

This time it goes slow and sweet. He pulls me on top of him, straddling him, holding my hands, eyes fastened on mine as I slowly rise and fall on his powerful cock. I can control how fast and how deep he goes, which is good because I'm tender. Even so, it feels so amazing that gradually I push down harder against him.

He releases my hands and reaches for my boobs, squeezing them, then tweaking the nipples. That shoots streamers of sensation right to where we're joined, and my breasts push into his palms.

"I love your breasts," he whispers. "So perfect. And sensitive."

I nod dreamily, my body a hot glow of pleasure.

He pulls me down to kiss me. Our mouths open to each other and his tongue slides in, hot and sleek against mine. He sucks my tongue gently, then pulls my bottom lip between his. The kisses are long and lush as he moves inside me. His body is so strong.

He wraps his arms around me and holds me tight as his hips power up against me. Then his hands slide down to my butt and hold me there, helping lift me as he fucks me. I bury my face in the side of his neck, gasping and groaning as he hits those sensitive places inside me. If I move a little, I can get the pressure I need, on my clit . . . right there. "Don't stop. Oh yeah, right there . . ."

"Damn that's hot."

I have a vague thought that I'm being completely selfish by focusing on my own pleasure, concentrating on the feelings twisting up inside me, feeling my body tighten on Jacob's cock.

"I love that," he gasps.

Okay, maybe not entirely selfish—he likes it too. And why shouldn't I make sure I come? Actually, I don't know if I can stop it. I reach for it . . . higher . . . oh God, so high . . . and I lose my mind as my orgasm explodes in a nearly painful burst. I hear faint cries that are mine, distant and high-pitched

Then Jacob flips me onto my back, so easily, still inside me, pounding into me in delicious hard strokes that draw out the pleasure, heat radiating from my center in waves.

"You're amazing, Sky," he pants long moments later. "Fucking amazing."

"I think we already agreed this is amazing."

He rolls me on top again and gives my butt a little swat that makes me smile.

It's true, though. I haven't been with tons of guys, but this is kind of like pyrotechnics and shock waves and crazy chemical combustion compared to the others. "Red hot. Increasing the temperature of a body allows it to emit more energy overall."

After a short silence, he chokes out a laugh. "Very good. I'm impressed." He squeezes me.

This time when he withdraws from me I wince, and his forehead furrows. He brushes my hair back. "You okay?"

"Oh yeah. I might not be able to walk tomorrow, but I'm okay."

"Damn." He bites his lips but pride gleams in his eyes and I laugh and shove at his shoulder.

"Ass."

He grins and smooches me. Then his smile fades. "Do we, uh, need to talk about this? In light of our, uh, arrangement?"

All I want to do is go to sleep. "I guess we should." I'm not sure what he's going to say and I'm not sure myself. "This fake boyfriend/girlfriend thing clearly didn't require this level of commitment."

His lips quirk. "Probably not. But hey, it'll make things more realistic, right?"

Somewhere in the back of my brain is the thought that adding sex to this "relationship" probably isn't a good idea. I've heard of friends with benefits arrangements, and somehow it always seems that someone ends up hurt.

But I'm so damn overjoyed and relieved that the sex was so fantastic. I was totally into it—in fact, begging for it . . .and I had three freakin' orgasms! How can I put a stop to that? Plus, Jacob is a cocky ass sometimes, but over the last few weeks he's kind of grown on me. We have fun together, even apart from the smoking hot sex, and this seems to work for both of us. If he was into partying all the time, it might be a problem, but he's really working hard on school, so our "study dates" benefit both of us. And I was also being honest when I said I'm starting to like hockey. Jacob's skill on the ice continues to impress me and I've already admitted watching him makes me hot.

"Right." I meet his eyes. "But . . ."

"What?"

"Don't take this the wrong way, but people think we're really together. If you cheat on me and humiliate me, I will hurt you."

His eyebrows fly up and his mouth drops open. "I wouldn't do that."

"You might meet someone you want to have a real relationship with."

He frowns.

"I'm just saying, if you do, tell me."

His frown darkens and he lifts his chin. "Well, same for you."

I want to roll my eyes, because I can't see that happening, but I nod. "Okay."

"Okay. We're on the same page here."

"Yep." I have to stop myself from asking when we can boink again, because, wow.

Jacob again leaves the bed to get rid of the condom. This time when he comes back he says regretfully, "I guess I better go."

I sigh and roll to face him, my eyes heavy. "I guess. I have to work in the morning." I start to push the covers back, but he stops me.

"Stay in bed. You look like you're half-asleep."

"I think I am." I lie back on the pillow and smile at him. "I was going to see you to the door."

"I can find my way. So. I'll talk to you tomorrow."

"Okay. Night, Jacob."

He kisses my forehead, another of his surprisingly sweet moves. "Night, Sky."

Chapter 16

Jacob

Buck and I have discovered a mutual fascination with the Science Channel show *How It's Made*. The weirder the stuff, the better. I should be studying, but this show rocks, and also since Buck wants to watch it with me, I don't want to reject him. I'm getting to know the guys better, hanging out after practices and games, but I still feel like an outsider at times.

We're watching an episode that starts with frozen perogies.

"What the fuck are perogies?" Buck dunks a tortilla chip into salsa. We're treating ourselves with binge TV shows, junk food and shots of tequila.

I gape at him. "You don't know what perogies are?"

"Nope."

"Jesus. Every Canadian knows what perogies are. They're Ukrainian and they're fucking awesome."

He narrows his eyes at me. "I thought Canadians were French, not Ukrainian."

One of the other Canadians on the team is French, Pascal Bouchard, known as Butch. I laugh. "You're bullshitting me."

He grins. "Okay, I know you're not all French."

"Watch the show. Let's see how they put those delicious little pillows of dough and potato together." I munch on some chips. "I have to confess, I've

116

never had homemade perogies. My mom buys those frozen ones in huge bags at Costco."

After the perogies, we learn about diesel engines.

"What would you be if you couldn't play hockey?" I ask, then toss back another tequila shot.

Buck contemplates that. "Maybe a soccer player—no, a pilot. I've always wanted to learn how to fly."

I nod in approval. "That's cool."

"What about you?"

"I'd be an engineer. Maybe a mechanical engineer."

Then they're showing us how golf clubs are made. "That's my backup plan!" I lean forward. "Pro golfer."

"You any good?"

"Hell yeah." I give him an offended frown.

"What's your handicap?"

"Five."

"Huh. Same here." Buck lifts his chin. "We need to play."

"Golf's for the off-season."

"Right. As soon as we win the Frozen Four, you and I are hitting the links."

"You're on, dude."

We watch a few more episodes, at which time I realize I'm staring blearily at the TV screen. The tequila shots have snuck up on me with motherfucking stealth.

"I'm wasted, man," I tell Buck.

He grins, a loose, mellow grin. "Me too." He stretches his legs out in front of him, feet on the coffee table, hands behind his head. "So tell me . . . why'd you come to Bayard?"

"It's a good school. Great hockey program."

"Yeah, yeah, but why *any* school down here? If you were some hot prospect up in Canada, why wouldn't you stay there?"

It's obviously the tequila that makes me think it's a good idea to spill my guts to Buck. I spew a brief version of the story.

"That blows, man." Buck gives me an unfocused but sympathetic look.

"You believe me?"

He frowns. "Yeah. Why wouldn't I?"

I shrug and pick a crumb of tortilla chip off the front of my shirt. "Lots of people didn't." I don't want to tell him how much that hurt and pissed me off. "You don't even know me."

He's silent for a moment. "I know you're not a rapist."

This strikes me as funny and I start laughing. "That's high praise." I guess from him it's better than nothing.

Surprisingly, he laughs too. "Yeah, that didn't sound good, did it?"

"So, now you know." I almost don't want to give him this much power, but I say, "I'd rather no one else knows about this."

Buck lays a hand over his heart. "I wouldn't fucking tell."

I swallow. "Okay. Thanks."

"Hey. I'll share my own ugly story with you. That way you'll have something over me too."

"A good basis for a lasting friendship—blackmail."

Buck laughs. "Yanno, Flash, I'm kinda getting to like you."

"Gee thanks. Okay, what's your story?" I'm thinking he probably did something embarrassing with a chick, like pass out while he was getting a BJ, or accidentally text his mom something meant for his girlfriend.

"Okay. My dad was murdered when I was six years old."

"Jesus." I stare at him, my tequila haze suddenly vanished.

"Yeah." He shrugs. "I don't remember a whole lot, but I know it was never really investigated and they never found who did it. All my life, I grew up thinking it was some kind of robbery gone wrong."

I nod slowly and pour myself another shot. Then I pour him another shot.

"Thanks. Then about four years ago, I found out that it was actually my uncle who killed him. My mother's brother, not his own. Apparently they both had drug problems and my dad owed him money."

My gut tightens painfully. This is awful.

"So my family life wasn't exactly all happy TV sitcom family."

I know he's from Buffalo, but for some reason I thought he came from a well-off family, I guess because of how he likes to dress and the stuff he has.

"After my dad died, my mom didn't have much and I grew up in a pretty rough neighborhood with a lot of crime. I couldn't wait to get out of there. So that's my ugly secret that nobody knows."

"And I thought mine was bad." I frown. "You seem to have done okay, despite all that crap."

"Thank fuck for hockey." He grimaces. "It was my way out of that garbage pit life. I always knew I wanted better and I worked my ass off to get out of there."

I lift my shot glass to him. "And you did it, bro."

"Not yet, I haven't. I mean, yeah, I got out, but I want more. That's why I hafta get drafted. I gotta make it into the NHL."

I nod. "Me too."

"Why?" Buck eyes me with owlish curiosity.

"I just do." I shrug. "Without hockey . . . I got nothin'."

"Eh, you got golf, man! Or engineering. Hey! You could write episodes of *How It's Made*."

I snort-laugh. "Right."

"You got no worries, man. You'll be drafted, for sure."

"Not so sure of that." I grimace. "I had to pull out of the draft last spring because of all the shit that went down. What if I'm still in the bad books?"

"Seriously? A guy with talent like you have? Teams don't care about crap like that. They want someone who can score goals and win games. Make money for them. That's the bottom line."

"So cynical for one so young."

"Phhht. Realistic is what I am. Come on. You'll be drafted."

"So will you."

Buck reaches over and clinks his glass against mine. Tequila sloshes out, but whatever. We tip them back.

Next thing I know, there's a lot of hooting laughter and yelling.

"What? What?" I try to wake up and lift my head to peer around. Where am I? What's going on? Who's . . . ? Jesus fuck, I'm cuddled up against Buck on the couch.

"You look so cute together." Rocket is killing himself laughing. "You been hiding something from us?"

That's pretty hilarious, since we just shared our deepest, darkest secrets with each other in a drunken exchange. And then apparently passed out. I scrub a hand over my face, feeling out of it, my mouth all dry and stuck shut. "Yeah, now you know our secret."

"Why him?" Soupy frowns at Buck. "I'm hotter than he is."

"In your dreams, dude." I smirk at Soupy.

Buck squints, then frowns at me. "You're dreaming about me?"

"Yeah, man. Every night." I lean in and make kissy noises. The guys crack up all over again, Soupy collapsing into a chair. Tears run down his face.

"Get the fuck away from me." Buck shoves at me.

"If that's what you want." I shake my head and stand, a little wobbly. "I need more sleep. Hitting the sack."

"Alone?" Rocket taunts me as I climb the stairs.

I show him my middle finger over my shoulder and he cracks up again.

The next morning Buck and I meet up in the kitchen, both grabbing bottles of water out of the fridge to wash down our painkillers.

"Shit." Buck rubs his forehead. "What were we thinking?"

"We weren't. Fuck, my head hurts."

"Mine too."

Our eyes meet and we crack up.

Knowing Buck's past actually makes me like him more. He's had his struggles too, and I kind of get why he dresses so well, sort of like a costume or a mask, trying to escape the life he had growing up.

Seriously, nothing is a better bonding experience than getting drunk and then being hungover together.

Chapter 17

Skylar

JACOB and I are studying for mid-terms in the kitchen at my place. I'm struggling with quantum mechanics. Honestly, the talk of light waves being a combination of oscillating electric and magnetic fields makes my head spin. This shit makes no sense at all and I want to pick up my textbook and hurl it through the window. As I imagine doing that, Jacob covers one my hands with his.

"Relax, babe."

I turn my gaze to his, pressure building inside me. "Easy for you to say." He's already aced three mid-term exams apparently without even breaking a sweat.

He stands and moves around behind my chair. His big hands drop onto my shoulders and he starts massaging. "Jesus. You've got rocks here."

I groan at the feeling of his hands on my tight muscles. "Oh my God."

He kneads and squeezes, finding spots of exquisite pain that he gently works until they release.

"Wow," I breathe. "You're good at this."

"I love getting a massage. I guess I've picked up a few things."

He digs his thumbs into my spine, down between my shoulder blades. I whimper.

"Okay?"

"Oh yeah. More than okay."

He continues to work on me, up my neck, back to my shoulder. "You're killing yourself, Sky," he murmurs. "Are you sure this is what you want?"

His question makes me tense again, and he squeezes my upper arms.

I release a long breath and let my head fall forward. His fingertips find two spots at the base of my skull that are tender. "I have to do this."

"Why?"

"I told you. My sister's going to be a doctor."

He massages my neck more. "Do you think your parents won't love you if you don't become a doctor like her?"

Tension grips me again and my head snaps up.

"It's okay," he soothes, gliding his hands along the tops of my shoulders. "Tell me."

I struggle to find the words. I don't want to talk about it, but he asked, and . . . it's Jacob. "They'll be disappointed. Every time I don't do as well as Elisha, they're disappointed. They've paid a lot of money for me to come here, and if I don't do it . . . well, they won't hate me, but I can't stand the thought of letting them down. Of being *less* in their eyes."

I hear a low growl in his throat. "That's bullshit."

I close my eyes. "I'm sorry. But it's true."

"You aren't less than your sister."

"Sure I am." My throat tightens. "I just want them to look at me with the same kind of pride they look at her. I want them to brag to their friends about both their smart daughters, not just one."

"They fucking do that?" His hands go still.

"Yes. They probably don't even realize it. All I ever got growing up was, *Your sister got an A in this course. Your sister was the class valedictorian when she graduated. Your sister got a full scholarship to Bayard, and then Harvard.*"

"Christ." His hands go still on my shoulders. "Your sister sounds pretty damn annoying."

I choke on a laugh. "Well, yeah, but she wasn't doing it on purpose. She's just a super overachiever and my parents apparently wanted two kids like that. Even my A wasn't as good as her A+. I got a partial scholarship because I busted my butt, but it's still costing my parents a lot of money to send me here and they never let me forget it, always reminding me they didn't have to pay for Elisha to go to Bayard. Last year when I told them I'd flunked two courses and would have to take them over, they were so upset. I stayed here all summer to take the classes again. I worked so I could pay for them myself, to try to make up for flunking. And so my parents would keep paying for me to come back this year."

Jacob makes a low noise in his throat.

"That's why I have to do it. They'll consider it a waste if I don't become a doctor."

"I can't get my head around that. They should be proud of you no matter what you decide to do. And you're not your sister, you're a different person. You should just be yourself, Sky. Because you're pretty damn amazing. And they should want you to be happy."

I don't think I've ever heard them say that. I swallow through a tight throat, my chest aching. "Do your parents want you to be happy?"

"Yeah." He pauses, his fingers still working on my less-tight muscles. "They've done a lot for me so I can achieve my goals."

"To play hockey."

"Yeah. Hockey costs money. They don't have a lot, but they made sure I had equipment and registered for minor league hockey. We lived just outside Kamloops, so when I got older, there were hours of driving back and forth to games and tournaments. Then when we realized I was actually pretty good, they let me move away from home when I was sixteen. It was hard on them, especially my mom. They sacrificed a lot."

I nod, my throat squeezing.

"They also believe in me," he adds quietly. "Which is the best thing of all they could give me. Last year, I kinda screwed up and they still supported me."

"Your parents sound awesome."

"They're coming in a couple of weeks. You can meet them."

"Ah . . . for your birthday?"

"Yeah."

Meeting Jacob's parents sounds like a "real girlfriend" thing to do. Also celebrating his birthday with him is a "real girlfriend" thing to do. This is awkward. But I don't say anything right now.

"How's that? Better?" He lays his big hands on my shoulders.

"So much better."

He lowers his hands to give my boobs a squeeze.

"Jacob!"

He laughs as he drops back into his seat. "Sorry, I couldn't resist. And you love it when I fondle your boobs."

I smile. I really do.

He leans forward and I meet his eyes. "Seriously, Sky. You should be doing what makes you happy. Not what will make your parents happy."

I gaze at him as I process this. "But they're my parents."

"Yeah, I get that."

But he has a point.

"You know what you should be doing?"

I shake my head slowly, my eyes fastened on his.

"Teaching. You're an amazing teacher."

I blink at him. "What?"

"The training you did. I told you before how you rocked it. You were so great."

I shrug. "I didn't even know what I was doing. It was my first time."

"See? You did know what you were doing. You were reading everybody in that room and adjusting what you did to hold their interest. You got everyone comfortable and involved, even when it wasn't a super comfortable topic. You were funny and . . . engaged . . . and . . ." He appears to search for words. "Human."

I smile. "Human. A high compliment."

He grins. "You know what I mean. There are teachers that are intimidating. Sometimes they don't seem like they're really human."

"I know what you mean." My chest warms. "Thank you. I did enjoy it." My mind is turning in circles, thinking about what he said. "But I don't really like kids that much."

He laughs. "Seriously? How much time have you spent around kids?"

"Not much," I admit. "I babysat a little in high school."

"Well, you could try it. Or you could teach high school."

I picture that, and surprisingly, I find this idea ridiculously appealing.

"The class you like the most is psychology," he says. "What else would you take if you could take anything? What were your favorite subjects in school?"

"Not physics." He smiles at my joke. "Um, I loved history and geography. I'd love to travel and see the places I learned about. Especially Europe."

"Yeah. That would be cool."

I stare into the distance and my stomach knots up. The weight of the unfathomable physics and chemistry suddenly seems unbearable. Like I've reached the point where I just can't do it anymore.

And even if I do, it'll be for what? My parents will still be disappointed in me. I'm never going to get a full scholarship to Harvard. Even if I had the marks, I need to do some kind of extra-curricular medical work. I love what I'm doing at SAPAP, but I don't think that's going to cut it to get into medical school. I know this and yet haven't made any efforts to find something appropriate.

A teacher. What would my parents think of that?

And should I care?

I do care what my parents think. Of course I want their approval. Is that wrong? Or do I need to grow up and make my own decisions?

"What if . . ." I hesitate. "What if I change my major and my parents decide they're not going to foot the bill for a prestigious college just so I can be a teacher?"

His eyes go shadowy. "You think they'd do that?"

I shrug. "It's definitely possible."

"Well." He shoves a hand into his hair. "I guess there are other options. Student loans, maybe?"

"Another part-time job." I grimace. "Or switching schools."

Our eyes meet and his face is somber. "That would suck."

My stomach feels like a knotted-up ball of yarn. "Yeah, it kind of would." I'm thinking about him, which is stupid because I know he wants to be drafted this year and might not even be back next year. There is no way in hell I should be making decisions about my future based on him. Especially since we are fake dating.

"I need to think about it," I tell him. "But . . . thanks, Jacob."

He nods. "Okay. Let's see if we can get another hour of work in. If we do, we can reward ourselves with donuts."

"You brought donuts?"

"Yep."

"Oooh, you devil. You know my weaknesses."

"Donuts, coffee, cherry Kool-Aid and chocolate-covered almonds."

I blink down at my book. Wow. He does know me.

Thursday night is Halloween and we're going to a sorority party. Jacob was enthusiastic about a costume for the party, but he was determined we should go as a couple. We looked at some Pinterest pictures for inspiration. Neither of us wanted to spend a lot of money, so here we are dressed as a Hawaiian vacation couple.

A trip to the dollar store the other day loaded us up with leis and flowery necklaces, which we're both wearing. I've got a fake flower in my hair and I'm wearing a cheap grass skirt over a pair of tight running shorts, with a bright pink bikini top. Jacob is wearing shorts with a wildly colored, tropical-flowered shirt open over his bare chest. My heart gives an extra beat at how hot he looks.

His eyes warm as he studies my costume. "You look sexy, babe."

"Thanks. So do you. But we're going to freeze."

He laughs. "Wear a warm coat. It'll probably be warm in the party."

"Probably."

The party is crazy. Music is blasting when we walk in—"Spooky Scary Skeletons." The house is dark and packed with bodies in all kinds of costumes, some cute, some sexy, some downright terrifying.

I edge closer to Jacob. "I hate it when I can't recognize people. It creeps me out."

"Hey." He slides his arm around me. "S'okay, baby, I'm here with you." He gives my waist a squeeze that reassures me.

The music changes to "Monster Mash." Jacob grins and grabs my hand and pulls me toward a bunch of people dancing.

My eyes go wide. We've never danced together in the weeks we've been fake dating. Taking both my hands in his, he pulls me near then steps back.

"Hey, you know how to dance."

His grin goes wicked. "You know I do, baby."

We find the rhythm and he spins me around into his arms then back out. Our eyes meet and we share a smile. My head starts bopping as I get into the beat of the music. The song ends too quickly, my heart beating a little faster, my skin warming.

"See, no worries about freezing." Jacob touches a finger to my cleavage in the bikini top through the layers of leis.

"Nope."

"The Time Warp" from *Rocky Horror Picture Show* is playing now. With shouts of delight, people swarm the makeshift dance floor. Jacob and I laugh and move to the music as people crowd around us, singing along with the song, yelling out the chorus with big arm movements. I shake my hips and do a circle with my hands in the air, and when I face Jacob his lips curve with amusement and his eyes blaze. He gives me a nod of approval as he moves in perfect time to the music.

He's an athlete and I guess it makes sense that he's a good dancer—he's fit and coordinated—so I don't know why this surprises me. I like it.

We dance to "She Wolf" by Shakira, and then the music changes, slowing down, to "You and Me" by Lifehouse. Jacob pulls me up against him and sets both his hands on my hips. I drape my arms over his shoulders, my eyes fastened on his, like the song says, and our bodies move together. He smiles into my eyes. "You like dancing?"

I nod.

After the slow, sexy dance, we take a break, both of us breathing quicker and a little flushed. Jacob spots some of his hockey buddies and we join them. Them, and the puck bunnies surrounding them.

Ack, did I actually just think that? I lectured Ella on how the term "puck bunny" is demeaning and slut shaming, and then I think something like that. These could be perfectly nice girls interested in the Bears for reasons other than the fact they're hockey players.

Giant spiders and cobwebs hang from the ceiling above us and a skeleton sits on a chair in the corner. These sorority gals have gone all out for this party.

"Jacob!" A girl turns to him and eyes his chest. "Hi! Love the costume."

And she actually slides her hand over his bare chest.

A yellow witch hat perches on her head, a tiny black-and-yellow bikini top reveals a lot of cleavage and her black-and-yellow skirt barely covers her ass cheeks. I hear Hunter murmur, "Whoa. Cooch alert."

I bug my eyes out at him and he laughs.

I turn my gaze back to this . . . er, witch, and give her an icy glare.

She ignores me and continues to caress Jacob. "Wow, your abs are amazing."

"Thanks."

He's not moving away, just grinning at her.

"How'd you do on that STURB test?" Blink, blink. Rub.

"Uh . . . good. Hey, Julie, have you met my girlfriend, Skylar?"

Julie flicks a glance my way. Her lips twist up.

I insert myself between her and Jacob and wrap my arms around his waist. "Hi, Julie. Nice to meet you." I give her a big phony smile.

She rolls her eyes, but shrugs and leaves.

"She's in one of your engineering classes?"

Jacob lets out a breath and hugs me. "Yeah."

I give him a wry smile. "You're welcome. Every girl on campus is going to hate me by the end of this year."

"Oh, come on. Not every girl."

I make a choking noise. "I can't believe you're admitting that."

He laughs.

Skimpy costumes abound at this party, and I guess I can't talk since I'm wearing a grass skirt and bikini top. But these girls keep coming on to Jacob and it's pissing me off. I'm not in my comfort zone having to be a badass bitch. I'd rather be making friends with them. Well, some of them.

"I'm hungry. Let's find some food."

There's a big table in the dining room loaded with food, some of it disgusting-looking. We pick up mini pizzas, the cheese and two olives making them resemble mummy faces, but I pass on something that looks like intestines and move to chips and dip in a small hollowed-out pumpkin.

I run into a few people I know from classes and introduce Jacob. The guys get into a hockey discussion. It should be boring, because I don't really know much about hockey, except I'm fascinated to listen to Jacob talk about it. He's so knowledgeable and well spoken, and these guys are hanging on his every word.

"I have to say the DeWitt Center is pretty awesome." He smiles. "I mean, it's the fans. They're great. Really makes it a crazy, noisy environment. That gives us a huge boost and I think it's intimidating for other teams to play here."

Jacob leaves to use the bathroom and I talk to Portia about one of our profs.

"I didn't even want to take this course," Portia says. "But I had him last year, and omigod, he makes everything so much more interesting. He's so brilliant and funny. I felt crazy signing up for his class just because it was him teaching it, but I'm so glad I did."

Jeez, she sounds like she's in love with him. "He is good," I admit. But nothing is going to make me love quantum mechanics.

"One of my mentors told me that you take a course for who's teaching it, because the prof is what makes or breaks a class."

"But you can't pick every course because of who teaches it. I mean, you have to meet certain requirements, right?"

"Well, yeah, but if there's a choice . . . go for the good prof."

Good teachers are important. Could I really do that?

I ponder this for a moment, then . . . uh-oh. Jacob has been gone a while . . . hopefully he hasn't been waylaid by some girls. Although he wasn't trying all that hard to get away from Julie earlier.

Oh my God, now I'm thinking like he is, that every girl is after him.

"Hey, Skylar."

I turn to see Justin from my psych class. I smile at him. We've sat next to each other a few times and he's really funny. "Hi, Justin. How are you?"

"Great."

"I like the costume."

He looks down at his police uniform. "Not very original, but it works." He moves closer. "*Your* costume's awesome." He gaze moves down over my boobs and then he touches one of the leis. "Should I make a bad joke about wanting to get laid?"

"Not if you want to walk out of here on unbroken legs."

Justin's head whips around to see Jacob standing behind him, all big and tall. Jacob lifts one eyebrow and stares him down. I blink and my hand goes to my throat. Whoa.

"Just a joke, man." Justin frowns. He glances at me questioningly.

"Uh, this is my boyfriend." I nearly choke on the word. "Jacob Flass. Justin's in my Research Methods class."

Jacob lifts his chin and narrows his eyes.

"Uh, yeah, good to meet you, man." Justin shoots me a regretful grimace. "See you around, Skylar."

"Yeah. See you."

Justin vanishes.

I glare at Jacob. "What the hell was that?"

"What?" He frowns at me. "I was protecting you."

"I don't need protecting."

His lips thin. "Are you saying you're interested in that guy?"

His rudeness and overbearing attitude annoy me for some reason and what comes out of my mouth next is probably not well thought out. "Maybe I am."

Chapter 18

Jacob

I suck in air between my teeth at Skylar's response.

She glares at me. "You didn't need to be rude to him. He's a friend."

Blood runs hot through my veins and I have to relax my hands. Okay, okay, I know Skylar's not really my girlfriend. But she can't be flirting with others guys when I'm not around. We both agreed we wouldn't do that.

Which in no way explains the magnitude of my anger.

He had his eyes all over her and he was touching her. Touching her lei anyway, and making a dirty joke about it, and she might be interested in him, and . . . fuck.

I'm fucking jealous.

I shake my head. What. The. Hell.

"Where were you for so long, anyway?" She lifts her chin. "With one of the many girls stalking you?"

I shake my head. "For Chrissake, no."

"You didn't seem too upset about Julie feeling up your abs."

She's jealous too. And being jealous and angry is not conducive to having a calm, rational conversation. Because I was about to throw down something that couldn't be taken back. I was about to ask her if she wants out of this deal. And I'm too afraid to hear her answer to ask that question.

"Let's go."

"What?"

"Let's go." I take hold of her arm. "We're not having this discussion right here and now."

She starts to argue with me, but then she huffs out a huge long-suffering sigh. "Fine."

My anger is fading already. I can have a quick temper, but it's usually over just as quickly. Drop the gloves, land a few punches, get it all out and then it's done.

I'm talking hockey, of course. I am not going to punch Skylar. But the testosterone and adrenaline and possessiveness pumping through me definitely makes me want to do something else to her.

The drive home is silent, the air in my truck thick. Once we get back to her place and we're inside, she tosses her coat over a chair and turns to face me, arms crossed, hip cocked, lips pouting. "Okay," she says. "What was that?"

"I was rude. You're right. I apologize."

She blinks and her arms drop to her sides. Then she plants her hands on her hips. And damn, she's so goddamn gorgeous, bare legs beneath that ridiculous grass skirt, the smooth curves of her torso in the bikini top, her long hair flowing down her bare back. Christ. My dick stands up and salutes her beauty. I wish we were on a beach in Hawaii and I could stretch out on the sand next to her in that tiny pink bikini and rub coconut-scented sunscreen over every inch of her body and then . . .

"Jacob?"

I blink. "Yeah?"

"What are you doing?"

"Fantasizing about doing you on a tropical beach."

Her eyes go wide, then hazy. "Oh."

We stare at each other, and the air goes electric around us. The backs of my thighs tingle and my dick hurts. Then she's in my arms and our mouths are fused.

"Damn." I pull her bottom lip into my mouth, then her top lip. She moans and we kiss again, openmouthed, tongues sliding. She's plastered against me, arms wrapped around me, mouth devouring mine, and I'm devouring her back. "Damn, baby."

"Shut up and kiss me."

My mouth twitches but I comply. We need to talk, but hell, I'd way rather do this.

I back her up against the wall and slap my hands on either side of her head, pressing my hips into hers. She moans into my mouth and her hands slip under my shirt to my bare skin.

"You know what should happen now?"

She licks her bottom lip and looks up at me with heavy-lidded eyes. "Fucking? A blow job?"

"Aaaah." I groan and kiss her again, fast and hard, my dick twitching at two of my favorite words. "Okay, that wasn't what I was thinking, but now that you say it, hell yeah."

She gives a breathy laugh. "What were you thinking?"

"I was thinking you should totally do a hula dance for me."

"Oh. Hmm. I'm not sure I know how to do one."

I step back and spin her around like I did earlier, then release her. "Okay, baby, bust a move."

She giggles, and damn me if she doesn't start swaying her hips in a graceful rhythm. She moves her arms and it looks pretty good to me. Except, hey, she's moving away from me, across the room . . . I smile and follow her and she turns her back on me and gives her ass a twitch, shaking that grass skirt, and it damn near sends me to my knees.

I pick up speed to catch up to her but she casts a flirty look over her shoulder then breaks into a run toward the stairs.

Hell yeah, I chase her.

She gets onto the first step when I wrap my arms around her waist and lift her right off her feet. We're both laughing, and fuck, I'm turned on as hell.

"Where do you think you're going?" I growl into her ear.

"My bedroom."

I nuzzle her hair and bring one forearm up right under her lush tits. "You made my dick so hard it hurts."

"I'm sorry?"

I give a low laugh and catch her earlobe in my lips. "No you're not, you little tease. Damn, that was hot."

She grinds her ass back against me. "Okay, that's it. Now you get that fucking."

"Finally."

We both laugh again as I carry her up the stairs.

I don't think I've ever laughed so much with a stiffy as I have with Skylar.

I kick her bedroom door shut and lower her feet to the floor. She immediately turns in my arms and plasters herself against me again. Goddamn, I love how hot for me she is.

She runs her hands up over my chest.

"You were jealous when Julie was touching me earlier, weren't you?"

She pauses. "Okay, yes." Then she narrows her eyes. "You can wipe that shit-eating grin off your face."

I bark out a laugh. "S'okay, baby. I admit I was jealous too when Dustin was all over you."

"Justin."

"Whatever."

It occurs to me that we really shouldn't be jealous of each other since this is just an arrangement, but that thought burns to a crisp in my brain with an audible sizzle as Skylar goes down on her knees in front of me.

"Whoa, baby."

She's working open my shorts but she needs to be careful or my wang is gonna hit her right in the face. I'm as hard as a fucking goalpost.

Her soft little hands are on me then, my baggy shorts dropping to the floor, my boxers down around my thighs.

"Oh yeah." Her breathless words sound admiring. I swell even more in her hand. "Your cock is so beautiful, Jacob."

I should make some smart-ass comment, but I can't even speak.

"Seriously. So big." She gives me a long, slow stroke. "So hard. Smooth here." She kisses the tip.

"Ungh." I slide my hands into her hair. "Baby . . . can we do this lying down?"

She peers up at me, eyes big. "Sure . . ."

I haul her up and steer her over to the bed. I ditch my boxers and shirt then leap onto the bed and stretch out.

She regards me with amusement. "You're keeping those on?" She gestures at the flowery garlands still around my neck.

I'm sure I look ridiculous. "Yeah."

Her lips twitch. "Okay. Whatever trips your trigger."

I snort-laugh. "Oh baby, you have no idea. Get over here."

Still wearing her grass skirt and leis, she climbs on the bed and kneels between my legs. She reaches for me and strokes. My dick is a throbbing spike in her hand and lust pulses in my balls.

Then sweet baby Jesus, she bends forward and her long gold hair falls all around her face and my cock. It tickles my thighs and I can't stop the groan that climbs my throat. "Oh fuck yeah."

Her mouth around me is hot and silky, her tongue agile and slick. But the visual . . . dear God, her hair all over me, swishing across my belly . . . damn. It's my hottest spank bank fantasy come to life and it's even better than when I imagined it.

Hoping she's okay with this, I reach for her hair and pull it all around and over one shoulder. With her lips still wrapped around my aching dick, she peers up at me. I take her hair and rub it over my shaft. Another groan escapes me.

She drops fascinated eyes to my hand holding her hair. "You like that?" she whispers.

"Fuck yeah. I've been fantasizing about your hair since the night we met."

"Oooh." She squeezes her thighs together. "Here. Let me."

She slides a hand down the tail of hair I have gathered up and I let go. Leaning closer, she wraps her hair around my dick and then slides it up and down.

"Fuuuuuuuck."

The fingers of her other hand tickle my balls, nearly blowing the top of my head off. My thighs spread even wider and she caresses my sack, which is pulled up tight beneath my shaft.

She has to make an adjustment to the hair, then she's stroking me with it again. Sensation wraps around my cock, pleasure licking over every nerve ending in my body like flames.

She swipes her tongue over her bottom lip and looks up at me again. "How's that?"

"So hot. Dying here, babe."

"Good. I like doing this do you." She leans down to kiss my lower belly, right above my pubes. Jesus.

"If you like my hair on your dick, what about my breasts?"

I can't breathe. My lungs have seized up completely. My head spins.

"I've never done it, but I've heard . . ."

"Fuck yeah." My vocabulary is seriously limited right now. But I think I'm getting my feelings across.

She quickly shifts onto her butt and reaches behind her for the fastener of her bikini top. Then her tits spill out, so perfect and round, her nipples hard little points. I'm panting like a dog in a heat wave.

She lies back, pulling the leis to one side. "Come here," she invites me in a throaty voice. "Come fuck my tits."

I could weep I'm so overcome. My dick leaps up eagerly and I shove up and knee walk until I'm straddling her body. She pushes those sweet mounds together and I slide my cock between them.

"Mmm. Too dry." She waves a hand at the bedside table.

I well know there's a bottle of lube in there, which we don't use often, but she once gave me a most awesome hand job using it, which made it fantastically . . . fantastic. I grab it and squeeze some onto my dick, watching her watch me, her lips parted, a pulse fluttering wildly in her throat.

"There we go." I toss the bottle aside and stroke myself, getting my dick all nice and lubed up. Then I resume the position and slide between her tits.

Again, it feels a-fucking-mazing, but it's the visual that makes it extra hot, like our own porn movie, up close and personal. Then our eyes meet and the intensity makes my brain short circuit. The fact that she loves this as much as I do is enough to make me worship her for the rest of my life.

"I'm gonna come," I gasp, my ass tightening, my balls squeezing. "You want me to stop?"

"No. Do it. Come on my tits."

Jesus Christ. The words alone send me over. I hold my cock, my vision going dark, a roaring in my ears. I vaguely hear her murmurs of pleasure and the words "Oh my God," but my heart is hammering, my blood pounding in my veins. Pleasure races up my spine, burning through my chest, and my cock surges as I come in violent, wrenching spasms.

When I can pry my eyelids open, I gaze down at my come on her gorgeous chest. I swallow hard. It's so dirty and hot, and when she trails her fingers through it and then licks them off, I can't even . . . I groan and collapse, resting my head on her belly, trying to wrap my arms around her hips. "You're the best girlfriend in the world."

"Fake girlfriend."

What the fuck ever.

I try to catch my breath. A while later I say, "Sorry."

She strokes my hair. "What for?"

"Ladies come first."

She laughs. "Such a gentleman."

I lift my head. "I am."

Her smile softens. "I know you are."

"I just . . . you got me all horned up with that hula dance, and then down on your knees, and then your hair . . ." My voice cracks embarrassingly, and I cough. "And then . . ."

"Yeah." Her fingers slip through my hair. "I know you'll make it up to me. Because if we're keeping an orgasm score, I'm winning."

I huff out a laugh and lay my head back down. Her fingers feel so nice smoothing my hair. "You know I will, baby. Just give me a minute."

I could almost fall asleep, but then again that sweet pussy is so near my face. I have to get her out of her clothes. She's topless . . . but maybe I should clean her up first. Yeah, that's a good idea.

"Be right back." I drag my ass off the bed and jog across the hall to the bathroom. I'm in the hall and naked when it strikes me this might be dangerous. I'm wearing nothing but flowered garlands draped around my neck. But no one else is around. I grab a washcloth and run some warm water over it, then return to the bedroom with it and a towel. She's still a sexy topless hula dancer wearing a sultry smile and my semen. Hot.

I slowly drag the cloth over her breasts, between them, under them, cleaning her all off. Her nipples contract even harder and tiny goosebumps raise up on her smooth, wet flesh. "You're cold. Better dry you off." I use the towel, but after that I can't resist touching her more, shaping and squeezing those exquisite tits. "So beautiful. Look at you." I lean down to suck on a nipple. Her abs tighten. I give a firm tug and she shudders, holding my shoulders. "Like that?"

"I love it." She moans and her legs move restlessly.

I close my eyes and enjoy the feel of her nipple against my tongue, then nip at it with my teeth. I move to the other one while my fingers toy with the first wet nipple, pinching and tugging it. Her whimpers increase in tempo and her hips are lifting.

"Does that sweet pussy need some attention?" I lick her nipple.

"Yes. Please. It hurts . . ."

"I made your pussy hurt, baby?"

"Yes. God yes."

"Mmm. I'll kiss it better. But gotta get this sexy hula skirt off you."

I rise up on my knees to untie and get rid of it, then pull off the stretchy little shorts and her thong panties. Now we're both wearing nothing but flowers. I grin.

"Wish I had a picture of this."

"No way."

"I know, I know." I shake my head ruefully. "Maybe one day you'll trust me enough to take some sexy pics."

She bites her lip and our eyes meet and for a few seconds we're probably both thinking that's never gonna happen. Again, I push that thought aside and focus on the heaven in front of me, all pink and plump and smooth.

"Wanna make you feel good." I position myself between her thighs. She pushes up onto her elbows to watch with hazy eyes, hair all over the place. I kiss the inside of one leg where the skin is thin and tender, closing my eyes and drawing in a breath through my nose. She smells fantastic, her usual apple and vanilla and flowers mingled with her unique female perfume. It makes me nuts, makes my dick harden all over again and my balls ache.

She's watching me still, biting her lower lip, a flush staining her chest and climbing into her cheeks, that sweet and sexy blush. I nibble her inner thigh, giving a nip with lips and then so gently with my teeth. I press a kiss to the crease where her leg meets her hip, then I lick and suck her other thigh.

She's panting now, quick little breaths that I love. "Jacob . . . please."

"What, baby?" I'm teasing her, kissing her legs, knowing where she needs to be touched. But it's fun and I know the hotter I get her, the better her orgasm will be.

I start playing with my fingers, stroking over her. She seems so tiny and soft. I like watching this too, my big hand on her pussy. "Are you wet, hmm?"

"Why don't you check?"

"Cute." I slant her a smile and see the gleam in her eyes. "All right, then." I dip my fingers into her folds. "Oh yeah. So wet. All for me."

"Yeah. For you."

I fucking love that. I slick up her girl lube and rub over her skin, all around her clit, and she makes a hissing noise. A smile tugs at my mouth.

I push my middle finger inside her. She's tight and hot and I ease in deeper, deeper, until I can stroke inside her and her body twitches hard. She falls flat on her back and grips the bedcovers.

"There?" I whisper. "How's that?"

"Oh God yes. That's amazing."

Now I can let myself taste her. I lick up and down, around where my finger penetrates her, tasting her sweetness, teasing around her clit.

"Please," she begs again. "I need to come." Her hand rises and rubs over the top of my head, and her hips roll against my mouth in a needy rhythm.

I play a little longer, with slow strokes of my tongue and soft suckling kisses. I reach up and squeeze one tit, holding it as I open my mouth on her pussy, then pinching her nipple. Her hips lift again and again. Finally, I lick over her clit. She jerks against my mouth and her inner muscles squeeze my finger. "Ready, baby?"

"I'm beyond ready, oh my God, Jacob . . . keep doing that . . . right there . . ."

I work my finger in and out faster, fucking her with it, tonguing her clit, and she comes apart against my mouth in a long, shuddering orgasm, hoarse cries falling from her lips. It's epic.

I close my lips over her swelling clit and suck as she writhes. She grabs my head and gently pushes. "Stop. Oh God."

I lift my head and smile with satisfaction.

"Oh wow. Wow. You did good, Jacob."

I kiss her lower belly. "I'm glad."

I get Skylar under the covers and then slide in against her. "Wish you had a bigger bed."

She cuddles into me, all warm and soft. "Me too."

I eye the space. "A king bed probably wouldn't even fit in here."

"Probably not."

"Sometimes we could get it on in my bed."

I feel her smile against my chest. "I guess."

I caress her hair, still stoked about what she did earlier. "Next weekend is my birthday."

"Right."

"My parents are coming."

"Mmm. I remember you said that."

"I, uh, told them I was seeing someone."

She tenses a little. "Yeah?"

"Yeah. I thought it would make them feel more comfortable about how I'm doing here if I had a girlfriend."

"Oh no . . . you don't . . ."

"Yeah. They want to take us out for dinner on Saturday night."

"Oh, Jacob. That's not fair to them. To make them think—"

I kiss her forehead. "It'll be fine. It'll set their minds at ease. They might not even be back this year, and . . . well, we'll figure it out."

"I don't know . . ."

"Seriously. They're nice people. It'll be fine."

She sighs against me. "Okay."

Chapter 19

Skylar

I'M at Jacob's home game Friday night. His parents are here somewhere, but since they just arrived late this afternoon, I haven't met them. I didn't want to meet them at all (well, that's not entirely true; I'm actually pretty curious about them) but when Jacob said he thinks they'll feel better about how things are going for him here, knowing he has a girlfriend, I kind of got sucked into that. I do feel a little guilty about the pretense. But it'll probably be the only time I'll ever meet them. And the truth is, Jacob and I *are* friends now.

I watch Jacob on the ice, as usual turned on by his athleticism, intensity and fierce aggression. I love how he's such a leader out there, yelling at his teammates, setting up plays.

I know he wants to play well tonight since his parents are here.

The action is down in the Bears' end, and Jacob has the puck behind the net. He's playing with it, not moving, looking up the ice. "Go!" I yell, along with others in the crowd. Then I see players changing and realize that's why he's delaying there. A big Knights defenseman circles around in front of the net, keeping an eye on Jacob. As Jacob starts out from behind the net, the Knight swings his stick at John Alfredson, the Bears' goalie, hitting him right in the head. John drops to the ice.

My eyes widen in horror but I don't think a lot of people saw it because everyone's watching Jacob. Did Jacob see it?

He passes the puck up the ice to Buck, but stops, spins around and rushes at the Knight who just hit John, dropping his gloves.

Screaming Jesus, he's going to fight that hulk.

I close my eyes as my heart climbs into my throat. But I have to watch. They're yelling at each other, although I can't hear exactly what they're saying. I'm sure it's laced with profanities and insults. I know hitting the goalie like that is absolutely dirty. And Jacob is standing up for his teammate.

They raise their fists and circle around each other until finally Jacob lashes out with a fist and the other guy grabs him. They're wrestling, punching, yanking jerseys, and the Knight's helmet goes flying off. Jacob lands a few good punches and then throws the guy to the ice, landing on top of him. The crowd roars with approval.

I cover my mouth with my hands. Holy duck fuck, this is so dangerous. They're on sharp blades, on ice, punching each other. Luckily that Knight player's head doesn't hit the ice without his helmet on. That could be so bad. My stomach tightens painfully, watching this brutality. Damn, I hate this part of the game.

The other players are cheering their guys on, but once they're down, the linesmen step in and pull Jacob off his opponent. He doesn't really resist. He's made his point.

The linesman pushes Jacob toward the penalty box and the other player gets up, apparently not hurt. He's got a hand to his face, though, and as he makes his way to the other penalty box he's shouting at Jacob, who turns and yells back, this time clear as anything, "No, you're the fucking asshole for hitting the fucking goalie, *moron!*"

The guy's name on his jersey is "Morin" and fans snicker about this.

Everyone starts clapping and cheering for Jacob, who clearly won the fight. I watch him stomp into the penalty box and throw himself down on the bench, breathing hard. He takes his helmet off and a trainer hands over a towel that Jacob uses to wipe his face, and then his visor. I can see the set of his jaw and his narrowed eyes, his face flushed—he's pissed.

And gorgeous.

And I'm a mess. A terrified, relieved, angry, proud mess.

He sits for five minutes for fighting, clearly anxious to get back out there. I'd rather watch him than the game. But the fight seems to have energized the Bears, who score two unanswered goals and win the game four-two.

Ella and I are heading home after the game, although she tried to convince me to go to Curly's, and Jacob is going visit with his parents. Tomorrow night we're having dinner with them to celebrate his birthday, which is Sunday. That is freaking me the hell out. Having to make conversation with Mr. and Mrs. Flass while pretending to be Jacob's girlfriend—gah! Why is he making me do this?

Okay, okay, he's not making me. He just has this charming ability to always get his own way. It's mildly annoying.

Saturday evening I'm stressed about what to wear. We're going to Rudy's Public House, which is a fun kind of place with steaks and burgers, nothing fancy. Again, I'm not sure why I care this much about what they think of me. I could wear my shortest skirt and highest heels and a top cut down to my navel and it wouldn't matter.

I drag Ella into my room to help and this is no act.

She studies my closet, pulls out a black dress, then puts it back. Finally she says, "Jeans. With boots and . . . this top." She pulls out a plain black long-sleeved T. "And my big black and gray scarf. Hang on."

Hmm. Okay, with the scarf it won't look so plain. I do love that scarf. I strip off my yoga pants and hoodie and pull on my skinny jeans. Ella returns with the scarf and I finish dressing, then wrap it around my neck in a big cowl, the corners hanging loose.

She adjusts the ends. "There. Casual but put together. With your black boots, it's perfect."

"Thank you. I don't know why I was so flustered about it."

"Hey. It's Jacob's parents. I get it."

I swallow my sigh.

Jacob arrives then to pick me up. I sit on the couch to zip up my boots and then I grab my black pea coat, which luckily the scarf also goes with. "I think I'm wearing too much black. I look like I'm going to a funeral."

Jacob laughs and kisses my forehead. "You look gorgeous, gorgeous."

"They're going to think I'm emo."

"I don't think they know what emo is."

His parents are staying at a hotel, so they're meeting us at the restaurant.

"Did they enjoy the game last night?"

He makes a disgusted noise. "They said they did, but fuck, I can't believe I got in a fight."

"You were defending your goalie. Plus, you motivated the team. Look how it turned out."

"Yeah." He grins. "You're becoming quite the hockey fan."

"Hmm. Except I hated seeing you fight."

"Yeah? Worried about me?"

"Maybe a little." I chew on my bottom lip. Then I change the subject. "So. Yesterday I went to talk to my faculty advisor about changing my major."

Jacob's head snaps around. "Really?"

"Yes. You made me think about it. She was really supportive and helpful."

"So are you doing it?"

"I haven't for sure decided, but . . . I'm leaning that way. I feel like I need to talk to my parents first, though. I can do that at Thanksgiving when I'm home."

He frowns out the windshield. "What if they try to talk you out of it?"

I nibble my bottom lip. "That could happen. Or they'll guilt me into keeping my major."

"You're an adult, Sky. I think you should make your own decisions. And yeah, I get that they're helping you financially. But it's not like you're changing your major to basket weaving or something. And you got good advice from someone who knows. That's the mature, responsible thing to do. Plus you're the one who has to live with your decision."

As usual, he's pretty smart for a jock.

Mr. and Mrs. Flass are already there, seated on one side of the booth; they both slide out and stand to greet us. My stomach has a herd of butterflies flapping around inside it, but I smile and shake hands with them, while the words *this is crazy, this is crazy* spin around in my head.

"It's lovely to meet you, Skylar." Mrs. Flass smiles warmly at me, her eyes sparkling behind stylish, dark-framed glasses.

Jacob has her eyes, but the rest of him comes from his dad, a handsome man with the same chiseled cheekbones, and dimple in his square chin. He's tall and fit, with only a bit of gray in his brown hair. Mrs. Flass has shiny, shoulder-length chestnut hair. She's small and curvy and very pretty.

Jacob takes my jacket and hangs it on a hook near our table. I slip into the dark red leather booth first, putting me directly across from Mr. Flass. Jacob sits next to me and sets a warm hand on my thigh.

I think he means this to be reassuring. Which then makes me wonder if I look that nervous. Oh my God. I take in a long, slow breath and let it out, surveying the dark wood paneling and floors, and the mellow, low-hanging lights above each table.

Mr. and Mrs. Flass make conversation by asking me what courses I'm taking and what my major is. I tell them I'm working on a science degree, but then I stop before saying I want to get into med school. "Actually, I'm rethinking my major."

Jacob's hand squeezes my thigh but I don't look at him.

"There's lots of time to figure it all out," Mrs. Flass says. "You're young."

I know she's right, but I feel like at nearly twenty, I should have it all figured out and it bugs me that I don't. But I smile and nod.

They ask Jacob questions about his own classes, although clearly they keep in touch and also got caught up on a lot last night after the game. They talk about hockey and his roommates, who they met earlier today when they went to see his place.

"They seem like good guys," Mr. Flass says.

Jacob grins. "Looks can be deceiving."

We exchange a smile.

"Seriously, they're decent." He doesn't tell his parents how he thought they hated him and I know it's because he doesn't want them to worry. He wants them to think everything is great here at Bayard, including his new girlfriend.

So I give him that. We discuss my volunteer work at SAPAP, which I'm always happy to talk about. Jacob tells his parents about the training and compliments me again, which makes my cheeks heat to what is probably tomato red.

"Is that how you two met?" Mrs. Flass asks, looking between us.

We share another look, and as if we've read each other's thoughts, we both say, "Yes."

In the end, it turns out to be a fun evening. My burger is delicious. Mr. and Mrs. Flass are both funny, and of course Jacob is too, and we laugh a lot as they tell him stories about what his younger sister has been up to back home in Kamloops.

Outside the restaurant, Jacob's parents give me hugs, which is nice. I really like them.

"I hope we'll see you again soon, Skylar," Mrs. Flass says. "It's been so nice to meet you."

"I hope so too." Whether this is likely is another matter, but I actually mean it.

Jacob and I climb into his truck and he drives toward our neighborhood. "Well," he says, "that was great. They like you."

"I like them too. Hopefully they don't get too invested in our relationship, though."

My insides tighten. Saying that makes me feel weirdly sad. Hopefully *I'm* not getting too invested in our relationship.

After a short pause, Jacob says, "Yeah. True."

I watch him drive. Even the way he drives is sexy, the easy way he holds the steering wheel and checks for traffic as he changes lanes. He drives fast but I always feel safe because he seems so in control of the vehicle.

This reminds me of watching him play hockey and how in control and skilled he is, and it reminds me that last night after the game was the first time I've watched him play when we didn't go back to either my place or his and bang our brains out.

"Um . . ."

He glances at me. "Yeah?"

"I'm kind of . . . turned on."

His head whips around, then turns back to the windshield. *"From meeting my parents?"*

I choke. "No! God no." I wheeze. "From watching you drive."

He shoots me an amused look. "Babe. Seriously?"

Heat floods into my face, which is still not as hot as between my legs. "Seriously."

"Want me to pull over?"

I lick my bottom lip. "Um . . ."

"Jesus."

"No, that would be crazy." I pause. "I've never had sex in a car."

He hammers on the brakes, lurching me forward against my seatbelt. With a quick flick of the lever, he signals a turn and pulls off Center Drive. Then he steps on the gas.

"Where are we going?"

"You'll see."

He makes another turn and enters a park. It's dark and quiet, and he drives to the end of the parking lot, away from the only streetlamp that illuminates it. Beneath a tree spreading its bare black branches across the deep blue sky, he parks the truck.

My belly does a flip as he turns to look at me. His smile is wicked and panty melting. "Seriously?"

"Oh yeah." He leans across and kisses me, hard and long. His tongue licks over my bottom lip as he draws back. "Come over here."

"There's not much room."

"This is as far back as the seat goes. I have long legs." He shifts in the seat.

I undo my seatbelt, and since it's now nice and warm in the truck, I pull my arms out of my jacket and leave it there as I crawl over. Straddling his lap, I'm not sure how this is going to work, since we're both wearing a lot of clothes, but I place my palms on his stubbled cheeks and lean down to kiss him. He grips my hips and kisses me back, taking control of it, his tongue sliding into my mouth and playing with mine.

One hand tangles in my hair and tugs my head back. His lips glide over my throat and suck gently. I make a noise that might be a protest but I really don't care if he leaves a mark. He licks me there.

"This is in the way." He gives my big scarf a tug and unwraps it. Then he kisses me again on the neck, laying a string of soft openmouthed kisses down to the neckline of my shirt. He tugs it aside to continue his exploration.

He cups my breasts in both hands, gently molding them to his palms. "Love these beauties."

"That feels so good." My back arches to press into his hands and I bash into the steering wheel. "Ouch."

"Sorry, baby."

"Not you." I giggle. "It's a little squishy."

He lifts his hips and nudges his erection into me. "Hey, take that back. It's not little. And it's definitely not squishy."

I collapse into laughter against his chest, my hair all around us. Jacob's big body shakes with laughter too and his hand cups the back of my head.

I finally stop giggling and lift my head. Our eyes meet and we share a smile. Something turns over in my chest at the warm affection I see in his eyes. I'm feeling that too, for him. And suddenly I want him even more.

"Do me," I whisper. "Right here."

"I'm trying. Stop laughing."

"You're the one who made the joke."

"Yeah, I'm pretty damn funny, aren't I?"

I grin as another laugh bubbles up.

"Did I harsh the glow, babe?" He grabs the hem of my shirt and whisks it up and over my head, and I'm sitting on his lap in a black lace demi bra. "Ah, okay. Nope." He traces his fingertips along the top edge, which is so low my nipples almost show. And then he tugs that lace edge down with both hands, exposing me to him. His eyes devour me. "Sweet."

Heat spreads through my body. Jacob bends his head to suck my nipples, and warm streams of pleasure ripple through me right to my core. "I'm aching for you," I whisper.

"Me too, baby. Feel how hard I am for you."

"Mmm. Not squishy at all." I move against him, and damn, I can't help it, but I start laughing again.

His lips twitch too and he brushes his mouth over mine.

"That's what I'm going to call your junk from now on. Squishy."

"Don't you fuckin' dare."

"It's like a sarcastic nickname." I kiss his jaw. "Because you're so the exact opposite of squishy."

"Damn right."

My heart swells up so big I almost can't breathe, and I'm still so turned on. I grind against him.

"Getting these jeans off is gonna be a challenge." Jacob flicks open the button. "Lift up, baby."

It takes some work and possibly a couple of bruises, but we manage to get them down my legs. I push off one boot and pull that foot out. The other doesn't matter. I help Jacob open his jeans and reach into them. "Squishy," I murmur. "I need you."

Jacob chokes on another laugh but his cock swells in my hand. I love how he feels, so hot and hard. I stroke his rigid length while he pulls a condom from the ashtray.

I lift an eyebrow at him.

"What? It's important to have safe sex wherever you are."

"I guess I can't argue with that."

He has the condom on in a flash and then his big hands on my waist lift me again. I reach for him to help guide him inside me, lowering myself slowly onto him. "Oh God." It's like he's thrusting up so deep he's pushing all the air out of my lungs.

"Oh fuck." He lets out a deep groan, lifting me so I slide up his shaft. I'm so wet, he glides through me, then I plunge down onto him again. I adjust my position to get better balance and then I can take over, rising and falling on him.

"So deep. So deep." I press a hand to my abdomen and squeeze my inner muscles around him.

"I love when you do that. Christ."

My breasts are in his face and he buries his face between them. His cock slides in and out of me. I move up and down. He kisses and nips at my cleavage, making appreciative noises.

"What do you need, babe?" He tugs a nipple with his lips and my abs tighten.

So considerate. He's an amazing lover. "I need you to touch me."

He slips a hand between us and finds my clit with his thumb. "There? Good?"

He hits the exact spot. "You really know how to put it in the slot."

He chokes on another laugh. "You're killing me, Sky. Jesus."

I smile, but I'm getting close. Tension's twisting inside me, dark and beautiful. "Don't stop."

I close my eyes and let sensation take over, his cock tunneling in and out of me, stroking sensitive nerve endings inside me, his thumb working magic on my clit, all of it pulling up tight and high and . . . "Yeah." My body tightens and then the tensions breaks, pleasure coursing through me in hot, delicious waves. "Oh *yeah.*"

"There you go, sweetness. So sweet." He kisses my mouth. "Sweet and sexy."

I'm pulsing around him and he's fucking up into me with fast, hard thrusts and then he goes still and I feel him, a flutter inside me, as he comes too.

Then we collapse together in a sweaty, rumpled pile of sated exhaustion.

Chapter 20

Jacob

I'm sitting in the locker room taping my stick. Daft Punk is blasting around us and the other guys are doing their stuff to get ready. I like hanging out here in the locker room for a while before practices. It's good to spend time together as a team. I'm getting to know these guys better and better.

I've already warmed up on the bike and done some weights and I'm ready to hit the ice. It's what I wait for every day.

Our next game is against our archrival, the Harvard Crimson, and we talk about what to expect from them.

"They've really kicked their offense into high gear the last couple of games," Coach tells us. "They've got their senior star Paul Black back in the lineup, and a power-packed top line. Last game they combined for eleven points."

Fuck.

"We're going to need tight defense. After practice we'll look at some plays."

Then we put on our equipment and practice jerseys and hit the ice. This is it—skating, hitting the puck. I love it.

After we warm up and do a few stretches, our assistant coach Art Backes gets us doing some give and go shooting. We line up outside the blue line, Art in the corner. My turn. I pass the puck to Art, skate toward the net for the pass back and make a quick shot. It has to be fast. I nail it.

"Good, good!" Then, "Eyes up, stick on the ice, ready for the pass!" Art yells at Jimmy.

At the end of practice, the coaches get us all in a circle on one knee at center ice, and then team captain Franco yells, "Dance off!"

My mouth drops open. What the fuck?

"Rookies go first." Franco points at me.

Is he serious? I stare at him, but everyone's hollering at me to get up and dance, and the coaches are grinning.

Then the music starts over the sound system, Walk the Moon singing "Shut Up and Dance." It's a quick, catchy beat, and what the hell, I like dancing. So I push up onto both blades and glide to the center of the circle. I slide my stick across the ice and drop my helmet and go for it, arms in the air, thrusting my hips, then a spin. It's a little tough to show off my moves with all my gear on, but I give it my best shot.

The guys cheer and Coach shouts, "Now Churchill!"

I lift my arms as the guys tap their sticks on the ice, gliding over to the circle while a red-faced Danny Churchill takes my place.

It's fucking hilarious, and cuts through some of the intensity of the practice and our upcoming game. Because dammit, hockey should be fun.

Even Black Jack dances, but he's clearly not into it. If he'd just loosen up and have fun, it wouldn't feel so awkward, but he only does a few perfunctory moves and then skates off. I meet Buck's eyes and he makes a face.

By the time everyone else has had a turn making a fool of themselves, my abs hurt from laughing so much.

It's five o'clock when we're done, but Buck and I stay on the ice a little longer and practice tipping the puck in. We've been playing on a line together the last few games and things are really clicking. Franco on the right wing plays the same kind of gritty game I do, we both go in hard on the forecheck and drive the net, and the three of us all seem to read each other and find each other.

After we're finished, we head back to the locker room. I do more stretches, and my ice bath, which is painful. I'm told it's good for reducing muscle inflammation, but I'm actually skeptical of it. Then I jump in the hot shower, which feels fucking fantastic after that. We watch some videos, and Coach points out problems and things we need to work on. He also points out some good things, which makes me respect him as a coach.

As I leave the DeWitt Center I pull out my cellphone to turn it on and check the time. We have strict rules about no cellphone use from the minute we step into the center until we leave. It's nearly six-thirty. I debate going for something to eat, but study table is happening at the Herbert J. Kane Academic Center for all college athletes.

I don't have to go, because I'm not a freshman, and I'm not in poor academic standing—yet—but I like to go when I can. I find it motivating to be around others who are working hard. In the weight room, there's a little competitive edge between me and the other guys that pushes me to try harder. On the ice, same thing. And I'm finding when I'm studying with a bunch of other elite athletes—one guy here is an Olympic swimmer—it makes me want to do better.

So I find a spot and open my laptop to go over some lecture notes from earlier. I let out a sigh. Sitting in classes all morning is difficult. Going to practice when I have all that pent-up energy feels good. Now coming here, somewhere so quiet and still, and trying to focus again on schoolwork at the end of the day when I'm tired, is fucking hard. It'd be so easy to just say fuck it and go home and veg in front of the TV with a video game or a movie. But I have to push through this.

My phone buzzes with a text message a while later. Quite a while later. I'm impressed to see I've been focused on schoolwork for nearly two hours. Go me.

It's Skylar.

Hey, where are you?

I text her back with my location. *Where are you?*

Just getting off work. Hungry?

Starving.

Be there in ten.

I smile and set my phone down. I heave a sigh and rub the back of my neck. This week has been crazy. It feels like every minute of my day is scheduled with something—early classes, practices, meetings, studying and squeezing in time to solicit donations for the pizza fundraiser. I know there are perks to this gig, like the awesome training facility, the coaching staff I'm learning so much from, the strength and conditioning coach who's making me so much fitter, the trainer who gives me massages . . . but it's not exactly easy.

Skylar arrives with a big paper sack from the Taste of Heaven Diner in her hands and waves at me. I pack up my stuff and join her in the lounge area, where she hands me a Styrofoam take-out container holding a burger and fries. It smells fantastic.

"Thank you." I pick up the burger and take a huge bite.

She opens her own container of a salad with some kind of spicy chicken slices on top.

I eye it. "That looks good."

Her lips quirk. "Want to try some?"

"You can have some fries."

She grins and hands me her fork to spear some chicken and salad, then helps herself to a couple of fries. "You need ketchup."

"I don't like ketchup."

"What?" She stares at me as if I just told her I like to kick puppies with my skates on.

I shrug. "I'm a salt and vinegar kind of guy. But you can hardly ever get vinegar down here. So I just go with salt."

"Huh."

She passes me a container of chocolate milk and I take a long pull. The fact that she knows I love chocolate milk makes something inside my chest go soft. "Thanks. This is great."

"Long day?"

"Yeah."

We talk about our days as we eat. She laughs at my story about the dance-off after practice, then we pack things up and throw it in the trash before walking outside to our respective vehicles. I walk with Skylar to her car and we pause before she gets in. She tugs her scarf up around her chin in the chilly night air.

"Won't see you until next week. We leave tomorrow for Boston. Our first road trip."

"Right." She nods. "Good luck."

"Thanks." I find I don't want to say good night to her. I don't want to leave her. I've hardly seen her this week and now we're going on a road trip and I won't see her until next week.

Jesus. She keeps reminding me this isn't a real relationship and it's starting to bug me. I mean, I *know* it's not real. Except why do I feel like something's squeezing my chest at the idea of leaving her?

We'll chat on Facebook probably, when I have time.

I need to get a grip here, so I give her a quick kiss good night. She flashes a smile before climbing into her car.

I watch her drive away and then jog across the parking lot to my truck. Our three and a half hour flight to Boston leaves at six a.m. and I need sleep.

A road trip is a bonding experience for a team. We're forced into close proximity for three whole days. We're on the plane together, hanging in the airport together, going for dinner together. It forces us to get to each other better—especially the guys like me who are new to the team.

And then there's the game, our first in an opponent's rink. My first game wearing the white away jersey instead of the black home jersey. I know our rink is hard for other teams to play in, but there's an intimidation factor playing here at Harvard. Friday night, we lose, which blows. But it definitely makes us come together as a team, and that's good. We learn more about each other and what we can do when we're faced with adversity.

Saturday night, we manage to pull out a win, two-one. We almost had a shutout for Alfie, but somehow the Crimson tipped one in with only a minute on the clock. But Alfie's a good sport about it, saying how happy he is for the win and how well we played in front of him. Coach's tight defensive play is paying off for us.

I try to get some studying done on the plane on the way home. We're heading into the last few weeks of classes before exams and then Christmas. Somehow I pulled off a couple of As, a B+ and some Bs on my mid-terms, so I don't feel quite as much pressure. I think I have to thank Skylar and all our study dates for those marks. I only wish she felt better about her own classes. She was so bummed when she got a C on her physics mid-term. I've helped her as much as I can, and as much as she'll let me. She's pretty stubborn and determined to do this, but man, it's just not her thing. I wish she'd stand up to her parents and do what she really wants to. I think she'd be a lot happier.

I have to admire her determination, though. She's a tough, sweet little cookie. The weekend was too busy to think much about her, but now I'm on my way home . . . fuck, I miss her. I'm excited to see her but also a little worried that maybe this fake dating thing is getting a little too intense.

Chapter 21

Skylar

"WE NEED A CHICK PERSPECTIVE ON THIS."

I look up at Grady. I'm in the kitchen at Jacob's house with him. Ben, Grady and Hunter have just walked in.

"On what?"

"Scrotum reduction surgery."

I choke on my latte. *"What?"*

"Scrotum reduction surgery."

"Uh . . . is that really a thing?"

"Yeah." Hunter slants Grady a frown. "There are legitimate reasons to have it done."

I blink. "I guess there could be."

"Girls get boob jobs." Ben folds his arms across his broad chest. "Now guys are getting nut jobs?"

I burst out laughing at that.

"You know what I mean," he says.

"We are not having this conversation," Jacob announces, frowning. "You are not discussing your balls with Skylar."

"I'm talking hypothetically," Grady says. "Do girls care what guys' balls look like?"

I nearly choke again, but I'm also laughing. "Well, I'm only one girl . . ."

"Yeah, but you're smart. And hot."

6

66

I grin at Grady while Jacob scowls more. "Personally, the most important thing is cleanliness."

They all nod seriously.

"What about shaving?" Hunter asks.

Every other guy winces. I shrug, my lips rolled in to stop my smile as I glance at Jacob. "Um . . . sure. But no stubble."

They nod again.

"Does size matter?" Ben lifts an eyebrow.

I shift in my chair. "Not to me." Now I have to studiously not look at Jacob, because what I really want to tell them is, Jacob's balls are perfect. I love fondling them, teasing them, licking and sucking them . . . I have to squeeze my thighs together on a burst of lust.

"What if they're really low hanging?" Hunter asks. "Hypothetically."

"Stop talking," Jacob says.

"You stop talking," Hunter says.

I giggle. "I don't think there's anything wrong with low hanging. Hypothetically speaking."

Jacob groans.

"A little slap action during doggy style," Grady says. "Girls like that, right?"

"Find your silence. Please," Jacob says. Then he grabs my hand. "We're leaving."

I can't stop laughing. These guys aren't being offensive; they're cute and funny despite the nature of our conversation. "Wait, I need to use the bathroom."

He releases my hand and I hustle down the hall and into the main floor bathroom. I'm sitting on the toilet when I spy the empty toilet paper holder. "Damn." I open the doors of the vanity beneath the sink, but there's none there. "Oh my God."

Then I see the stack of fast food napkins on top of the vanity. Wendy's. Subway. Dairy Queen.

"Seriously?" I cannot believe this. I use a couple of the napkins, which is not the most pleasant experience, hoping they don't plug the toilet.

After I wash my hands, I grab the unused napkins and stalk back to the kitchen. I hold them up. "Guys. This is an atrocity."

They all exchange guilty looks, but shrug. "Oops," Jacob says. "Didn't have time to go shopping, so we found those."

156

Grady bites his lip. "They work, right?"

"Oh my God. Go buy some toilet paper!"

"Sorry, Skylar."

Ben's sincere apology makes me smile. Okay, it's kind of funny as well as pathetic. I'm grinning and shaking my head as Jacob leads me out. "Where are we going?"

"Your place. You're not allowed to hang out here anymore with those idiots."

I giggle. "They're kind of fun."

Jacob is smiling too.

"Oh sweet screaming Jesus."

I flop onto my back and fling my arms up over my head, my body quivering from an explosive orgasm. Jacob's naked beside me, breathing fast, and he lays his hand on my thigh and squeezes.

"Yeah," he pants. "That."

I smile drowsily. I've never been so content or lethargic. I'm not sure if I'll ever move again.

Jacob rolls toward me. "I don't want to leave," he murmurs in my ear. "Okay if I stay?"

I don't want him to leave either. "Yes."

I've never spent the whole night with a guy, and it feels intimate and special and sexy. I wake up briefly a couple of times in the night, and I listen to his breathing and savor the heat his body emanates. Once he reaches for me when somehow we separate, not that we can get far apart in my double bed, but he's still sleeping, which makes my heart turn over in my chest, and I snuggle in and go back to sleep.

I'm sound asleep and warm and cozy in Jacob's arms when the door of my bedroom opens and bangs against the wall. My fuzzy brain tries to make sense of this. What time is it? Is it morning? I have to work at noon at the diner. Did I sleep in? What's going on?

Jacob stirs beside me and lifts his head. "What the fuck?"

Ella is standing there staring at us, her face contorted. She appears to be having difficulty speaking.

"Um, Ella, what's going on?" I pull the covers up over my bare boobs. I don't usually sleep naked, but then, I don't usually have people walking into my room without even knocking.

Ella glances at Jacob, squeezes her eyes shut briefly then turns her gaze to me again. "You slept with him."

"Uh, yeah." I clutch the covers, giving Jacob a sidelong glance. Ella's upset about this? The girl who's been sleeping her way through the male student body? Also, she knows I've slept with Jacob.

"Not Jacob." She slashes a dismissive hand through the air. "Brendan!"

The name hangs there between us. The air in the room goes thick and very still. My insides seize up.

Ella holds up a cellphone and takes a step closer, and I can see tears in her eyes. "You slept with Brendan. I read the texts he sent you after."

"What?" I give my head a shake.

"When I was home that weekend, Brendan's mom gave me his cell phone. They thought it was lost, but they found it in his things. It was dead and they didn't have a charger, but it's the same as mine. She asked me to see if I could find anything that would give them some clue about why . . . why he did it." Tears slide down her face. "I didn't want to look at it, because I was afraid, but finally I charged the phone and today I read the texts. You slept with him and then rejected him, and that's—" Her voice breaks on a sob. "That's why he killed himself."

I stare at her in horror, my fingers tightening on the covers. I don't even know what to say to this. Because it's true.

Chapter 22

Jacob

I DON'T KNOW what the fuck is happening here. My head's still cloudy with sleep, struggling to wake up and figure out what is going on. Not to mention, I'm sporting serious morning wood.

I remember Skylar talking about her friend Brendan, who committed suicide. That's what this is about. But holy shit, Ella is furious. And Skylar is sitting there openmouthed and not saying a word.

"Uh, maybe we could have a few minutes to get dressed," I say to Ella. "Then you two can talk about this."

"I don't want to talk about it!" Ella yells, glaring at Skylar. "I'm done with you. How could you do that? It's all your fault that he's . . ." She sobs again. "Gone." She makes a terrible choking, crying noise that has my guts twisting.

I look between the two women, horrified.

Skylar's face is pale and crumpled. Now she's crying too. "It wasn't my fault," she says in a shaky voice. "It wasn't."

"Yes, it was! You broke his heart and he was devastated. Why? Why did you do that? How could you?" Ella sniffles and swipes a hand across her wet face. "I loved him so much."

Skylar's body jerks next to me. "What do you mean?" she says slowly. "You loved Brendan? More than as just a friend?" She sounds bewildered.

"Yes!"

"You never told me that, Ella."

"I thought you figured it out. And then you slept with him! How could you do that?"

Skylar stares at her friend and the pain in her eyes makes me sit up and slide an arm around her.

"You are dead to me." Ella spits the words out. "We can never be friends again." She spins around and stalks out of the bedroom. Seconds later, her own bedroom door slams shut.

Skylar is trembling in my arms. "Oh my God. Oh my God." She covers her face with her hands and bends her head. Now she's sobbing—hard, painful-sounding noises. My guts cramp up even more. Christ, this is awful. I don't understand a lot of it, but it's awful.

"It's okay, baby." I caress her hair. "It's okay."

"No." Her head moves. "No, it's not okay. Oh my God." Her body shudders with more sobs. I feel helpless and a little panicky. This is *way* outside my comfort zone. Skylar is crying so hard I'm afraid she's going to hurt herself.

I wrap my arms around her, because it's the only way I can think of to help her, and rock her a little as she cries. Maybe when she calms down, she'll want to talk about it. Truthfully, I'm kind of dreading that. This sort of scene scares the living crap out of me and I honestly have an urge to jump out of bed and get the hell out of there.

But I can't do that to her. She's distraught, as much as Ella was when she came in. They're best friends. There has to be a way to make this better. Maybe I can help figure it out. Probably not, because I'm an idiot when it comes to female emotions. But whatever—I can't leave Skylar like this.

She turns into me, still crying, her arms going around my neck and clinging to me. "I'm sorry," she whispers moments later, when her sobs have eased. "I'm so sorry."

"Don't apologize." I smooth a hand up and down her bare back. "I'm not sure what's going on, but you don't have to apologize."

She swallows and nods, her hair all down around her face and I keep holding her. I give her more time and then she pulls away and draws in a shaky breath. She shoves her hair back but doesn't meet my eyes.

I reach for some Kleenex on the table beside the bed and hand them to her. She wipes her eyes and blows her nose. Her face is strawberry red and her eyes are puffy. She's still so beautiful, though. My heart squeezes at her misery.

"Want to talk about it?"

She closes her eyes, anguish etched on her face. "God."

It wasn't a no. I mull that over and decide to press a bit. "You didn't know Ella was in love with Brendan?"

"No." She shakes her head. "God, no. We were friends, all three of us. We were friends in high school and we all ended up here at Bayard so we stuck together. We were just friends."

"Did you really sleep with him?" I have to say, I'm not thrilled about this, but I already know she's slept with other guys, and hell, I've slept with other girls, so it's really a non-issue. Not to mention, the poor guy's no longer with us.

She swallows and her lips tremble. She meets my eyes briefly, then looks away.

"It's okay if you did," I tell her gallantly. I *think* it's gallant. I know I have to say it even if I don't like the idea of her sleeping with other guys.

"It wasn't like that," she whispers. She twists the soggy Kleenex up in her hands, nearly shredding it.

I narrow my eyes. "What does that mean?"

"I don't know if I can talk about it."

My insides twist up into knots again, suddenly afraid of what she's going to say. I hold my breath and keep petting her back. "You can talk to me, baby."

She gives a tiny nod, her head bent. "I didn't want to have sex with him."

Oh fuck. Fuck me sideways with a chainsaw. Nausea rolls inside me. I can't even speak.

Her voice is low and wobbly as she continues. "We were at his place one night doing homework. Then we had a couple of beers. Maybe he had more than me, I . . . was a little drunk, but not, like, passed out or anything. Ella wasn't there. He . . ." Her voice chokes up. "He started trying to kiss me. He said he loved me. I told him I didn't feel the same way, and I was sorry. He kept kissing me and I told him to stop and I was pushing him away, but he wouldn't listen, and . . . I didn't want to do it, but somehow we ended up having sex." A small sob escapes her. "After, I lay there for a while, then I got up and left. The last words I ever said to him were 'I hate you.' "

She takes another breath. "The next day he texted me and said he was sorry and he loved me, and could we talk about it. I didn't answer him and he kept texting me. I ignored his texts, I didn't know what to do. I didn't want to tell Ella, because they were friends." Her voice wobbles. "At first I was kind of . . . in shock. Almost numb. I was ignoring him and trying to pretend it never happened. And then three days later he . . . he hung himself." Another sob escapes her.

"Jesus Christ, Skylar. You can't blame yourself for that."

She lifts her head and I stare down into her beautiful, tear-streaked face, the anguish there making my heart hurt. "Of course I blamed myself. I totally felt like it was my fault."

"No." I shake my head, my jaw set. This I know. "It was not your fault."

"If I'd accepted his apology or talked to him, maybe it wouldn't have happened." She gazes up at me with tear-drenched eyes. "If I'd reported what happened, maybe he would have got the help he needed, even though he would have been in trouble. I was sure he killed himself because of me. I didn't know what to do. I didn't tell anyone what happened, not even the police. I know I should have, but I couldn't. Brendan was a good guy, and a good friend . . . how was I supposed to tell people what he'd done?" She swallows. "His parents would hate me if they knew. What Ella said . . . that it was my fault . . . I believed that at first. God, I felt so guilty. I understand why Ella sees it that way."

Christ. Jesus Christ.

"She doesn't know the whole story. It wasn't your fault." I don't know much about suicide but I know that much. My skin is burning and my guts are rolling. I hold Skylar tighter, squeezing my eyes shut.

"I know that now." She sniffs. "I do. But it took a while for me to get there . . . and still, sometimes, I question myself. Brendan was always kind of a moody guy. He'd get down, but usually he was crazy fun. I didn't realize he'd been struggling with bipolar disorder for a while. Then I felt guilty for not knowing."

"He raped you. You should not feel guilty."

Damn, I didn't even need to go for all that awareness training to know that.

She gives another tiny nod. "I didn't even want to admit it was rape, at first. I kept telling myself I could have stopped him. That I didn't try hard enough to stop him. I could have fought back more and . . . and I don't know why I didn't. He wasn't violent. But . . . I didn't want to do it. I told him that. I told him to stop and he didn't." She bows her head.

I close my eyes on another wave of sick that rises up inside me. I don't know if I can stand the thought of Skylar being hurt like that. For a moment, I'm consumed with black rage.

"I was having nightmares and panic attacks. I was a spaced-out zombie. I felt so alone and hopeless. Then I just couldn't live like that anymore. I needed help. I was determined that I wasn't going to let what happened define me. When I talked to the counselor, the first thing I had to do was admit how angry I was at Brendan. Which was hard, because . . . he was dead." She takes a couple of slow breaths, fighting for control.

"Well, I'll tell you this . . ." I narrow my eyes at her. "He didn't really love you."

Her forehead creases and her lips part. "What?"

"A guy who loved you wouldn't have forced you to have sex with him."

She stares at me wordlessly and then her face changes and she gives a slow nod. "Oh my God. You're right, Jacob." Then the corners of her mouth droop again. "He was my friend."

"You probably don't want to think that the guy who was your friend was an asshole."

She jerks her head up and down again.

"And you lost someone you care about, which sucks." I blow out a breath. "Wow, baby. That's a helluva lot to deal with."

"Now I've lost Ella too."

"You need to tell her what happened."

"No!" She draws back, her mouth in a circle of horror. "I can't tell her! I can never tell her."

I stare at Skylar. I'm not sure what to say. To me it seems obvious.

"What good would it do? It will just ruin her memories of Brendan, and for what?"

"Um . . . so you two can be friends again?"

She stares across the bedroom, her eyes vacant. "If she blames me now, she'll still blame me even if she knows what Brendan did. I blamed myself. I get it." Her bottom lip quivers. "And if she blames me, then our friendship is over."

She turns and buries her face in the side of my neck again. I just hold her because it's all I can do. I have no words to make this right. Skylar's in pain, and I'm feeling it too, my chest burning, and I can't fucking fix it and I hate that.

"I'm sorry." Skylar mumbles the words into my neck.

"For what, baby?"

"For all this drama. This wasn't part of the deal."

I let her words sink in. She's right. This is the last thing I need right now.

She glances toward her alarm clock and her eyes fly open wide. "Oh my God! I have to be at the diner by noon."

It's after eleven and we're still in bed, naked. Skylar is scrambling out from the covers.

"You okay to go to work, baby?"

She makes a face. "I have to be. Shit. I'm a mess and . . ." She blows out a breath. "Shit."

"What time do you work till?"

"Six."

"Want me to drive you?"

"No. That's okay."

I slide out of bed too and look around for my clothes. I really need to take a leak, but I can't walk across the hall naked here.

Skylar pulls out a pair of striped Hello Kitty boy shorts and steps into them. I grab my boxers and jeans from the chair where I tossed them last night and pull them on. I'd like to stay and watch her finish dressing but my bladder is protesting so I say, "Be right back," and hurry to the bathroom. Ella's door is still firmly closed and I wince remembering the earlier scene.

When I return to Skylar's room, she's already dressed in her hot waitress uniform with the tight pink dress and little apron. I set my hands on her waist. "Have I told you how sexy this outfit is?"

She gives me a wan smile. "No. One of your friends did, though."

I smooch her lips.

She takes her turn in the bathroom, coming back with her hair brushed into a neat ponytail and wearing makeup that attempts to cover her swollen eyes. I'm worried about her. She's calm but still distracted and visibly upset. She's trying hard not to show it, but it's obvious to me. I don't have much choice but to leave her there, though.

I go to a drive-through and pick up a breakfast sandwich and a big coffee on my way home. I have a fuck-ton of homework to do. Now we're into the season, it's even more of a challenge to balance all the practices and workouts and classes and homework. Science may come easy to me, but that doesn't mean there's not a lot of work to do, with reading and assignments. And we have another game tonight, which means being at the arena early and then home late.

But I'm distracted too as I crack open my laptop and try to make sense of some notes. I keep thinking about what I heard—that Skylar's best friend forced her to have sex with him. It makes my gut and chest burn with helpless fury. I have the awful thought that it's good he's not around, because if he were, I would kick his loser ass. Then shame washes through me because the guy was so messed up he took his own life, and that's never right.

Stuff that I learned during the training sessions comes back to me too. Consent and intimate-partner violence. They weren't intimate partners, but they were friends and Skylar trusted him. He betrayed that trust.

This makes it all seem so much more real.

And it also makes me think back to what happened at that party last spring.

I've been avoiding thinking about it, because I'd really rather not. But I keep thinking about going upstairs to the bedroom at that house with Ace and Crash, and Brittany. Brittany was a little drunk that night. I didn't think she was that bad, but now, looking back, maybe she was drunker than I realized. She was all laughing and flirty and telling us she wanted a hat trick—meaning sex with three hockey players at the same time—and it all sounded hot to a bunch of horny young guys. Including me.

I'd heard other guys talk about group sex. I'd fantasized about it. Every guy fantasizes about a threesome with two girls, or even the odd orgy. Here was my chance to actually experience it.

But deep inside me, I must have known it wasn't the right thing to do. She was eighteen years old and a little drunk and we were three big, strong guys. It was a crazy position to put herself in. I asked her if she was sure that was what she wanted and she laughed and said of course. Then I tried to tell the guys we shouldn't be doing it, but Brittany was already taking her clothes off and grabbing at Ace, and there was no stopping her. I'm now willing to admit I felt misgivings, which was why I left. And then she accused us all of raping her.

I guess I'll never know what really happened. Maybe she changed her mind and didn't want to go through with it, but if she had, I'd like to think my teammates would have stopped. I don't think they were so drunk that they wouldn't have realized she wanted to stop . . . were they? I'd also like to think they weren't such assholes that if she'd asked them to stop they wouldn't have. I asked them outright if she'd changed her mind, and they denied it, and I want to believe them, but I wasn't there so I'll never really know.

Guilt and doubts coming crashing back on me, making my stomach roll, squeezing the air out of my lungs.

I'd been bitter because it was Ace and Crash who'd had sex with her, but I was punished along with them. I kept telling myself I was an innocent bystander, and because I'd gotten the hell out of there, it was nothing to do with me. But now the word "bystander" has a whole different meaning.

I shouldn't have left. I should've put a stop to it. I know that now.

I slump into my chair and lean my head back. I guess this is the moment I'm supposed to have. It's why I'm here. To fucking learn from my mistakes. And thanks to Skylar, I guess I have.

Skylar.

Her friend raped her. It makes me want to punch something. And now she and her best friend have had a huge fight over it. Skylar's been worried about Ella, about her emotional state, and wow, now we know Ella was secretly in love with Brendan—no wonder she was so devastated by his death. But it pisses me off that Ella blames Skylar for Brendan's death. *He* was the one who screwed up and probably—hopefully—felt guilty about it. *He* was the one who took his own life, perhaps because of it. But Ella doesn't know that.

What a mess.

I try once more to focus on Hooke's law, but a feeling of hot pressure is building inside me. Too much. Too much to do. Too much to think about. Too many emotions I don't want to feel.

I close my eyes and suck in a long breath. Having Skylar as my fake girl-friend was supposed to help so I'd be able to focus on hockey and school. It wasn't supposed to mess me up even more.

Skylar is right. This wasn't supposed to be part of the deal. I don't need all this. I need to be focused, most of all on my hockey so the scouts who are coming to games this year are taking notice of me, and for the right reasons. I have to get drafted this year, which means fulfilling my part of the deal with Bayard—staying out of trouble and getting decent grades.

A panicky pressure swells inside me. Yeah, I can't deal with this. I should throw up my hands and back off and let her deal with her problems. I recognize this is selfish . . . but Jesus, I've got my own problems and goals. I can't deal with all of her problems too.

Chapter 23

Skylar

IT'S DEFINITELY hard to focus at work. I screw up a couple of orders, which probably loses me tips that I need. I can't stop thinking about it all—how upset Ella was this morning, how horrible that night with Brendan was, how sympathetic and understanding Jacob was.

I never wanted to tell him about that. I never wanted to tell *anyone* about it. I told Frances, the counselor I saw, and that was it. But now I realize this is a huge secret I've been carrying around, and it's been the wall between Ella and me all along.

And now she knows.

But she doesn't know all of it. Jacob thinks I should tell her the truth. I go back and forth over this in my mind, trying to figure out what to do. What the consequences of telling her would be, good or bad. What the consequences of *not* telling her would be.

Taisha nudges me. "Hey, girl, table twelve is trying to get your attention."

"What? Huh?" I look around. "Oh!" Damn, I promised them their check ten minutes ago. I hurry over to leave it on the table, apologizing profusely. Their frowns tell me that's another tip lost.

I sigh and move to the next table to see if they need anything else. They ask for refills of ice water. "Sure thing."

I walk back to the kitchen, but on the way I get stopped by another table, asking for more syrup for their pancakes, which I quickly get for them.

I lean against the counter, lost in my thoughts again. My stomach is a mass of twisted nerves. I've picked at a hangnail on my thumb until it's bleeding. I thought I was getting past the guilt and grief, but it's all swelling up inside me, making me feel like I'm going to burst out of my skin. I can't stand feeling this way, but I don't know what to do about it.

Maybe I need to make another appointment with Frances.

Or maybe I need to take a few minutes and remember some of the strategies she taught me, about controlling my breathing, controlling my thoughts, my self-talk.

Taisha stops in front of me, frowning. "Table ten is still waiting for water."

"Shit." I close my eyes and jump forward to get a pitcher. "I forgot."

"You okay, hon?" Taisha eyes me, her forehead wrinkled. "You don't look so good, actually. Late night last night?"

It was a late night, by the time Jacob and I fell asleep after trying out numerous positions and I had three orgasms. But that's not what the problem is. "Sort of." I rush over to pour ice water into glasses, once more apologizing.

I seriously need to focus here. I'm being paid to do a job, and screwing up isn't good for my tips or for the diner. I dig deep for the strength I need to shut my mind off to my problems and concentrate on work.

By the end of my shift, I'm drained. I walk slowly to my car. The cold air chills my face and the pale sky looks like it's ready to release snowflakes.

I start the engine and let it idle for a minute. Now I have to admit I'm afraid to go home. Because Ella will be there.

She said she's done with me, and I'm dead to her. I rub my chest where it burns. She can't mean that. We've been best friends since middle school. Yes, there's been this divide between us since Brendan died, and it's only now becoming clear to me why that is. I thought it was her behavior that was driving the wedge between us, but now I can see it's more than that. It's the huge secret I've been keeping from her.

I don't know how to fix this.

I lean my head on the steering wheel, my eyes burning, my throat aching. Then I pull in a shaky breath and lift my head. I have to try to talk to Ella.

In the house, I knock on her closed bedroom door. I lean my forehead against it and wait, but there's no answer. She doesn't usually keep her door closed if she's not in there. Paranoia grabs hold of me. She was really upset this morning, and after what happened with Brendan . . . I open the door and peek in.

Nope. The room is empty.

I quietly close the door and walk into my own room. I can hear music from behind Natalie's closed bedroom door but it doesn't seem likely Ella's in there with her. Looks like Brooklyn is out too. In my room I sink down onto my unmade bed and stare at the floor, not sure if I'm relieved or disappointed that Ella's not here to talk things out.

Ella doesn't come home all night. That's not exactly unusual for her lately.

I don't hear from Jacob either. That is unusual for a Saturday night. He almost always has games Saturday night, and he likes when I go to them, but tonight I have no one to go with and I'm not going alone. And Jacob hasn't texted to see if I'll be there. I kind of thought I might hear from him, even if only to see I was okay after that scene this morning. Whatever.

I don't sleep well, listening for Ella to come home. I guess I'm still affected by what happened with Brendan and it's making me worry about her. I keep telling myself she's not going to do anything extreme.

I'm in the kitchen Sunday morning making myself coffee when she arrives home. She passes by the kitchen door on her way upstairs. Her makeup is smudged, her hair a mess, and she's still wearing a tight, short red dress. My stomach tightens, but I call out, "Ella!"

She ignores me.

I move to the bottom of the stairs. "Ella, we need to talk."

"Nope. We really don't."

She doesn't even look at me and disappears into her room.

Great. Is this what it's going to be like for the rest of the school year? It's only November.

I haven't felt such a sense of bleak desolation since Brendan died. With heavy steps I climb the stairs to my room and shut myself in there.

I have lots to do. I have homework and some research, and tasks for the pizza fundraiser, as well as the frat chat we're planning for January.

But I find myself lying on my bed staring at the ceiling.

I roll off my bed and sit at my desk in front of my computer. I check the hockey team website to see how the game went last night. They lost, five-three. Ugh.

I send Jacob a text message. *Hey, sorry about the loss.*

It takes him a while to reply. *Yeah, it sucks, but oh well.*

I wait a while longer, debating what else to say to him. Should I ask him what he's doing today? Or is that weird? We've been spending a lot of time together and I've been thinking that things are changing between us. We keep talking about our deal and how this isn't anything real, but I have to admit, it feels real to me.

I care about him.

I might even . . . love him.

Then he messages, *How are you? Doing okay?*

I stare at my phone, smoothing my thumb across the screen as I again deliberate over how to respond. In the end, I lie. *Yeah, I'm okay.*

Good.

And that's the end of our conversation.

I sit there for a long time holding the phone. Then I rise and walk over to the dresser to plug it in to charge. I stand there with my hands gripping the edge of the dresser, staring at myself in the mirror.

My eyes are still bloodshot and swollen, my nose is still pink. My hair's in a lank ponytail from work.

I feel so alone. Tears spring to my eyes again.

How did my world get so fucked-up in the space of a day? And what do I do about it?

This week is Thanksgiving and I've planned to go home for the long weekend. I don't know whether this is fortuitous or crappy timing.

When I still haven't heard from Jacob by Tuesday night, I know I have to call him. I get his voicemail and leave a message. "Hey. It's me. I, uh, haven't heard from you all week, and I just wanted to let you know I'm going home tomorrow night. For Thanksgiving. Not sure what your plans are . . ." I have this crazy impulse to invite him to come home with me, but that's . . . crazy. He doesn't have family here though, and campus will be largely deserted over the long weekend and I hate the thought of him feeling alone. But I don't say this because I'm filled with uncertainty about what's going on with us.

Of course I've wondered if this is because he found out I slept with Brendan. Or because Brendan raped me, if we're going to be perfectly

171

honest about what happened. Has this changed how Jacob sees me? How he feels about me?

That makes me want to throw up.

I went for the counseling. I know what happened doesn't change who I am. I know it wasn't my fault. I know I'm still a good person.

But I'd be lying if I said I'm sure Jacob knows this.

I finish my voicemail message. "Anyway, I won't be around. Give me a call if you want."

I end the call and distract myself by starting to pack a few things in a suitcase. I discover I desperately need to do laundry, so I gather up some things and trudge downstairs to the small laundry room off the kitchen.

Doing laundry reminds me of Jacob's laundry lessons and his pride in knowing to separate whites from darks, and I smile.

My phone chimes in my bra as I'm dumping clothes into the washing machine. I fish it out and see it's Jacob. "Hi!"

"Hey, Sky. How's it going?"

Once again, I have to pause before I can answer. The truth is, things are shitty. Ella's avoiding me, Natalie and Brooklyn are acting weird, which makes me think Ella has talked to them and poisoned them against me, and he hasn't called for days. Finally I say, "Kind of crappy, actually."

"Oh."

This doesn't sound good. Like, maybe he wanted to hear that everything was all sunshine and lollipops and fucking rainbow-colored unicorns or something. Well, it's not.

"Sorry to hear that," he says.

I don't even know what to say to that. "Have you been busy this week?"

"I'm always busy." He sighs.

This is the truth. I know how intense his schedule is. "What are you doing for the long weekend?" I gather up my courage. "If you're not doing anything, you could come home with me."

Dense silence fills my ear. Finally he says, "Hey, no need for that. I'm good here. It's not Thanksgiving for us Canucks, so I'm going to hang out with Barks and Butch." The other Canadians on the team—Adam Barker and Pascal Bouchard.

"Ah."

"But thanks for the invitation. You have fun visiting your family."

Have fun? Uh, not likely. "Thanks, I will."

I slide my phone back into my bra. My stomach cramps up and I stare into space.

No need for that.

Right. Because he wanted to show his parents he was happy and settling in fine here with a girlfriend, but there's no need to impress my parents. And that's what this is all about—a fake girlfriend to keep the puck bunnies away and keep his parents from worrying about him far from home at a new school.

He just very effectively reminded me of that. God, I was so stupid to issue that invitation, as if we were really dating or something. What an idiot.

I need to add detergent to the machine. I do that mindlessly, then wander out to the living room, sink down onto the couch and cover my face with my hands.

I can't stop the tears that flow.

I've started to have real feelings for Jacob. And I was stupid enough to think he might feel the same. I'm more than an idiot. I'm delusional.

My throat burns and my chest aches.

The front door opens and I quickly swipe away tears as Ella and Nat walk in.

"Hi, Skylar." Natalie gives me an offhand greeting. Ella deliberately turns away and walks into the kitchen. Even though I'm sitting there crying. She doesn't care.

Nat pauses awkwardly, glances at Ella, then walks upstairs.

I sit there alone, clutching soggy, crumpled Kleenex.

I haven't felt this horrible since right after Brendan died, when I was so sunk into helpless despair. There's no worse feeling in the world than being alone like this. Feeling like I've lost every friend, that they're excluding me and avoiding me, and that includes Jacob.

So yeah, going home to see my parents seems like a great idea right now.

Chapter 24

Skylar

IT STARTS SNOWING as I reach Syracuse. My hands are tight on the steering wheel because it's dark and now the roads are getting slippery. I was anxious even before I left Ridgedale, knowing I have to have a difficult conversation with my parents this weekend. I pull into our driveway with relief, flexing my fingers. Whew. Made it.

I lug my suitcase into the house, dropping it on the hardwood floor inside the front door. As I shut the door, Mom appears from the kitchen, wiping her hands on a dish towel.

"Skylar! You're here! Hi, honey!"

We hug, and my throat thickens. I wish . . . I wish I could turn to my parents for comfort instead of instantly feeling small and inferior. Because I really need some comfort.

"Dad's in the family room watching TV. Come on in and say hi."

I follow her down the hall, through the kitchen, which is open to a big family room.

Dad looks up and sees me and smiles. He stands and holds his arms out, and I give him a hug too. "So, college girl, how are things?"

"Not bad."

Actually, things couldn't be much worse. Okay, I could be failing my courses; yes, that would be worse. Thankfully I don't have to tell them that again. But I am going to have to tell them I want to change my major.

It's late but Mom heats up some leftovers for me to eat, even though I tell her I'm not hungry. We get caught up with news we haven't shared in phone calls or emails, but I'm painfully aware there's so much I'm not telling them. Do I mention Jacob? He's been a big part of my life the last couple of months. But what do I say? *There's this guy I'm pretending is my boyfriend and we're having hot sex.* Yeah, right.

I also can't tell them about my fight with Ella, because they don't know what happened with Brendan and me.

So basically I feel awkward and stiff.

Elisha's arriving from Boston in the morning, and I really am tired, so I'm not making an excuse when I tell them I want to go to bed early. In my bedroom, I look around at the furnishings that are so familiar to me. Most of my personal things are in Ridgedale now, but I pick up the stuffed dog sitting on the dresser, the dog I got when I was a kid because it looks exactly like the real dog we had back then, who has now gone to doggy heaven. "Smokey." I give the dog a cuddle. Maybe Smokey should come back to college with me. I need all the hugs I can get.

I spend the weekend in Elisha's shadow. She's beautiful and confident and tells us about the praise one of her profs heaped on her for some work she did, the research she's doing, and the new guy she's seeing, which thrills my parents, although they are a little concerned that she'll be distracted from her studies. I don't know why; Elisha barely had to study in high school or for her undergrad degree. She's just that smart.

The C I got on my on physics mid-term is nothing to brag about and I'm sure not going to tell them what a mess my life is, when Elisha's is so perfect.

Sitting in my room Saturday night, propped up against pillows in bed, with my laptop on my knees, I remember what Jacob said . . . that I should just be myself.

Would things be different if I was taking courses I love? If I was passionate about what I was doing and proud of it? If I wasn't trying to be like Elisha?

I've spent my whole life trying to be like her. But I should just be myself.

I have to tell my parents that I'm going to be a teacher instead of a doctor.

Which probably means that along with everyone else in my life, they're going to be mad at me.

I hate feeling like this. I need to take control of my life and fix things.

I like to plan, so I open a Word document and start typing. I write out all my feelings and questions. I write out a script for how I'm going to tell my parents. I've been procrastinating all weekend and tomorrow's my last day here.

I make a list of their possible reactions, brainstorming everything I can think of. Then I try to come up with a plan to deal with each of those scenarios. Student loans are a viable option. Starting my career in debt isn't ideal, but hey, tons of people do it.

Then I think about Jacob and Ella.

I type out my plan for dealing with Jacob. I won't call him. I'll wait to hear from him. He's the one who needs a fake girlfriend, so he can contact me when he needs me. And when he does, I'll be friendly. I imagine how I'll feel the next time I see him, if he even wants to see me. We'll go to a party or something together. I'll do what I have to do—make sure girls there know I'm his girlfriend. But I'll also make a point of mingling more.

I need more friends.

Ella and Brendan and I stuck pretty close together in our freshman year. Then after Brendan died, I didn't feel much like socializing. So I haven't made new friends at Bayard. Natalie and Brooklyn seemed to be potential friends, until this shit hit the fan with Ella.

I make a list of people I know who I could be friends with. There's Grace and Leah at SAPAP. I could ask them to go out for coffee or to a movie one night. There's Taisha at the diner. She probably has her own group of friends, but maybe we could go out after we get off work sometime. There's Justin in my psych class. He was being friendly to me that night at the party when Jacob got all jealous.

Jacob *had* been jealous.

My fingers go very still on the keyboard. I really thought he was starting to feel more for me. He admitted he was jealous. Was he just being a dick because some other guy was interested? Or does he really care?

I set my laptop aside and roll over onto my side, knees pulled up. Probably it's stupid to get my hopes up about that.

I have a plan. And I'm going to stick to it.

Sunday morning I go to church with the fam and then we go out for lunch. This is a good time to break the news to them because if it doesn't go well, I'm leaving right after lunch, anyway.

"So. I need to talk to you about something," I announce after we've ordered.

"What is it, honey?" Mom lifts her eyebrows.

"School." I square my shoulders and lift my chin. "I'm not going to try to get into med school."

Elisha gasps. Mom and Dad blink at me. Mom's face falls. "Why not?" Her forehead creases. "Are you having trouble with your classes? You're not failing again, are you?"

The only time in my life I ever failed courses was last year, but Mom makes it sound like I do it all the time. She knows that the college entrance courses I did in high school were hard for me, especially math and physics, and how frustrated I got, but I never failed.

"The reason I failed last year was because of what happened with Brendan."

"I know you were upset about that, honey, but you still should have buckled down and—"

"He raped me."

Oh dear God. Did I really just say that?

My eyes fly open wide and I stare at my parents. Their mouths drop open and silence expands painfully around us as the noise of the restaurants recedes.

Whoa. *That* wasn't part of my plan.

I pick up my coffee cup with trembling hands and take a sip. The hot liquid sloshes onto my lip, scalding me.

"Brendan raped you, Skylar?" Elisha asks softly, almost disbelievingly, from beside me.

"What the hell?" Dad's face is red and his mouth tightens.

"Dave." Mom reaches out and lays a hand on his rigid forearm.

Our casual lunch has become tense and painful.

"I shouldn't have blurted that out." I stare down at my coffee. "I'm sorry. I just . . . last year when I failed those two courses, it wasn't only because Brendan committed suicide. It was a lot more than that. You make it sound like I didn't try hard enough, but . . . I was dealing with a lot of stuff."

Elisha squeezes my hand. "Skylar. Are you okay?"

I blink rapidly a few times. "I'm kind of . . . not." I glance at her. "I went for counseling. I'm dealing with it. But never mind. We don't have to talk about it."

"Why are you giving up on med school?" Elisha persists. "Are you dropping out of school?"

"No!" I pull in a long breath and let it out. "No, not at all. I've been trying to figure out what I want to do with my life. I'm not enjoying most of my courses. Jacob . . ." Ah shit.

"Who's Jacob?" Elisha asks.

"A guy I've been . . . seeing."

She gives a delighted laugh. "Hey! Why didn't you say something sooner? I was talking about Tony all weekend, and you didn't say a word."

I can't explain why, so I shrug. "It's not that serious. Anyway, he made me realize how much I enjoy delivering training as part of my volunteer work, and that teaching would be a good career choice for me."

"Skylar, changing your major is a big decision," Mom says. "You shouldn't do something rash just because your courses are hard."

She'd rather talk about that than the rape. Rape is not an easy thing to discuss. I get that. But it burns a little.

I tip my head to one side as I meet her eyes. "It's not that they're hard, Mom. I'm used to working hard. It's because being a doctor isn't what I really want to do with my life. It's what *Elisha* wants to do. I wanted you to be as proud of me as you are of her."

Mom's forehead creases and Elisha makes a soft sound of dismay beside me.

"Skylar," Mom says. "Of course we're proud of you."

I bow my head. Her words don't really sound all full of pride. But I nod.

I tell them about my meeting with my faculty advisor and how supportive she is of my choices. "It's only my sophomore year. There's time for me to make this change. Lots of people don't figure out exactly what they want to do right away."

"Why the hell are we talking about this?" Dad asks, his lips and jaw tight. "You just told us . . . Christ." He stops and presses his lips together.

Oh man, I've really screwed this up. My stomach clenches. "I'm sorry, Dad."

"Jesus! You don't apologize for something like that!" He takes a deep breath. "Let's talk about this at home."

The waitress arrives with a big tray with our lunches on it. I've lost my appetite, but I spoon up some of the beer-and-cheese soup, and play with my salad. Nobody else is eating much either.

178

We finish our lunches with some stilted conversation and drive home. The snow that fell a couple of days ago is melting, the sky a painful clear blue, water dripping from tree branches, the streets slushy.

Once we're in the house, there's an excruciating, uncomfortable silence. So I jump in. "I know how hard it is to talk about something like rape." I bite my lip. "I've only told . . . two people about this, ever." Jacob is one of them. "I probably should have told more people after it happened, but it was . . . painful."

Dad closes his eyes and his hands clench into fists and when I look over at Mom, tears are running down her face. I know other survivors who've never told their family what happened to them. This was one of my fears—that they would be so upset. And that would upset me all over again. And I wasn't sure if I could handle that.

We move into the family room. I have no intention of sharing too many details, but I tell them briefly what happened, and all my confused and guilty feelings afterward. This is disturbing and confusing to them, with Brendan's suicide having happened so soon after it occurred, and it's hard for me too, emotion welling up inside me.

I can see my parents are struggling, especially Dad, who's not so good at talking about emotional things. His eyes are red and he doesn't say much.

"I wish you had told us," Mom says.

She doesn't understand how complicated my feelings were right after. "It wasn't that easy," I say quietly. "There were a lot of reasons. I knew you'd be upset and worried about me. And I was afraid people would blame me for Brendan's death."

"Bullshit."

My gaze snaps to Dad's face, his jaw tight and his eyes blazing.

"He knew he did a terrible thing," Dad continues. "You are not responsible for that."

I nod, my throat aching. "I also felt like I'd be letting you down. But then I let you down anyway, failing those courses."

"Oh my God." More tears stream down Mom's face. "Skylar." She closes her eyes briefly and her mouth tightens. "I'm so sorry. Come here." She stands and moves toward me with her arms outstretched.

Without thinking, I move too and I'm in her tight embrace. Her body is trembling and her arms squeeze me.

"I know you've sacrificed a lot for me to go to a good school." I try to keep my voice steady. "I wanted to do well and make you proud. And I plan to be a damn good teacher. But if you don't want to help me with that, I understand."

"Skylar. Honey." She strokes my hair. "How could you even think that? Of course we'll support you in whatever you want to do. Right now the most important thing is that you're okay. I'm so sorry you didn't feel you could come to us when you needed to."

My throat thickens and now I really can't talk.

"I'm glad you told somebody and got help. I'm proud of you, honey. What a strong, amazing woman you are."

This time her words are sincere and my heart squeezes. I manage to choke out, "Thanks, Mom."

As I drive back to Ridgedale later that afternoon, I'm lighter, my muscles looser. I don't know how my parents feel about my decision to become a teacher. Maybe they're disappointed. But I've been honest with them—and with myself—and that's a relief. And I know they care about me.

Maybe this means I really do need to tell Ella about what happened. Because there's an even bigger wall between us now and being honest with her is probably the only thing that's ever going to knock it down. That wasn't part of the plan I drew up last night, but now I think it should be. Maybe she still won't want to be friends with me, but I'll be okay. I'm going to make new friends and move on. Like I have from the other crap.

When I get home, I see a light under Ella's bedroom door. She's home. I should do this now, while my resolve is firm. I set my suitcase on my bed, wipe damp palms over my jeans and cross to her room to knock on the door.

"Come in."

She must think it's Brooklyn or Natalie. I open the door and step inside. "Hi."

She looks up from her computer. "Oh. Skylar. Hey." She gives me a funny look.

"Can we talk? Actually, forget I asked that. I'm not asking, I'm telling you, I need to talk to you about what happened. There are some things you need to hear."

"Funny. There are some things you need to hear too."

I frown. "Like what?"

"Like . . . this." She turns her laptop toward me. "It's about your boyfriend."

180

I blink but don't move. "Jacob? What about him?"

"The things you learn with a Google search. I can't believe you didn't Google him when you started going out."

I guess some people do that. Jacob and I are Facebook friends, and I did look back through his timeline and check out his photos from when we first met, just out of curiosity. But I didn't feel a need to Google him. I know where he's from, where he played hockey before, what his family's like.

"Why are *you* Googling him?" I squint at Ella.

"Honestly? I have no idea. But I found out some interesting stuff. And I think you need to know about it."

I take a step closer. A sense of dread fills me, dark and cold.

"Your boyfriend was involved in a gang rape back in Saskatoon. Wherever that is." She shrugs.

Those words make ice water run through my veins. I freeze and stare at her. "What?"

"Read the news article. There are a bunch of them. It was big news up in Canada."

My insides snarl into painful knots. My skin goes cold and clammy. This can't be true.

I manage to walk over to Ella's desk. I bend slightly to read the screen. It takes me a few tries to absorb the words I'm reading.

It's true.

My stomach heaves and saliva pools in my mouth. My head swims. Jeez, I'm about to vomit. I can't do that. I swallow. And swallow again. Try to clear my vision. I straighten and look at Ella. "Why are you doing this?"

Her eyes widen. "Hey, don't shoot the messenger. It's not like I made this up. I just happened to find it. And I thought you should know."

"So glad you care." I mean it in a sarcastic way, but my voice is flat. "You've had a funny way of showing it."

Her eyes cloud. After a moment, she says, "What did you want to talk about?"

I close my eyes. I can't do this now. "You know what I want to talk about. But . . . I can't. I . . . I have to go . . ."

I dash into the bathroom and puke my guts up. Then I curl up on the bathroom floor and sob.

Chapter 25

Jacob

I COULDN'T GO HOME with Skylar for Thanksgiving. Things have been getting too serious between us. I can't take on all her problems and stay focused on my own goals. Some time apart will be good, and when she gets back, I'll let her know that maybe I don't need a fake girlfriend around as much anymore. I don't even know why she invited me. She knows we're not real. Maybe she was just trying to be nice. We *are* friends. Friends who bang each other's brains out any chance we get, mind you.

And I do care about her.

Christ. I care about her way too much. This can't be happening now. I had my goals so clearly set out in front of me when I came to Bayard. This is all about making it into the NHL after I screwed up so badly last year. Fear squeezes my insides in a cold grip, that fear of not making it I've had ever since then. Only now it's even worse, because I'm not only afraid for me, I'm afraid for Skylar.

Fuck. I lean back in my chair and let my head fall back, my hands curling into fists.

I was curious to meet her family, the ones who've fucked up Skylar's view of herself. She thinks they're not proud of her. I'm dying to find out if that can be true. If I went home with her and checked out the sitch, I'd be able to reassure her they really do love her and are proud of her.

And if they aren't, I could kick their asses.

Metaphorically, of course.

I sigh. I'm never going to meet her family.

A heaviness settles in my gut.

The truth is, I've had a hard time concentrating on anything for the last week. Since that morning Ella stormed into Sky's room, I've been worried sick about Sky. She says she's okay, but I'm not so sure, considering how upset she was.

And she has every right to feel upset. I'm still furious about what that motherfucker did to her. And then cowardly took his own life rather than face up to what he'd done.

And I'm pissed at Ella too. What kind of friend is she to unload all that onto Skylar and not even give her a chance to talk about it? She had no idea what happened. Hopefully Skylar and Ella have talked about it and now she does know and everything is okay, like Skylar said. Or as okay as they can be, given what happened with their friend.

Things are quiet on campus over the holiday weekend, but there are a few activities going on for those of us not going away. Thanksgiving is a big deal down here. We get a turkey dinner with all the trimmings at the dining hall. Turkey dinner is one of my favorite things ever—I especially love gravy. I missed Canadian Thanksgiving, which falls mid-October, and I might not be able to go home for Christmas because we're playing in a big tournament in Florida right after that, and I'm not sure my parents have enough money for me to fly home.

Florida sounds awesome at Christmas. Right?

Sure.

I go over to Butch's place to spend the day with him and Barks. While we're watching football games, eating junk food and drinking soda, I pick Butch's brain about being drafted and still playing college hockey. He got drafted by the San Jose Sharks in the second round last year, but chose to come back to Bayard and play another year.

"Why'd you do that?" I ask curiously.

"I wasn't ready for the NHL. I went to training camp but I knew I wasn't going to make it. My advisor convinced me I'd be better off playing here one more year, working on my strength and skills."

I nodded. "Who's your advisor?"

"Jeff Hodges." He grins. "Family friend."

"Wow." Jeff Hodges is a powerful agent who reps a lot of NHL players.

As college students, we're not allowed to have agents, but we can get informal advice about our careers. I met Jeff once and we had a good conversation. He'd be one of my top picks for an agent. "Great to have someone you trust giving you advice."

"Yeah. So this summer I'll go to training camp and we'll see what happens, but I think I've improved in a bunch of areas this year."

I make up for the junk food and soda by going for a long run, and then hitting the gym for a punishing workout. Then it's back to classes and practices Monday.

Skylar is never really out of my mind. There was a pretty big snowstorm on the weekend and I wonder how she made out on her drive there and back. When did she get back? *Did* she get back? What's she doing? Did she see her irritatingly perfect sister? Did she talk to her parents about changing her career plans? How did they take it?

I'm totally behind her on that idea and if they gave her grief, I could've been there to help out.

No. Not. My. Problem.

Coach works us extra hard at Monday's practice after a few days off. Despite having our asses kicked, everyone else is in a good mood after, I guess from all the turkey and gravy they ate.

"What's your problem?" Buck punches my shoulder.

"Ow! Fuck off." I glare at him. "What are you talking about?"

"You're moping."

"I don't mope."

"Oh yeah you do. And you know what? Sulking is a level two offense." He raises his eyebrows and nods.

"Oh Christ. What do I have to do? Kiss your ass?"

"You know you want to." He smirks and starts to turn around, sticking his butt out.

I snort. Now that I know him better I'm able to take his trash talk in stride.

Buck straightens, grinning. "No, you have to go out and start our cars for us so they're warm when we leave."

"Fuck you. That's what command start is for."

"I don't have command start." Soupy raises his hand.

Actually, neither do I; my truck is nothing fancy. But I know Buck does.

"I'm not doing it. I wasn't moping. Or sulking."

"Oh yeah? Check this out." Rocket shoves his phone in front of my face.

I glance wildly around. If Coach sees him with his phone out, he'll be in trouble. But it's only us players right now.

I frown at the screen. Somehow he took a picture of me, a few minutes ago, sitting on the bench in front of my cubby, staring at the shin pad in my hands, looking like I've just been told the NHL no longer exists and hockey has been outlawed.

"Shit."

Everyone starts laughing. I hold my hand out. "Keys."

Soupy tosses me his keys, as do a couple of other guys and I pull on my jacket, a tuque and scarf and jog out to the parking lot.

I need to get my shit together. I can't be all sad and mopey. I need to be focused and tough.

As the week goes on and I still haven't talked to Skylar, I find myself with a strange tightness in my gut. I'm edgy and restless and irritable. Concentrating on schoolwork is getting harder and harder.

Saturday night is our last game of the semester, against the Mavericks from University of Nebraska at Omaha. Normally I'd make sure Skylar's going to the game. There's a rock in my stomach as I step on the ice for warm-up, not having called her. I can't stop myself from scanning the stands to see if she's there.

I don't see her.

My legs are stiff and heavy tonight and it takes everything I've got to focus. I've used all the techniques I learned: Visualization, picturing processes that will happen in the game and acting them out in my mind. Becoming the character I want to be when I step on the ice. Before the game, I had my iPod earbuds in, listening to 50 Cent singing "Ready for War," which usually revs me up. I used my strategies of narrowing my focus—first when I walk through the arena doors, symbolically leaving shit behind, outside the arena, and then prioritizing my thoughts even more when I step onto the ice. I put my equipment on in the same order I always do, using that routine to create a feeling of security and consistency. I've done it all because I know I'm not at my best and I'm pissed off at myself. I don't let anything interfere with hockey.

I have a moment in the game when the puck hits my stick and I can see a clear break to the net. I put on speed, leaving behind the two D-men. I fake the Maverick's goalie with a move to the left and he comes out, way out. The whole fucking net is open to me, it's the easiest goddamn shot ever, but when I shoot, the puck goes wide of the net. The collective groan of disappointment in the arena hits me in the chest. I skate to the bench, shaking my head.

We lose three-two.

I know I'm not supposed to relive my mistakes, but dammit, if I'd gotten that goal . . . Ah well.

After the game, the guys are all going to Curly's. I tag along, even though I'm grouchy. Maybe a beer or two will help my mood.

We grab a couple of tables and order. I'm looking around, checking out everyone who's there, still with a faint hope that I'll see Skylar. Although I don't know why she'd come when I haven't invited her. I mean, it's a free world and anyone can go to this bar, but . . . it's kind of our team hangout.

There are lots of other girls there, though. They're approaching our table, and the guys invite a few of them to join us.

Then I see Ella walk in.

Every nerve ending in my body goes on alert. If Ella's here, Skylar probably is too. But as I watch her, I see she's with Natalie. Not Skylar.

I swallow and look down at the beer bottle in my hands.

What is wrong with me?

Black Jack looks over at Ella and Nat. I don't like the look in his eyes as he assesses them.

"Aren't those your girlfriend's friends?" he asks me.

I glance over. "Yeah."

"Where is Skylar?" Buck asks. "She coming?"

"I don't know."

Buck frowns. "You two break up?"

I shrug and lift the bottle to my lips. "Just cooling off a bit."

Apparently she got that I wanted to cool things off when I turned down her invitation to go home with her for Thanksgiving, because I haven't heard from her.

"Huh." Buck gives me a puzzled squint. "I thought you were really into her."

"Her friend's hot," Black Jack says.

Buck rolls his eyes. "That slut sleeps with anything with a dick."

I straighten my spine. "Hey."

Black Jack grins lewdly. "It's true."

It kind of is, but . . . "That's an ugly name. Girls can enjoy sex as much as guys."

"Hey, I don't disagree."

"Then don't call them names like that."

Buck's smile disappears and his forehead creases. "Sorry, man."

"Guys can sleep with as many girls as they want and they don't get called sluts."

"Nah. They get called man-whores."

I shake my head. "I'm outta here."

"Already?"

"Yeah. The mood I'm in, I'm doing you all a favor."

Buck gives me a long look but nods, and I push away from the table to leave.

I sit in my truck for a few minutes. I can't stop thinking about Skylar. This is nuts. I need to see her.

I end up parked in front of her house. There are still lights on, so some-one's up.

I'm not sure what I'm doing there. I'm not sure what I want from her. All I know is . . . I miss her, with an empty, gnawing ache deep inside me.

I ring the bell and wait, hands in my pockets. It's only a minute before Skylar peeks through the high window, but after that it takes forever for her to respond. I'm almost at the point of wondering if she's going to ignore me when the door opens.

She stands aside and lets me in. I pause in the small foyer and study her.

She closes the door but hovers near it. Her small face is drawn into sad lines, her lips are pressed together and her eyes are cool. "Jacob."

"Hi." I swallow. "How are you?"

"Good." Her forehead furrows. "What are you doing here?"

I look past her, then around, then back at her. Then I just say it. "I miss you."

Her gaze goes icy. "You miss me."

I nod. "Yeah."

"I haven't heard from you for two weeks. You just decided this now?"

I swallow a sigh. "Um, yeah. I've been a dick."

She gives a hard laugh. "Okay, glad I don't have to tell you that."

I rub my face.

"Look, if you're here for a late night booty call, sorry, but I can't do that."

Booty call? What the fuck? "That's what you think?"

"Why else would you show up at one in the morning? After a game, which as we know, makes you want to fuck."

I stare at her.

She crosses her arms and glares at me.

I guess I deserve this. But I hate it. I really have missed her. I want her in my life. Not for booty calls, although I have to say her booty is the finest and the calls are fan-fucking-tastic. But she's fun to be with. She makes me laugh. She's sweet and caring. She's been through hell and hasn't let it get her down; instead she took a fucked-up situation and turned it into helping other people. And she knows me. She sees past the tough bravado and cocky 'tude, sees my fears and insecurities, and she still likes me.

Or maybe that should be past tense. Because she sure doesn't look like she's very fond of me right now.

"I'm sorry?" Well, that's the lamest apology in the history of apologies.

She arches a brow. "Sorry for what?"

I swipe a hand over my face again, and shift my feet. I sigh. "For so much, Sky."

"Never mind." She shakes her head. "You need to leave. I don't want to ever see you again."

My mouth falls open. I know I was a jerk for not calling, but . . . wow.

She closes her eyes briefly. "I found out what happened." She lifts her chin and meets my eyes, and hers are sharp with gold glints. "Why you're here. Why you got kicked off your team up in Saskatoon."

Every muscle in my body tightens. The room shrinks around me. "How'd you find that out?"

"On the Internet. Ella actually showed it to me." She gives a laugh that almost sounds like a sob. "She hasn't spoken to me for nearly two weeks either, but she seemed happy to fill me in on *that* story."

"She hasn't spoken to you?" I frown. "Not at all?"

Her bottom lip quivers. "Nope. She's still pissed at me." She shrugs, but her throat works. "Whatever."

"Didn't you tell her the truth about what happened? What Brendan did?"

"She doesn't want to hear about it." She rolls her eyes. "Nice change of subject, though."

"Ah, right." I shove my hands in my jacket pockets.

"You never told me about that, Jacob. You never told me you raped a girl."

Fuck! "I did not!" I shout the words, horrified.

"It was in all the news. They kicked you off the team."

I stare at her, pulling a hand out of my pocket to rub my aching stomach.

She shakes her head. "I can't believe that. Stupid me. And stupid me for . . . oh, never mind. Just go. Please." She opens the door.

"No, let me tell you what happened, Sky. Please. You don't know the whole story."

"I don't want to know the whole story." She shakes her head. "Get. Out."

A gajillion thoughts are tumbling around in my head. She actually believes I raped someone. She's not the first one, but she's the first person who really knows me who believes it. My parents believed me. My friends at home believed me. Buck even believed me when I told him. But Skylar . . . the person I think knows me the best . . . she doesn't believe me.

My belly muscles go rigid, hot pressure building inside me. My chest feels like someone just drilled a puck into it.

I know I screwed up, but not nearly as badly as she thinks I did. And I know my attitude has changed after being here, being with her, going through that training. But I was so tired of defending myself, after that happened, trying to explain the truth to people who didn't believe me. That shit hurt. And I'm not going to do it now. If she thinks that little of me, then she's not the friend I thought she was.

I make my feet move. "I can't believe you think so little of me, without hearing my side of things. I'm out." I stride away, not looking at her.

Chapter 26

Skylar

CLASSES ARE DONE and it's study period, with exams starting later this week. I just want to get it done with. Some of the pressure has eased, knowing that I just have to get through this and next semester will be different. I've already got my courses picked out and I'm thrilled with them. I've heard good things about the profs. I want to get on with it. And yet, I can't blow things off this semester. I still want to do well.

Which tells me something. The pressure to do well wasn't just coming from my parents—it was coming from inside me.

How about that.

I got a long email from my mom, telling me that they never expected me to be a doctor like Elisha and that they would support whatever I want to do. She said she was shocked when I said that, the day we had lunch after church, because she thought I wanted to be a doctor. She apologized for making me feel I had to be like Elisha, because they love me and are as proud of me as they are of her. I can still think of so many times they made me feel I didn't live up, but I can now also see that I was putting pressure on myself. Pressure to try to be as good as Elisha, when really I am as good as her . . . I'm just different.

Mom also asked how they could support me after the rape and I sent her some links to websites she and Dad could go to for information.

The night classes end is our pizza fundraiser at Santorelli's. We've got

190

some great prize donations—thanks in large part to Jacob. Santorelli's is donating the pizza, which is being sold at a cheaper-than-usual price to entice all the students in. Of course, they're ordering drinks and other stuff too, so the restaurant is still making money.

The Italian restaurant is crowded, everyone letting loose a little before exams start. A lot of the Bears are there, hanging out, laughing with people, signing the affirmative consent pledge. And I know there are a lot of other people there because of that. It makes my chest hurt to see this. Jacob really came through.

He's there too, sitting at the table with Grace, selling silent auction tickets and charming people into spending more money than they wanted to, with his easy smile and chin dimple. I can't stop looking at him. Doubts have been nudging me. I remember the stiff, hurt look on his face when he walked out.

I wish I had more to do, but things are so well organized, the event is practically running itself.

With a glass of lemonade in my hand, I lean against the wall, talking to Grace.

"This is going great," she says happily. "You did a fantastic job, Skylar."

"Thanks."

She bumps my hip. "And Jacob did a ton of work. He's so awesome."

I say nothing and inspect my drink.

"Hey. You okay?"

"Oh yeah." People keep asking me that, so clearly I don't look okay. I have to do a better job of keeping my happy face on. I give her a wide smile. "So after our last exam, we're going out to celebrate, right?"

"Right!"

We discovered we both finish the afternoon of the twentieth, and our plan is to go straight from the exam to the bar. I think I might not stop drinking until New Year's.

Ha. I'm exaggerating, of course. Sort of.

But I've been sticking to my plan, trying to make new friends and move on with my life.

"I need another piece of pizza." Grace pushes away from the wall. "Want one?"

"Yeah. Sure. Pepperoni."

I haven't had much appetite lately, but I'm faking that tonight too. And Santorelli's pizza really is the best.

I glance over at the ticket table and this time my gaze collides with Jacob's, who's watching me. He doesn't look happy right at that moment either.

An ache blooms in my chest, a throbbing longing. I miss him so much.

I can't take my eyes off him.

I hate him.

No, I don't.

Fuck, I'm mixed up.

It's so hard to stop thinking about him, and what he did. Or what he was accused of. After I tortured myself by Googling him and reading everything there was to find about that incident, I learned that there wasn't enough evidence to lay charges. He claimed he wasn't even there. There were some people who confirmed he went upstairs with that girl and his teammates. There were also some who said they'd seen him leave shortly after. So it was never proven that he did anything. He did get kicked off his hockey team, though.

I hate him, but I find myself aching for him. Then reminding myself he's an asshole and deserves everything he's gotten.

I close my eyes against a wave of pain, turning away from him.

"Skylar."

I look up and he's standing there in front of me.

"Hi."

I can't even talk. My throat thickens and a burning rushes up my esophagus.

He looks pretty much like I feel—conflicted and miserable. "I wish you'd talk to me," he says quietly.

"There's nothing to say."

"*I* have some things to say."

I shake my head and turn away from him.

"Wait." He curls a hand over my arm, gently. "Did you tell your parents about changing your major when you were home at Thanksgiving?"

I stare at him. "Yes."

"How did they take it?"

"Well, they say they'll support me in whatever I want to do." I bite my lip. "I also told them what happened with Brendan."

"Jesus."

I give a dry laugh. "It wasn't my intention, but I think that might've made the news about changing my major a little less disturbing." I shrug. "They say their main concern is that I'm okay."

"Of course it is. It should be."

I nod.

He pauses again, his gaze intent on me. "I really am sorry, Sky. I never wanted to hurt you."

My spine stiffens with pride. "You haven't hurt me."

"Oh. Right. Okay, then."

"Thanks for helping out tonight."

Grace returns then and hands me a plate with a piece of pizza on it. "Hey, Jacob. How's it going?"

"Good. Done my shift." He bestows a gorgeous smile on Grace. "Seems like a successful evening."

"I think so! Thank you for all you did. It's so awesome having the hockey team here."

"Well." Jacob looks at me again. "I have to go. The guys are going out before we have to lock ourselves up to study."

I nod.

"See you, Jacob. And thanks again." Grace smiles at him.

He gives us a wave, gives me a long, tortured look that has my heart splintering into tiny pieces and walks out of the restaurant. I stare down at my pizza, my eyes burning. Damn.

I'm in bed reading. I've tried a couple of times to get to sleep and it's nearly one-thirty in the morning but I'm not sleepy. I hear the front door open and close and then slow footsteps coming up the stairs.

Usually I can tell by the steps who it is—Ella's are always quick, Natalie's are heavier and Brooklyn's are slow and measured. These steps are slow and uneven.

A soft knock on my door has my head turning. I frown. "Yeah?"

The door opens and Ella's head pokes in. I blink at her tear-streaked face and smudged eye makeup. Dropping my Kindle, I sit up straight. "Ella. Are you okay?"

She nods. "I am now."

"What happened?" I push my hands into the mattress, prepared to jump out of bed.

"Long story." She pauses. "Can we talk?"

My heart bumps. "Of course."

I chew on my bottom lip as she comes into my room, closing the door behind her. She sits on the foot of the bed. She's wearing a short black skirt, black boots and a loose flowered top. She reaches down and unzips the boots, pushes them off and lets them thud to the rug beside my bed.

I'm waiting.

"I went to Curly's tonight."

My lips push out. The Bears' hangout. Did she see Jacob?

"I was there with Jack Jones. He plays for the Bears."

I nod. I know who Jack is. I've met him a few times, and I think he's the only hockey player on the team I don't like.

"We were flirting and having fun, and making out a little. I drank too much." Her words are a little slurry, so I already figured that part out. "I was going to leave with him and then Jacob came up to us and started talking. He asked Jack if he wanted to stay for another drink."

I blink. At first I don't get it. Jacob was trying to get them to drink more?

"Jack said no, we were leaving. Then Jacob told Jack not to do it. He told Jack I was too drunk to be able to consent."

Oh. Now I get it. Jacob was using some of the Step In techniques to try to distract Jack. When that didn't work he got more direct.

"And then . . . Jack got pissed. And I started crying because . . . because . . . what have I been doing, Sky?"

Tears flood my eyes. "Oh, Ella." I reach for her hand and give it a squeeze.

"Jacob brought me home. I was a mess." A small sob escapes her. "I said an awful thing to him. When he first came up to us. Knowing what he'd been involved in . . ." She shakes her head. "Never mind. Even though I was a bitch to him, he looked after me and made sure I got home okay." She peeks up through wet eyelashes. "He told me I should talk to you about Brendan."

"Oh." My stomach cramps. My fingers start shaking and I curl them in my bedspread. " I've been trying to talk to you about it since that morning you read the text messages he sent me."

She nods. "I know. I didn't want to hear. I was so hurt, Sky. I loved him. I can't believe you didn't figure that out. And I can't believe you slept with him."

"I didn't. Exactly." I pause, willing myself to say the words. "He forced me."

Her mouth goes slack. "What?"

My inhalation is shaky. "We were at his place, studying. After, we had a couple of beers. I swear, Ella, he was just a friend to me. We were joking around and I don't know why . . . he told me he loved me and started kissing me."

"He was in love with you." She says the words with quiet resignation.

"No, Ella." I shake my head. Jacob made me realize this. "He didn't really love me. I don't know why he said he did." I pause. "I admit, I let him kiss me for a few minutes, I'm not sure why. Maybe I was curious. But there was nothing there, no attraction . . . it was weird. But when I tried to stop him, he wouldn't."

"No." She covers her mouth with her hands.

"Yes. He forced me down and . . . and . . . I told him no, I didn't want to do it. I've relived it so many times. I know I could have done things differently. I could have fought back harder. I don't know if he would have hurt me . . . he was strong and pretty determined and . . . I was afraid."

"He wouldn't do that." She stares at me, misery and disbelief etched on her face. "Brendan would never do something like that."

"And this is why I wasn't sure I should tell you." I make a face. "I know you don't want to believe that of him. Hell, I didn't want to believe it of him. We were friends, and I felt so betrayed and hurt after. I was so angry at him. That's why I wasn't answering his calls or his texts. I didn't want to see him. I felt so . . . violated, and I didn't know what to do."

"Skylar." Her voice breaks on the word. "Why didn't you tell me?"

I shake my head. "I couldn't tell anyone. I was so mixed up. He kept calling and texting me, saying he was sorry, and he loved me and he wanted to talk to me. I ignored him. I wouldn't talk to him. It was three days later . . . he committed suicide." Tears fill my eyes too now. "Then I really couldn't talk about it. The guilt was *killing* me, Ella. I felt I was responsible for him taking his life."

She bites her lip. I can see what she's thinking.

"You think so too." I look away. "That's okay. I know why you think that. But I know now that the only one responsible for him taking his own life was him. He must have felt so guilty about what he'd done. I felt horrible. I wanted to die myself. It was such a burden, eating away inside me."

"I don't know what to say."

I nod. "I know. It's complicated. I didn't want to tell you, even after you read those texts. Because he was our friend, and you loved him and he did a terrible thing. Jacob told me I should be honest with you, and when I went home for Thanksgiving, I did a lot of thinking. I told my family about it, and I realized I needed to tell you too. There's been this . . . this . . . *wall* between us ever since . . . because of that."

She nods. "I know. I felt it. Something was different, but I didn't know what."

"So. Now you do." I rub my mouth, watching her. "I didn't know you loved him and I certainly didn't do anything with the intent of hurting you. It was awful. But at least it's out there and I've been honest with you."

She sits there for a long moment, not meeting my eyes.

I pull in a deep breath. "I hope you can understand, Ella. Because I won't let people victim-blame me. I did enough of that myself, and when I was at my lowest and decided to get help, I vowed I wasn't going to allow anyone to do that to me. So if you can't get past it, then . . ." My throat squeezes shut. "Then we really can't be friends."

She slides off my bed. She seems less drunk now, but still she's a mess. "I really don't know what to think . . . or how to feel. I guess I need to process it."

I nod.

At my door, she pauses. "Skylar . . ."

"Yeah?"

"I looked at everything on Brendan's phone. To see if there was anything else . . . any other clue about why he committed suicide. There was something else going on with him. He emailed his psychiatrist the day he . . ." She swallows. ". . . raped you. Saying he was struggling. It sounded like . . . he'd cheated on a test and the prof caught him."

My eyes fly open wide and my hands go to my mouth. "What?"

She bites her lip. "He was upset about it. Worried about what was going to happen. They'd been making adjustments to his medications, but he felt it still wasn't right." She pauses. "He was supposed to see the psychiatrist Monday . . . but he never got there."

"Oh God."

"Yeah. But after that, there was nothing that indicated he wanted to kill himself. I saw him that weekend and he was really hyper and talkative. I asked him if he was okay and he said yes, he just hadn't slept well. But he never said anything, never even hinted . . . But I should have known . . . I had no idea that he was going to do that." She closes her eyes briefly. "And I felt guilty too, because maybe I should have . . . you know?"

"Yeah." My lip trembles. "I know, Ella."

"I just thought you should know that."

"Why didn't you tell me that sooner?"

"I'm sorry." She swallows and her face squeezes up. "I'm sorry. I was so angry at you. So hurt."

I have to bite hard on my bottom lip to keep it from quivering.

Still she doesn't leave. "That story about Jacob . . . I don't know what really happened. But . . . I think he's a good guy, Sky." Then she walks out of my room, quietly closing the door behind her.

My head is spinning like electrons generating magnetic fields. What does this mean? What was going on with Brendan? There was so much I hadn't known. Had he really cheated on a test? Dear God, why would he have done that? He was *not* a cheater. He must have been distraught about it.

Yes, he'd been hyper and chatty that night, jumping around in our conversation from one thing to another. I remember thinking it was like he was high on something, but we'd only had a couple of drinks. Damn. Tears slide down my cheeks and I palm them away.

I guess we'll never know the answers to our questions.

I have to say I feel a huge sense of relief at finally having told Ella the truth. She might hate me for being the messenger . . . like I was annoyed at her for telling me about Jacob's past. If she does, I think that will pass. I'm still not sure why she told me about Jacob—if her intent was to hurt me, that's really awful. If she was concerned about me . . . that's different. But it's not her fault it happened. It's not like she made up the story.

I think he's a good guy.

Jacob rescued Ella from one of his teammates. He made sure she got home safely when she was drunk. Even though she was the one who'd discovered his secret and told me. And even though she insulted him when he tried to help.

I slide back down into my bed and stare at the ceiling.

Yeah, he's a good guy.

I think back to when we met, how attracted I was to him despite the cocky arrogance that annoyed me. The glimpses of vulnerability I got—his fear of losing hockey. His belief that without it he was nothing. Now I understand why he was so afraid. He'd almost lost it all, and he had this second chance to make up for what happened.

My hunch that he was uncomfortable during the orientation training now makes sense. He was uncomfortable, because of what had happened. That night he came by, he denied that he'd raped anyone. The news articles had said there wasn't enough evidence to lay charges.

He didn't do it.

I close my eyes on a wave of sickness. I know Jacob Flass.

The first time we had sex, we didn't even actually do the deed. He was gentlemanly, and considerate, despite us both being so turned on and hot for each other. That was not the behavior of a rapist.

He's always been respectful of me. Never forced me to do anything. He makes me want him so much I can barely remember my own name, but I've always been a willing participant and he always makes sure of that. He helped me with the fundraiser and he actually got his hockey buddies—the ones he thought hated him—to come and sign affirmative consent pledges. And tonight, he looked out for my best friend.

It physically hurts that I believed he would do something like that. And when I think of the stricken look on his face that night when I told him I believed it, when I told him I never wanted to see him again, the pain intensifies to the point where I almost can't breathe.

I roll over and press my face into the pillows. God. What have I done?

He came over that night because he missed me, and I'm still pissed off about why I didn't hear from him, but he was trying to apologize for something and I never even let him really tell me what was going on. Maybe he *had* been trying to end things between us, but even so, I owe him an apology for thinking so little of him.

Chapter 27

Jacob

I DON'T KNOW what to do about this.

After dropping Ella off at home, wishing I could go in and see Skylar, then driving away feeling shitty, I'm at home in my room, stretched out on my bed, hands beneath my head.

I'm replaying the ugly scene in the bar. I stepped in and helped and I should be feeling good about that, and I guess I sort of do. But Black Jack was pissed and I saw the angry glare he gave me when he stormed out. He's a guy I'd rather not get on the wrong side of, and he's a teammate. But I can't help but be disgusted by how he acted. Disgusted by his sense of entitlement, that because Ella had been with other guys he was entitled to whatever he wanted from her.

I don't know what to do about it.

Maybe, like Skylar, who was hurt and turned it into helping others . . . maybe I can do the same. I made a mistake and I've learned from it . . . maybe I can turn that into educating others.

I've heard hints of that attitude of entitlement from other guys—a few others on the Bears, but also some of the football team. It makes me sick to think that other guys have the feeling that they're so special girls owe them sex. Maybe I've been living in the land of denial, but fuck . . . that's not right.

If only every player on the team could go through the training that I did.

Wait. Why couldn't they?

I stare at my ceiling. Why couldn't we do that kind of training for all the players? It would make them more aware, like it did me. It could make a difference.

I know the training was a pilot, and eventually all new students enrolled at Bayard will go through it. But how about now? How could we make that happen?

My mind is working. Churning. I know who I could ask how to make it happen—Skylar.

Fuck. We should be a team on this. We *could* be a team on this.

We should be a team.

My heart feels like it's sinking down to my toes. Skylar's a team player. I'm a team player. In hockey, you have to be a team player. We *were* a team. And I let her down. I let my team down.

I'm in love with her. She's the best thing that ever happened to me. And I fucking let her down. She was all alone, her best friend not speaking to her, worried about upsetting her parents with her choices, uncertain of her future, dealing with the fact that her friend raped her and then committed suicide, and I abandoned her too—when she needed someone most.

She's been through hell. Fuck me, I'm such an asshole. I was so concerned about my own needs. My own goals and priorities. What a fucking selfish dick I am.

I don't know if I can ever make things up to Skylar. She hates me for other reasons now, so I'm never going to get her back. But I can still make something good out of all this. And if I can't go to Skylar to help me make this happen, I know who I *can* go to—Victoria.

Okay. Okay. I can do this.

Two days later, I'm sitting in Victoria's office making my pitch. I did my research. I know my own anecdotal stories aren't going to cut it. But I'm also willing to share my story and open myself up to that judgment.

"A disproportionate number of sexual assaults on campus are committed by athletes." It's hard to talk about this. "Often in situations involving gang rape. I put myself in that position. I believe the girl involved in my situation absolutely wanted it, but I wasn't actually there when it happened and I'll never know for sure if she changed her mind. I know now I shouldn't have left. I should have made sure she was okay. And now I think there's a way to make a difference."

She studies me with serious eyes. "Go on, Jacob."

"I know how important athletics are to colleges. Sports bring in so much money to a school. I know it's important enough that they let me come here, knowing my past. I mean, I wasn't given a complete pass—I'm being held to some pretty high standards and expectations here. But still." I take a breath. "Athletic programs have bigger budgets and stronger recruiting efforts, and there's greater academic leniency for some athletes. For some guys, they think expectations and limits that apply to others don't apply to them."

She nods.

"We get lots of attention from lots of people. Maybe it makes us think we're above all those rules and limits. Plus, we're encouraged to be aggressive on the ice. Or the football field. Maybe that carries over to off it." I pause. "I was pretty bitter about what happened to me, because I knew of other situations where the athletes got away with it . . . and I didn't, even though I knew I didn't do anything and I believed my buddies didn't either. We were made an example of, and it made me angry, but now I can see I've learned from what happened. And I think I can help other guys learn, before they go through something like this and learn the hard way. Or before some other girl gets into a situation like that and gets hurt."

"And how would you do that, Jacob?"

"I think the place to start is with the coaches. Coaches have a pretty unique and powerful relationship with their players. If all the coaches went through the same training I did, it would make them more aware. Plus it would give them the tools to intervene when they see things that aren't appropriate. I think if they believe doing this would make their teams stronger, they'd be all in."

"You've really thought this through." Victoria regards me thoughtfully.

"Yes. I have." I hold her gaze steadily. "I think it's important. And then I think the athletes themselves could do modified versions of the training. We're kind of in unique situations, with the demands on our time and the other commitments we have, so it would need to look different. But someone like Skylar would know how to do that."

"Skylar." One eyebrow lifts.

"She's a great trainer. She has a gift for it . . . knowing how to reach her audience."

Victoria smiles. "That's great feedback." She goes silent and looks down at her desk, flipping a pen up and down. "I want to take this to the president and the executive officers and see what they say."

I'm not sure of what has to happen here, but that sounds like a next step. "If there's anything I can do to help with that process, I will."

She nods thoughtfully. "Yes. It might be good for you to be involved in the pitch. You're an athlete. You're in. That carries a lot of weight." She pauses and tilts her head to one side. "Are you prepared for the pushback you might get from your teammates? Other athletes?"

I hadn't even thought of that. Now I do. Yeah, I get that could happen. I think of Black Jack. I don't give a shit. "I can deal with it."

She smiles. "I'm pretty impressed with you right now, Jacob."

I shift in my chair and muster up a smile. "Thanks. It just feels like something I need to do."

"Okay. Let's talk about your schedule over the next week or so and see what we can set up."

As I walk out, Skylar is coming in.

Damn, she's so pretty, her long hair all gold and pink under a snowflake-dusted knit hat. Her cheeks are rosy, but her lips droop at the corners and her eyes are tired. When she sees me, she stops and her eyes widen.

Our gazes lock together and I'm taken back to that night, that house party where I saw her across the kitchen and our eyes met. If I could go back to that night, I'd accept her invitation to go upstairs and I would never let her go after that. She would've been mine, for real. Forever.

"Hi, Skylar." I can't take my eyes off her.

"Hi." Her lips part and her eyes are brimming, like she wants to say something. But there are people around us and I have to get to practice.

I hate it that she looks so sad. I don't know if any of it's because of me. I know she has a lot of other shit going on. But I hate it. With a last regretful look, I lift a hand and turn to leave. My chest aches and I sigh as I trudge out of the building and cross the Quad to the parking lot where I left my truck.

In the dressing room at the ice complex, I change into shorts and go into the gym to ride the bike for a while, warming up my leg muscles. We've got a lighter practice schedule this week, as guys are writing exams. Our next regular game isn't until January, but we have that tournament in Florida at the end of the month.

Some guys are there already, warming up, getting minor injuries looked at by the trainers and assistant coach. Alfie is reviewing some video with our assistant coach Art, nodding as Arty talks about butterfly recovery.

Black Jack walks in and his gaze lands on me right away. "Hey, asshole."

I ignore him. I don't answer to "asshole."

He walks up and stops in front of me. "What the fuck was that Saturday night?"

I look up at him. He's got a couple of inches on me when we're standing; with me sitting on the bench in front of my cubby, he's huge. My gut tenses. "That was you being an idiot."

"That was you cock-blocking me."

"That girl was drunk."

"She's a slop tart."

A red haze floats in front of my vision. "You're a douche." I surge to my feet, hands fisting.

"When did you turn into some kind of pussy? You think we don't know about you?"

Buck walks up behind Black Jack, his forehead creased and mouth tight. I meet his eyes briefly and he shakes his head, telling me he hasn't told anyone.

Whatever. It's all over the Internet. It's a wonder it's taken this long for it to come out.

I swallow. "You don't know shit about it."

"I know you watched a lamb roast. Your two buddies fucked that girl."

Okay, that's just wrong, because I wasn't even there when it happened, so I sure as hell didn't watch, and none of that made it into public news stories. How the fuck do rumors like that get started? And make it this far away?

"So where do you get off cock-blocking me, huh?"

"*She was drunk.*" I take a step toward him and we're nose to nose. "Are you that stupid? She was too drunk to consent. That's called *rape*, jackass."

Black Jack shrugs. "She wanted it. And if she tried to accuse me of rape, no one would believe her. I'm a hockey player. Chicks all want to fuck us."

I knew there was a reason I hate this guy. Red heat bursts inside me and without even thinking, my arm draws back and I lay my fist into his nose. Hard.

"Ow! Fuck!" Black Jack's hands go to his face and he staggers back.

Oh shit. He's bleeding.

I shake my throbbing hand.

Black Jack lowers his hands and stares at the blood, then lifts incredulous eyes to my face. "You did not just fucking do that." And he charges at me.

Buck grabs him, but Black Jack throws him off and then he's slamming me into the wooden cubby. My spine hits the edge of it and pain explodes through me. Then he tries to punch me.

I'm not a regular fighter, but I know how to throw down, and all the weights I've been doing since last spring have made me strong. The rush of adrenaline and fury through my bloodstream also helps, and I manage to shove him back and lay a few hits of my own, cracking one against his jaw. He lands one on my temple and I have to shake off dizziness.

Guys are all yelling and swarming around us now, running in from everywhere, and it's Buck and Soupy who manage to drag Black Jack away, while Rocket grabs my arms and says, "Easy, slugger."

I meet Buck's eyes, which are flashing, his face tight. "You okay?" he mouths.

I nod and my gaze goes back to Black Jack, blood streaming down his face, both of us glaring at each other, both our chests heaving. I want to pummel his ugly face. He is *such* a fucking asshole. Rage boils inside me.

I know the guys are stopping us from doing something really stupid, but good sense is washed away by hormones. I gulp air into my lungs.

Coach runs in and stands next to us, his face thunderous. "What the *fuck* is going on here?"

I flick my gaze to him, suddenly aware that it might be too late to stop me from doing something stupid. And I could be in deep shit.

I swallow, my throat constricted. Jesus. I'm the one who's supposed to be on my best behavior. I've been trying so hard to stay out of trouble and now I've screwed up and fought one of my own teammates, one of our senior players, possibly breaking his nose.

I am so fucked.

Chapter 28

Skylar

I WALK into the meeting room at SAPAP. I look at Victoria. "What was Jacob doing here?"

She smiles. "That guy is amazing."

My heart squeezes. I know that. And I screwed up.

"He came to put forward an idea to me. I'm not going to say much about it until I know we can do it, but I'm super excited about it." She pauses. "He was very complimentary to you."

"H-he was?"

"Yes. About your training skills." Her eyes crinkle up at the corners. "But we already knew that. You got excellent ratings on the feedback we collected from participants."

"Oh wow." My heart bumps against my breastbone. "That's so nice to hear."

Maybe he doesn't hate me . . .

I try to focus on the topic of our meeting, super curious about Jacob's proposal. What is he proposing to do?

I need to talk to him. If he doesn't hate me, at least I can apologize to him. He was right there in front of me and I wanted to do it, but this wasn't the time or place. I don't know what the right time or place is. I'm terrified, but determined.

I don't know what Jacob's schedule is like now that classes are done, and right now I have to get to a shift at the diner. Frustration mounts inside me, a feeling of hot pressure. I'll figure it out. Maybe after I get off work at ten I can find him and talk to him.

I rush home to grab a bite to eat and change into my uniform, and drive to the diner. Monday's aren't usually busy anyway, and tonight it's extra quiet, with most people studying for exams.

Then some of Jacob's teammates come in.

My quick assessment tells me he's not with them. Not that this would be the time or place to have our discussion either, but . . . I want to see him.

The guys are weirdly subdued. They greet me with polite smiles. "Hey, Skylar."

"Hi, guys. What can I get you?"

They place their orders, all of them having some variation of hamburger, and hand me their menus. When I return with drinks, they're talking quietly and seriously. I hear the words "suspension" and "injured" and "don't know if he can play in Florida."

Immediately my nerves go on alert. Are they talking about Jacob? Is he hurt? How would that have happened? Their last game was over a week ago and I know he wasn't hurt then. The suspension couldn't be him. He's a hard, physical player but not a dirty player. He hardly ever even takes penalties.

I want to ask, but bite my lip as I set drinks in front of them. But I meet Ben's eyes and his are full of concern. My insides tighten.

When I get back to the counter and turn around, Ben has followed me. "Hey," he says. "You heard from Flash?"

I smile wistfully at the nickname. "No. We don't, uh . . . I haven't talked to him for a while."

Ben frowns. "Yeah, he said you two were cooling off. But it seemed weird to me. You were crazy into each other."

"Yeah, well . . ." I swallow and drop my eyes. "Stuff happens."

Cooling off? That's what he told his friends?

"I guess it does. He's been pretty messed up the last few weeks, though."

My gaze snaps back up to his. "Messed up?"

"Yeah. Really down. Distracted. He played crappy those last two games against UN Omaha." He's eyeing me with a disturbing intensity. "Shit kinda hit the fan today."

"What? What happened?" I actually clutch his forearm, filled with dread and concern for Jacob.

"He got in a fight. With Black Jack."

"A fight? Oh dear God." I stare at Ben. "Is he okay?"

"Um, mostly. We're not sure what's going to happen to both of them. It sucks."

"What were they fighting about?" I can't comprehend this.

"Black Jack was being an asshole. He was giving Jacob shit about interfering with him and your friend Ella the other night."

I sense his disdain as he says "your friend Ella" and my back stiffens. We may never be best friends again, and she may be getting something of a rep on campus, but I still care about her.

"Flash wasn't taking his shit and . . . well, we pulled them off each other before one of them got killed or something, but Coach came in, and like I said, shit hit the fan."

"Oh no." I cover my mouth with both hands. My heart is racing and I can hardly think straight. "Oh my God." I suck in a breath. "Is he okay?"

"Yeah. A little banged up."

"Where is he?"

"At home." One corner of his mouth lifts. "Sulking alone in his room, like he has most of the last two weeks."

I bite my bottom lip. "I was going to go over after work, anyway. Now I will for sure."

Ben nods. "Good. I think he might like to see you."

"I'm not so sure of that," I whisper. "I . . . kind of screwed up."

Ben lifts an eyebrow. "How so?"

"I, uh, found out something about him . . ."

Ben's eyes narrow. "You heard about the rape accusation."

"You know?"

"Yeah. He told me a while back, one night we both got hammered on tequila watching *How It's Made*." His face tightens. "That really sucked for him. They made an example out of him and his buddies when that girl trashed them. It could've ended his hockey career."

"You believe he didn't rape her."

"Fuck yeah." Ben frowns at me. "I haven't known the dude very long, but he's the last guy who'd do something like that."

Shame heats my belly. "Yes. You're right."

I should've known that better than anyone.

"I mean, he admits he was there and he was going to . . . well, you should hear it from him." Ben eyes me with a cool expression. "You broke up with him because of that?"

Break up. How do you break up with someone who's not really your boyfriend? But I can't explain that to him. "Basically, yeah," I admit.

"He just fought with a guy who was saying ugly things about your friend, and women in general. Jesus." Ben gives me a disappointed look.

That burn in my belly intensifies. "I know I was wrong. I know what kind of guy he is. I need to tell him that, and apologize."

Ben eyes me and nods. "Good luck. And I say that because I think he really cares about you."

He turns and strides back to the table. He cares about Jacob. That makes my heart hurt. Jacob didn't even know these guys when he started at Bayard in September. He thought they hated him. They don't hate him.

And Ben thinks Jacob cares about me?

My eyes sting and I have to blink back tears as I go take orders at another table.

Taisha notices that I'm upset. "Hey, girl, you okay?"

"Yeah. Just a little shaken up about something that happened today."

I'd asked Taisha to go out for something to eat the other night. She and her friends already had plans to go for sushi, but she invited me along. It was fun hanging out with them. I told her a little about me and Jacob, that things were over and I was kind of bummed about it, so she was sympathetic.

"What happened?"

I tell her what I just heard about Jacob's fight. "I'm worried about him. If he gets suspended . . . I don't know what that'll mean for him. He's so worried about losing his hockey career . . . Long story."

I know how much this means to him, and now I know why he was so afraid of losing it all. Why he was trying so hard to stay out of trouble. Only . . . he got in a fight because some jerk was being an asshole about Ella.

Will he be suspended? He can't lose his hockey career because of that. It wouldn't be right.

"Go on. Go to him. I'll cover for you."

"You sure?"

"Yeah, I'm sure. It's dead here."

This is true. And right now Jacob's home alone because his housemates are here. I go to the break room and grab my purse and coat and race out of there.

Chapter 29

Jacob

I'VE LOST Skylar and now I've probably lost my hockey career.

Not only am I in danger of being suspended or kicked off the team, there's no way in hell I can concentrate on studying. I have two exams on Wednesday and I'm staring blankly at my notes, sitting at my desk in my room. The blasting music of Kanye West probably isn't helping me concentrate, but it suits my mood.

My head is aching and my right hand hurts like a mother, but apparently I didn't break anything when it connected with Black Jack's face. His nose, however, is definitely broken. This is not good.

Coach was pissed but calm when he met with me alone. He asked me to tell him what happened. I struggled with how much to say. I'm not a snitch, despite my loathing for Black Jack. But I admitted to hitting him. Coach listened without saying much. Then he nodded and said he'd have to discuss this with the head of the hockey program to see what should be done.

I get that.

I fucked up. Again.

It all got too much for me. I miss Skylar. It fucking hurts that she thinks so little of me, and I have to admit the reason it hurts so much is because I care. Goddammit. That night I went to see her I wanted to apologize for being a dick and getting scared and being selfish. I wanted to tell her how I really feel about her, hoping she might feel the same. What was happening between us wasn't an act, no matter how many times we said it was.

But she hates my guts and that makes me want to puke.

On top of that, I didn't play my best at the end of the season. Then that asshat Black Jack and his fucking ugly comments and sense of entitlement and . . . The worse thing is, I see a little of myself in that attitude.

Embarrassment heats my veins, remembering the night I met Skylar and I was talking about the girls who were after me. God. No wonder she hadn't been impressed with me. What a dipshit I was.

I lean my head back and close my eyes. Fuck. This is hopeless. I'm going to fail these exams and even if I don't get some kind of punishment for what happened today, I'll be out on my ass.

My eyes burn, like I'm about to cry.

Jesus. Sack up, dude. You can't just let this happen.

I was in a tough situation before and I fought my way out of it. I worked my ass off all summer to improve my mental and physical conditioning. I moved here where I knew no one, to play for an unknown team and take college courses. I fucking did it. I'm not going to give up now.

I rub my eyes and sit up straight.

I hear Skylar's voice telling me sometimes you have to work hard for the things you want. She's an example of that. Working her ass off to get good marks. Working her ass off to try to make her parents happy. Going through hell and coming out of it strong and brave and sweet.

My life was easy up until this year. I got myself into a bad situation and it threw a wrench into my plans. I never had to work so hard in my life as I have since Brittany accused me, Ace and Crash of raping her. I was bitter about that, bitter and angry and frustrated.

But maybe I've learned something about myself this year. Life was easy. I was talented. Everyone supported me. Then they didn't . . . and I had to do it on my own.

And I did.

I'm strong. Determined. Tough. I believed in myself when others didn't. Even Skylar, dammit.

I can do this. I have to do this. There are other ways to get into the NHL

. . .

"Jacob . . ."

I nearly fall off my chair at hearing her voice. I whip around and stare at her, standing in my bedroom doorway. "Sky." I blink. "What are you doing here?"

She stands there looking so damn beautiful. She clasps her hands in front of her and tension lines her face. Her black coat is open over her pink waitress uniform. "Sorry to just walk in." She's nearly yelling the words over my blasting music. "I rang the doorbell a couple of times and you didn't answer, but I knew you were home, so I decided to come in and . . ." She waves a hand. "I guess you didn't hear the bell over the music."

I reach over and turn it down. "Yeah. Guess not." I swivel in my chair again to face her. "Why are you here?"

She twists her fingers together. "I was going to come to see you anyway, but I talked to Ben at the diner, and he said that . . . you got in a fight today."

My jaw tightens. "Yeah."

She bites her bottom lip. So cute. "What happened?"

I curse under my breath. "It was so fucking stupid."

"Fighting usually is." Our eyes meet. "Unless it's, you know, on the ice and part of the game."

I smile at that. She hates fighting even on the ice, but somehow I've convinced her that it's part of the game. "Black Jack was pissed about my stepping in the other night with Ella." My forehead tightens. "I know you two aren't talking much . . . did you know about it?"

She nods slowly. "She came and talked to me that night. She told me what happened." The corners of her mouth turn down. "Thank you, Jacob. If you hadn't done that . . ." She closes her eyes.

I nod. "Well, Black Jack's pissed at me about it. He came into the dressing room and was mouthing off and I . . . lost it. I punched him in the nose. We threw down and . . ." I shrug and stare at the floor.

"Ben said you might be in trouble about it."

"Yeah. Coach is talking to the head of the program about what kind of disciplinary action needs to happen."

"Oh, Jacob."

"Yeah, I know." I rub the back of my neck. "I was supposed to stay out of trouble. Stupid thing is, I'm not a fighter. That wasn't the kind of trouble I ever envisioned getting into." I give a short laugh. "I guess we'll see what happens."

"What did Jack say?"

"Eh. Crude stuff. He's an asshole. Also he knows about me being accused of rape. He was a pig about it." I sigh. "I guess everyone knows about it now."

"Ben said he knew."

"Yeah." I narrow my eyes at her. "You two had quite the conversation, eh?"

One corner of her mouth lifts. "We talked a bit, yes."

"You said you were going to come over, anyway . . . ?"

"Right." She swallows. "I want to apologize to you. I know I hurt you when I believed that you had raped someone."

My insides start shaking. "You don't believe it anymore?"

"No." She meets my eyes, and hers are glowing. "You would never do something like that."

"How do you know that?" I lift my chin, my teeth set.

"Because I know you." She takes a step into my room. "You've always treated me so well. Considerate and gentle and . . . generous. I've heard the things you said in the training classes. And you stepped in and helped Ella." She takes a breath. "I got the impression you were uncomfortable with the training topics, and now I know why. But it wasn't because you were guilty."

I swallow, my throat thick. Her words mean so goddamn much to me. "Yeah, actually, it was."

She eyes me curiously.

"I came to realize I'd done something stupid, despite the fact that I never touched that girl. I swear to you, Skylar, she said she wanted to do it. I even asked her if she was sure and she just kept taking her clothes off."

She winces, but says, "Tell me about it."

I inhale slowly. "Okay. Last April, I was at a house party with a bunch of my teammates. The Warriors. We were drinking and there were a bunch of girls there. One of them—Brittany—wanted . . ." He swallows. "She wanted a hat trick. Meaning, she wanted to have sex with three hockey players at the same time. With my buddies Ace and Crash and me."

Her hand goes to her throat as she listens.

"We all went upstairs. There was lots of dirty talk and laughing and we all got naked."

She closes her eyes briefly and nods.

"I started to have misgivings about it. I didn't realize why at the time. I didn't feel comfortable with it. But Ace and Crash . . . went for it. I left to go take a leak, and when I went back in I just wanted to leave. I asked Brittany if she was sure . . . and I tried to tell the guys this wasn't a good idea . . . but it was too late, they were already . . . well, they were already apparently having a good time. I grabbed my clothes, and I . . . left." I pause. "I didn't have sex with her."

"Oh." She swallows.

"The next day Brittany went to the police with her parents and told them that we had gang-raped her."

Skylar's eyes widen.

"There was a big investigation. Ace, Crash and I were all suspended from the team. There was talk that every player who was at the party should be suspended, but that didn't end up happening. In the end, after they talked to other people at the party, there wasn't enough evidence to prosecute us. There were people there who saw her asking us. There were people who saw us all go upstairs, including me, but there were also people there who thought they saw me leaving. Crash and Ace admitted I wasn't there, and they maintained that Brittany wanted it. But still, we got kicked off the team. We'd made the playoffs. We had high hopes of going all the way. But the league wanted to make an example of us, because some other guys got in similar trouble and all got off. So we were out."

I bend my head, and embarrassed that my hands are shaking, I clasp them together. "I had to pull out of the draft because of it. I thought my hockey career was over." I pull air into my tight lungs. "But my coach and GM and my folks did some digging around, and pulled some strings, and they found this school that was willing to take me even with my baggage. As long as I stayed clean and kept my grades up."

"You didn't rape her."

"No. Lots of people didn't believe that. It pissed me off. Honestly I'm not sure if the team believed me. Even if they did, they were pissed that it happened and drew all that negative attention to them. It was a stupid thing for me to do. But they at least tried to help me out. Looking back . . ." I close my eyes and tip my head back. "I'll never know for sure what happened. Ace and Crash insisted she didn't say no, ever. But maybe she did. Maybe they were drunker than I thought. I want to believe those guys would have stopped if she said no, but . . ." I squeeze my eyes shut. "I've kind of been enlightened about some stuff since I came here." I open my eyes and meet hers. "After hearing what happened to you, I can't stand the idea that she might have been trying to get them to stop. And that I was responsible."

"How were you responsible?"

"I shouldn't have left. I had misgivings and I should have stayed and got them to stop. I should have known she might have been too drunk to consent." I suck in air. "The guilt is fucking killing me."

"Oh, Jacob." She bites her lip. "I understand why you feel that way. But you're not responsible for what happened. Like I'm not responsible for Brendan taking his own life."

"I could have done things differently."

"Yes. So could I."

I hold her gaze. "Yeah. I get it."

"I'm sorry. So sorry I didn't believe you at first." She swallows. "It's sort of a trigger for me, obviously. I wasn't thinking straight. I was all emotional about it. But when I thought about the kind of man you are . . . I knew."

My heart swells up huge in my chest. "Thank you."

"It's all . . . it's confusing. It's not black and white."

"What isn't?"

"Sex. Consent."

I huff out a laugh and rub the back of my neck. "No shit."

"I've seen the girls after you." She closes her eyes. "I don't like it, but I understand it. I saw the girls who went after the football players, the basketball players . . . now I'm one of them."

"Skylar. It's not like that with us."

"I know. I don't think it is. But it's hard to sort it all out . . . a woman's right to go after what she wants. To enjoy sex as much as she wants and not be called ugly names. And not be forced to do something she doesn't want to."

Fuck. My insides heat up. "I know what you're saying. I'm having a hard time figuring it all out too. It made me so glad I had you, and that I trusted you and you trusted me. At least you did, until I screwed up and got scared because I cared so damn much." I suck in a breath. "Anyway. Maybe you and I . . . maybe we can try to help other people make sense of it. That's why I went to Victoria today."

Skylar's eyebrows pucker. "I wondered what you were doing there."

I tell her about my ideas and she seems impressed.

"I wanted to work on that with you. But I thought I'd screwed it all up."

"I'm sorry. I reacted badly. I've been stressed and worried about Ella, and I was stressed and worried about you, even before that happened."

Sadness filters through me. "I know. I was acting like a dick. I'm sorry too, Sky." I pause. "This year's been tough. But now you know why. Why I have to stay out of trouble. Why I have to keep my marks up. Why I need to play my best hockey, so the scouts will see I'm good and forget about how I screwed up. So I can enter the draft this year."

"I know how much that means to you." She eyes me. "What's going to happen?"

"I don't know." I swallow, but I lift my chin. "Whatever happens, I'll figure out how to deal with it."

"Why did you stop calling me? Was it because of what happened with Brendan?"

"What?"

"Rape is a hard thing to deal with. Some guys see women as 'damaged goods' after that."

"Jesus Christ." I jump out of my chair, horrified that she thinks I would see her that way. "No! Is that what you thought?"

"It crossed my mind."

"Christ." I scrub my hands over my face. "Christ, no. No."

"Then . . . why? What happened?"

"I got scared." I move right in front of her and stare into her eyes. "Fuck. When you dropped all that knowledge on me about what happened with Brendan, that was heavy-duty shit. And then your best friend was mad at you, and I . . . felt overwhelmed. I kept telling myself those weren't my problems and I should back off and let you deal with them. I had enough problems of my own, trying to do well in my courses and play the best hockey I can and make up for what I did before. I thought that was the best thing to do."

"I understand."

"Yeah, you understand I'm an asshole." I rub my eyes. "I never . . . it was never about you. It was all about myself." I give a short laugh. "That was the most selfish thing I've ever done. But here's the thing, Sky. I couldn't stop thinking about you. Couldn't stop worrying about you. First, I thought you and Ella would talk and everything would be okay. When you told me she still wasn't speaking to you, I felt like shit. I was leaving you to deal with that all alone. I shouldn't have."

"You had no obligation to me, Jacob," she reminds me quietly. "We didn't have a real relationship."

"Yeah, about that." I meet her eyes. "I think we were both kidding ourselves about that."

"Wh-what do you mean?" Her eyes go big and glossy, her face wary but her eyes alight with . . . maybe . . . hope.

I take her hands. They're freezing cold and I rub them with both of mine. "Look, I think we need to be honest with each other."

"What do you mean?"

"I thought your problems weren't my problems and I could just back off, but Jesus, Sky, those were my problems. Because I care about you. And that kind of scared me too." I swallow hard. "We started off in a fake relationship. But that changed. For me. I thought maybe for you too." My heart is slamming against my ribs. I'm about to open myself up to a whole world of hurt and humiliation. "I care about you, Sky. Like a real girlfriend."

She closes her eyes and a tear slips out. Shit. I hope this isn't a replay of what happened with her and Brendan. But I won't be an asswipe like he was, if she's about to tell me we're just friends.

"If you don't feel the same, I understand," I quickly add, so she knows that.

"I do feel the same."

Relief pours through me, almost taking me down like the dirtiest slew foot. "Thank fuck." I tip her chin up and she opens her eyes and gives me a tremulous smile. "I let you down when you needed me, because I was a selfish prick. And then I was too pissed off to explain things to you when you found out about Brittany. You deserve so much better than me, Skylar. You're so sweet and giving and strong."

"Jacob." She lays a palm on my face, and I tilt my head into it because it feels so good. "I know you think that without hockey you're nothing. But that's not true. Look at how you've been doing in your courses. You could easily stay in college and get a degree. And the things you've done with the fundraiser—you draw people in and make them want to do more. You make it fun."

"Ah, baby." I reach for her hips and pull her close. Her bulky coat is too much between us, but we'll deal with that. "You know, I was thinking about stuff before you got here. I was kind of freaking out about losing you. About what happened today, how I'm gonna get through exams now, and what happens if I get suspended or something. But I realized, I can do it." I hold her gaze and the love that shines for me in her eyes makes me feel even stronger. "If I got through what happened in the spring, I can get through anything."

"Yes. You're right. And I'm here for you, Jacob. Whatever happens with the team . . . we'll figure it out. We'll make sure you play in the NHL."

My heart squeezes painfully. "Shit. You're here for me? *You're* the one who's been through hell. I look at you and what you overcame, and I feel . . . in awe. And I don't know if you even need me, but I'm here for you too."

"I do need you. I missed you so much."

"Me too. Damn, baby, me too." I crush her in my arms and find her mouth with mine. After a long kiss that I pour everything into, I lift my mouth from hers, but keep my nose touching hers. "Missed you so damn much."

I push the coat off her shoulders so I can feel her body in my arms, against me. Longing fills me, pushing at my skin, swelling inside me with aching intensity. I want her with me, always. In all ways.

"I've made so many mistakes," I whisper. "I don't know how you can even forgive me."

"I've made mistakes too. I should have reported Brendan, maybe gotten him the help he needed. I should have told Ella about what happened. Oh." She tells me what Ella told her about Brendan maybe cheating on a test and his medications not working.

"That doesn't excuse what he did to you," I say harshly.

"No, I know that. But it helps me . . . understand. It was also a mistake for me to try to be my sister. You told me to be myself, Jacob. You liked me for who I am, not who I think I should be. That meant so much to me." She brushes her mouth over mine. "But the thing about mistakes is, they don't define us. The only real mistake is not learning from them."

"Right." I let out a huge breath, full of gratitude and relief and love for this woman. "Skylar. I love you."

"Oh." She blinks at me and her bottom lip quivers. "Oh, Jacob. I love you too."

She slides her arms around my waist and tips her head back. I study her pale, beautiful face and glowing eyes, and love for her swells up inside me like a huge balloon. I step backwards toward my bed, pulling her with me. Her slow, knowing smile sends heat straight to my groin. I'm already half hard from holding her, but now my dick swells and twitches. "Damn, you're sexy."

I reach behind her to untie her little apron and drop it to the floor. Then I start with the top button of her pink dress. It's tight over her tits and her small waist, showing them off, and I watch as I reveal lush curves one button at a time. My mouth waters, my body tightens and I become impatient to get my hands on her. I work the rest of the buttons open faster until I can push the pink dress off her shoulders.

She's standing in front of me in a pink lace bra and the goddamn cutest little panties, pink flowers with ruffled edges. She's gorgeous, all smooth skin and slender curves.

"Now you," she murmurs, reaching for the hem of my hoodie. I help her yank it off over my head, along with the T-shirt beneath it. Her hands smooth over my pecs. She lingers on my nipples, sending a quick spear of pleasure straight to my groin, and my abs contract hard, which she notices, and she traces her fingertips down over my stomach. "You're beautiful too."

Heat rises in my cheeks but I like her compliment. I frame her face with my hands and touch my lips to hers. As I'm doing this, she reaches behind her for the fastener of her bra and then it's gone too. She moves into me, skin to skin. I crave the feel of her, every inch of her. We both gasp at the delicious shock of the contact, and need for her explodes inside me.

I slide my hands into her gorgeous hair and fist it as I kiss her, long, open-mouthed, seeking kisses, over and over. I slide my tongue into her mouth, rubbing it against hers, then lick her lips. "You taste so damn sweet." I want her so bad, all of her, the sweetness of her taste, the smell of her, the sounds of her soft sighs. "Want to be inside you, baby."

"Yes. Me too. Please." Her fingers dig into my back.

Emotion rises up inside me, almost closing off my breathing. I'm crazy about her, overwhelmed by the fact that she loves me too, so relieved, so thankful. I open my mouth wider on hers, kissing her deeper, swallowing the little noises she makes in her throat as she grabs my shoulders. Pressed against me, my chest to her breasts, belly to belly, it feels like she's trying to crawl inside me and I fucking love it. As always, our need for each other is equal.

I have to get the rest of my clothes off, so I release her and step back to shove my loose sweatpants down my thighs. I don't have underwear on, so when I kick them aside, I'm naked in front of her, my dick bobbing eagerly toward heaven.

Then she's in my arms again.

I nuzzle her ear, lick below it, tasting her skin, then sucking on it. Oh yeah. Yeah. This is it. My hands gather up her hair and I tug her head back and kiss her throat, then drag my tongue along her skin there. She shivers against me.

I let go of a handful of hair to cup one breast, her pebbled nipple hard, the rest of her so soft. She fills my hand perfectly, and her soft whimpers of pleasure make my body burn for her.

I bend her over my arm, lowering my mouth to her nipple. I close my lips on the tip then draw her deeper into my mouth. She clutches my shoulders, gasping, panting, crying out my name as I suck.

"Yeah." I lick her. "That feel good, baby?"

"Yes, oh God, yes." I lift my head and move to her other breast. Her hands slide into my hair to hold my head there and I take my time tasting her, using lips and tongue and teeth, making her quiver against me.

"Jacob. God."

"Love your breasts, Sky. Gorgeous. Perfect."

My hand glides down her back, over the curve of her ass, still in the frilly panties. "These are hot." I palm the undercurves of her ass cheeks and give a squeeze. Then I slide one hand lower, down her silky thigh, and lift her leg to my hip. My throbbing dick slips between her thighs, inside her panties, to her hot, wet folds, and I rub myself there, back and forth. A groan climbs my throat.

"Oh yeah. So wet, baby." I kiss her mouth again. I can't get enough of her. Flames burn over my skin and heat slides through my veins, an explosion building up inside me.

"Jacob." She gasps against my mouth, moving her hips to help stroke me. "I need you. Inside me."

"Yeah. Oh yeah." Tingles build at the base of my spine. "On the bed, baby."

I lower her leg to the floor and turn her toward the bed, my hands going back to the sweet curves of her ass. We fall together onto the bed. I wince at the jarring to my bruised back.

"What?" she whispers, going still.

"I'm okay. Got a few bruises from the fight, that's all."

"Oh, Jacob."

"Shh." Our mouths join, our legs twine and we wrap our arms around each other in a sizzling connection. I roll her onto her back and kiss her, long and deep and wet. Heat spirals inside me as her tongue slides into my mouth. I want this to go on forever but my dick is straining to be inside her.

"You want this, right?" I gaze down at her beautiful face, her hair spread around her on the pillow.

Her smile is blinding and beautiful as her hands touch my face. "Yes. I want this."

"Need a condom. Hang on." I lean over and grab a box of condoms from the bookshelf next to the bed, fumble one out and go up on my knees to suit up. "There we go."

She's watching me with big eyes, lips parted in excitement. "I love how you turn me on."

"I love it too, baby. So damn much. You make me feel . . . powerful."

She blinks and her lips curve into a slow smile as she lifts her knees for me.

I kneel between her legs to slide her panties off and her gaze travels over me, my chest, my abs, then down to my dick. I wrap one hand around it. Her breath hitches as I slide the head of it up and down over her pussy, slicking up her arousal. "Ah, Skylar."

She smiles. "Fuck me," she whispers. "Please."

Her body lifts toward me and then I slide into her, easing in, stretching her wide, filling her. A moan leaks from her lips as she watches me. When I'm balls-deep inside her, I pause, taking a couple of short breaths, then I lower myself over her. I slide one arm beneath her head and kiss her mouth, her cheek, her neck. I breathe in her scent, apple and vanilla and Skylar, and her hands run up and down my sides, then slip around to grip my ass. "Skylar." I kiss her ear. "Skylar."

She's everything at that moment. I move inside her and she holds on to me, her body tight around me, her thighs gripping my hips.

"I love you," she whispers, one hand sliding up my back and into my hair. "I love you so much."

"Love you too, baby." I roll my hips against her, thrusting into her deep, owning her.

I rise up onto my knees and gaze down at her. I cup her breasts and squeeze, then circle my hands around her narrow waist and hold her as I thrust into her harder still. Our eyes meet and hold and my heart swells in my chest at the love I see there. Pure joy and gratitude and overwhelming love for her rushes through me.

We stare into each other's eyes as I rock into her again, and again. Her hips lift to meet me, taking me deep, and the expression on her face mirrors my own feelings of gratitude and appreciation, devotion and worship. Heat pools in my groin and every nerve ending tightens. A ragged groan tears from my throat as sensation builds. I fall over her, one hand on her forehead, tipping her head back so I can find her mouth as I come.

Her body squeezes me, her arms and legs wrap around me too, and she cries out. Sensation explodes in me, racing up my spine, my balls contracting, my cock pulsing inside her in wrenching spasms. "Goddamn," I murmur against her lips and I feel them curve in response.

I bury my face in the side of her neck and we lay together panting for long moments. Her fingers dance across my back and she gives me slow, openmouthed kisses on my shoulder. Finally I rise up onto my elbows to peer down at her.

Her bottom lip trembles but she's smiling. "Thank you."

"Christ. Don't thank me. I don't deserve you."

Her smile goes crooked and she pets my back. "I'm not that special."

"Yes, you are." I groan as I lower my forehead to touch hers. "You are."

"You're the superstar hockey player."

"That means nothing."

"Aw, Jacob. It means everything to you."

"Nope." I kiss her soft mouth. "You mean everything to me."

"Oh." Her eyes get all shiny. "Damn you. You're making me cry again. I've cried enough."

"I'm sorry. I'll do whatever I have to, to make up to you for being such an idiot."

"You're doing a fine job so far."

Our mouths smile against each other.

It's true. Without her in my life . . . well, I hope I never have to find out how shitty that would be.

Chapter 30

Skylar

"I'm not going to tell Brendan's parents."

I look up at Ella standing in the door of my room.

Exams are done. I feel pretty good about how they went. Things between Ella and me are okay—subdued, but she's speaking to me. For the entire study period during exams, she hasn't gone out. She hasn't been drinking and she hasn't been partying. She still seems sad, but she's talking to me.

I nod slowly. "I wondered if you would. Come in." I'm sitting cross-legged on my bed with my laptop, looking at Facebook and Instagram now that exams are done.

She comes in and perches on the end of the bed. "I thought about telling them."

"You mean, about me? Or about Brendan cheating on a test?"

"Both." She sighs. "I know they want closure. But I don't think knowing what Brendan did would give them that. So I decided not to say anything."

"I feel a little guilty keeping the truth from them."

"I know. Me too. But I also don't want them to blame you." She meets my eyes. "Because I know it wasn't your fault." Her bottom lip trembles.

"Thank you, Ella." My throat tightens. I know that was a difficult thing for her to sort out. "I hope they'll find closure despite not knowing the truth."

223

"Yeah. And . . ." She straightens her shoulders. "I'm sorry about telling you about Jacob."

I blink. "Well, it's not like you made it up."

"I know, but . . . it was *how* I told you. And, shit, not knowing what had happened with you and Brendan . . . I had no idea how hard that was going to hit you. I'm so sorry."

"You didn't know."

"I should have. You should have told me. We're best friends."

I close my eyes briefly. "I should have told you. You're right."

We talk for a long time about what happened and how I was feeling, because Ella is experiencing some of the same emotions now.

"I'm going to see a counselor," she says. "I haven't been dealing with it very well."

My eyes widen. "Oh. Oh, that's good, Ella. It really helped me figure things out." I bite my lip. "I hope you can forgive Brendan."

She tips her head. "Have you?"

"I'm not sure." I mull that over. "But I think I'm on my way."

"God, Skylar."

I set my laptop aside and reach for her, and we hug for a long, silent moment. Then I draw back and wipe my eyes, trying to smile. "I'm heading over to Jacob's place to celebrate exams being done. Want to come?"

She gives me a teary smile back and nods. "Sure."

Natalie and Brooklyn have already gone home. It turns out they weren't taking Ella's side against me; she hadn't even told them exactly what happened. But they'd sensed the tension between Ella and me and weren't sure how to deal with it.

We arrive at Jacob's place to find a bunch of guys in the living room, some of them playing Xbox. Grady has already gone home, but Ben and Hunter are there, along with a few other players who haven't left yet.

Jacob tries to hide his surprise at seeing Ella with me, but bugs his eyes out at me behind her back when she walks in. "Okay?" he mouths.

I nod and smile. "I think so."

"Good." He wraps an arm around my neck and kisses my forehead. "Gonna miss you so much, Sky."

"I know. Me too." I slide my arms around him and hug him. "We'll talk, though."

"Yeah."

Jacob didn't get suspended for the fight. When the coaches interviewed the other guys who'd been present, they all said Jack had instigated it. They all told exactly what Jack had said. The coaching staff said it wasn't unusual in a team for players to cover for each other—but this case was unusual because often what happens is players are trying to cover up sexual harassment or bad behavior, but in this case they were trying to *expose* it.

The team management also heard from Victoria, who filled them in on the proposal Jacob had put forward that morning. Since his motivations were good, he got a stern lecture from his coach about appropriate behavior in the dressing room and that was the end of it. Luckily, Jacob only had some bruises to his back and his hand, and he'll be fine to play in the tournament in Florida.

His parents saved up money for a flight home for him for Christmas and he leaves in the morning. I'll probably go home tomorrow too. I've had some nice emails from Mom, and I'm not as anxious about going home as I was the last time, so that's good.

But I'm going to miss Jacob so much.

It's our last night together for weeks.

We join the others in the living room, where apparently Ella has just insulted Ben's clothing style.

"You're one to talk." He eyes her. "Was there a sale at Frederick's of Hollywood?"

"Ugh. Thanks for giving me a piece of your mind," Ella snaps. "I know you don't have much to spare."

Ben laughs. "Funny. I bet you complain about shit in your sleep."

"You'll never know."

"Damn straight I won't."

Ah. I wish my friend and Jacob's friend liked each other so we could all hang out. This kind of blows, but I don't know what we can do about it. I know Ben has formed an impression of Ella based on the way she'd been acting, and I can't blame him for that. And she doesn't like him because she thinks he's all full of himself with his hair and clothes and car, all BMOC.

"How did your presentation go today?" I ask Jacob.

This morning he and Victoria made a presentation to the college president and executive officers about his idea to do special awareness training for athletes.

He grins. "I killed it."

"Of course you did." I roll my eyes. But I'm smiling, because I know his cockiness is just an act. Underneath it, he has the same hopes and dreams and fears as any of us, despite his gifts and talents.

"Seriously. It went well. They seemed really interested, and with other stuff that's been in the news lately, they don't want shit like that happening here."

"No one does." I nod. "That's great." I go up on my toes and kiss him.

"Hey, that's a level one offense."

I look over at Ben, grinning at us. "What is?"

"Making out with your girlfriend in front of your buddies."

"Fine." Jacob laughs and starts toward the kitchen. "I'll get you a damn beer."

"It doesn't count when you're only doing it because you need one yourself!" Hunter yells after him.

"We were hardly making out." I throw a pillow at Hunter, who catches it with an athlete's quick reflexes and a grin. "It was just a kiss."

"Thank God you two made up," Ben says. "He was fucking moody as hell. Impossible to live with, not to mention useless on the ice."

"I was not useless," Jacob shouts from the kitchen.

Ben grins. "Whatever."

Jacob returns, carrying a bunch of beer bottles. "I'll bring you some Kool-Aid, babe."

"That's okay, I can get it."

"I'm up. Sit."

I lower myself into a chair. I love how he takes care of me. Even though I don't need taking care of. The thing is, we take care of each other. Whether we need it or not. Because that's what you do for someone you love.

Saying goodbye at the airport the next day might be one of the hardest things I've ever done. I have to remind myself of the challenges I've handled and come through stronger. But damn . . . I love Jacob so much. I feel like my heart is being torn out of my chest. I keep swallowing because my throat hurts so much. When he's about to go through security, he turns to me and we move together without speaking, our gazes joined.

"We can do this." He brushes his mouth over mine.

I go onto my toes and wrap my arms around his neck, finding his mouth again with mine. He hugs me back, pulling me up against him. Absorbing the heat and strength of his big body as I cling to him, I can't stop the tears that leak from my eyes, and the wetness is cool where my cheek presses against his.

"Don't cry, baby. Please." He squeezes me tighter. "It'll be okay. We'll Skype every day. You'll probably see more of me while we're apart than you do here."

I sob on a laugh. "Okay."

"Gonna miss you so much." He kisses me softly. "I love you, Sky."

"I love you too."

We kiss again, long and desperate. But I know he's right. It will only be a few weeks until we see each other again. We've been through a lot. We're both strong. We can do this. And I know at some point I have to let him go, let him get on that plane to go home. It takes everything I have to do that, to give him one last, lingering kiss, then move away.

"Bye, Jacob." I smile into his eyes, which look a little damp too. "Enjoy Christmas with your family."

"You too."

We've talked about it and we both feel like going home will be okay now. We've dealt with a lot of shit in the last few months. I'm actually looking forward to seeing my family, including my sister, and Jacob says he plans to talk to his parents about what he's learned and the program we'll be working on together in the New Year. I can only imagine how proud they'll be of him for doing that. My own heart still swells every time I think about it.

"I think I will." I pause, going serious. "You make me feel so loved, Jacob. You make me feel like someone who's worth loving."

"You are. God, Skylar. You are." His expression turns fierce warrior and I love that too.

"And so are you. And not just because you're a hot jock."

His eyes soften and warm with understanding, then he shoots me the cocky grin that attracted me to him across the kitchen that night we met. "But I am a hot jock."

"You're also a cocky ass." I plant my hand on his chest and give him a shove.

He walks backward, holding my gaze. "You love my ass."

My eyes bug out and I glance around. There are people all around us. I glare at him and he laughs and winks, then turns and gets in line.

I wait until he's through security. Once he picks up his backpack from the table and slings it over his shoulder, he turns. He's tall enough that he can see over the crowd as he scans the area and finds me. He lifts his arm and gives me a big wave and I fight back tears as I smile and wave at him too. Then I turn and walk through the terminal, my vision blurred, but I'm still smiling and my heart is full and happy despite the tears in my eyes.

Because I love him and he loves me and I'm so looking forward to next term, being with him, accomplishing things with him, our lives back on track and moving into the future together.

Thank you for reading Shut Out! Would you like a peek at Jacob and Skylar's future? Click here to join my mailing list and get bonus content!
https://view.flodesk.com/pages/6430269900e6d692adb1ca91d

And read on for an excerpt from Cross Check—what is happening with Ella? And is Ben really that perfect?

Acknowledgments

Researching and writing this book taught me so much. Mega-huge thanks to Christa Soule, who gave me so much guidance with this book. Your insights and knowledge made this story so much better, made Jacob and Skylar so much better, and probably made me better. Thank you also to beta readers Michele Harvey and Crystal Moyer—your feedback helped me keep going when I was worried this new adult adventure was a crazy idea for an "old lady" to attempt. I also want to thank my Chippy Chicks partners—Melanie Ting, Fortune Whelan, Stacey Agdern, and Danica Flynn—for the frank discussions we've had about events in the hockey world that mirror my story. Or that my story mirrors. And as always, thank you to my assistant Stacey Price, cover designer Dar Albert (you nailed this one!), Heather Roberts at 1852 Media, and of course you! Thank you for reading!

Cross Check Excerpt

Academic probation.

I bite my lip as I reread the letter in my hand, my stomach knotting.

At the end of each semester, the Academic Achievement Committee reviews the records of all students and takes appropriate action, including issuing warnings, placing students on probation, granting leaves of absence, advising students to withdraw, or suspending or expelling students.

Sitting on my bed in my room in the house I share with three friends, I drop my chin to my chest and squeeze my eyes shut.

I've already read the letter, but I tried to forget about it over the winter break. Now I'm back at college. Classes start tomorrow and shit just got real. I have to meet with my academic adviser next week and figure out how I'm going to pull my grades up.

This has never happened to me before. I may not have been a straight-A student in high school, but I never got below a B. Of course, I had my parents always on my back about getting my homework done, helping me with projects, and looking at every test and paper I brought home.

A knock on my bedroom door has me jerking my head up. I shove the letter under a pillow and call, "Come in!"

The door opens and Skylar bursts in. "Hey, you're awake."

"I am." I make myself smile at her. I've been faking smiling through the whole winter break so my family wouldn't guess how messed up I am.

Although yesterday, my brother Gareth had a "big brother talk" with me about my behavior last term, so he suspects. Ugh.

Our housemates, Brooklyn and Natalie, appear in the door too.

"Hi!" My smile widens. "You're back!"

"Just got here." Natalie moves into the room with a big smile that slips as she studies me. "Your aura is looking a little brown. Is everything okay?"

I blink. "Brown? Is that bad?" What am I saying? A brown aura *has* to be bad.

She perches on the side of my bed. "It can mean confusion or discouragement." She eyes me.

I'm a little skeptical of Natalie's ability to read auras, but right now she's nailed it. Hell yeah, I'm confused and discouraged.

"You usually have such a bright aura," Natalie continues. "Beautiful bright orange."

She's told me that means I am an outgoing social person who likes to party. Which is what got me into this confused and discouraged state. I summon all my energy to try to create a bright orange aura, imagining flames outlining my body. However, it appears I can't really fake that the way I faked being happy and carefree at home with my family. I need to deflect Natalie's attention from me. "How's *your* aura, Brook?" I joke.

Brooklyn grins, leaning against the door. "Very bright," she assures me. "Break was good."

"And we all know Skylar is beaming because she and Jacob are back together," I add.

Skylar laughs. Yeah, she's happy. It's so nice to see. "We're going ice-skating this afternoon," she says. "I came to invite you to go with us."

"Skating? Seriously?"

"Yeah. There's a pond in Seneca Park that they turn into a skating rink. Jacob thinks it would be fun to go there and skate just for fun."

Jacob is Skylar's new boyfriend. They were pretty much inseparable before Christmas, but were apart for a few weeks over the break, so their reunion yesterday was mega-steamy. Now they want to go skating? I'd think they'd want to stay holed up in a bedroom until classes start tomorrow. But Jacob's a hockey player for the college team, so I guess he likes skating.

"I don't have skates," I say.

"Neither do I, but we can rent them there."

"Who's going?"

"I don't know. A bunch of us."

"I'm not going." Brooklyn pushes away from the door. "I don't do cold."

I look at Natalie. She shrugs. "I might go."

I debate the invitation. I'm inclined to blow Skylar off. But to do what? I don't have homework, my mom did all my laundry while I was home for the break, and on a Sunday afternoon I'm probably not going to find a party to distract me from all the shit I want to be distracted from.

A lot of stuff went down last year, and things between Skylar and me were messed up. We've been best friends since middle school, but last term we had a falling out and for a while we weren't even speaking to each other. I know it was mostly my fault, and when I finally figured that out, I knew I had to work at repairing my friendship with her. That's one of my goals for this term, along with bringing up my marks before I get kicked out of school, or my parents find out about my academic probation and drag my ass home.

So because fixing things between Skylar and me is important, I find myself agreeing to go skating.

It turns out Natalie doesn't come either, so when Jacob picks us up, it's just Skylar and me. He drives us to the pretty park off the campus of Bayard College. It snowed recently and everything is pristine white, the black tree branches layered with white and the branches of dark evergreens holding big clumps of snow. The sky is clear blue, the sun bright, and it's hard to feel glum surrounded by so much light and freshness.

We enter a small but tall building with lots of windows. Inside there's a big stone fireplace and a bunch of picnic tables and benches. Jacob leads us over to a window where we can rent skates. I ask for size eights, hoping there's room for the thick socks I've donned. When I turn around to find a place to sit, I see Jacob's friend Ben waving at us.

Ugh.

I detest Ben Buckingham.

He's a pompous, pretentious ass who thinks he's all that, with his designer clothes and perfect hair and all the adulation that goes with being a star hockey player on campus. But even more than that, I despise him because he judges me.

I know he does. I've seen him at parties, watching me flirt with other guys, leave with other guys, and I can feel the waves of disdain coming from him. He thinks I'm a slutty tramp.

But that's *his* problem, because I'm not going to be ashamed of owning my sexuality.

I should have known he'd be coming along with Jacob, since they live together and play hockey together. I look around for Jacob's other friends, but Ben appears to be alone. Reluctantly, I cross the room toward him.

"Hi." I take a seat on the bench, not close to him. "Where's everyone?" Hopefully already out there skating.

"Nobody else wanted to come." He leans forward, elbows on his knees, already wearing his hockey skates.

Shit. When Skylar said a bunch of people were going skating, I figured I could handle it. Now this is just weird, with two couples, one of them being Ben and me, and we are definitely *not* a couple.

"How was your winter break?" I ask stiffly, pulling off my boots.

"Okay." He shrugs. "I went home to Buffalo for a few days."

"That's nice."

"Not really. But whatever."

His response makes me pause and flash him a curious look.

"And we had that tournament in Florida," he adds.

"I heard the Bears were runner-up."

"Yeah." He makes a face that clearly tells me he's not satisfied with being runner-up.

I guess when you're competitive, you don't like losing. Ever. "Well, win some, lose some."

His eyes flash with annoyance. Which makes me want to annoy him even more.

I take in his perfectly tousled brown hair, dark designer jeans, black pea jacket, and the scarf he wears looped perfectly around his neck, looking like he's here for a fashion photo shoot.

"Do you have a suit and tie under there? Who dresses like that to go skating?" I ask him, waving a hand up and down. In contrast, Jacob is wearing a knit cap and a plaid scarf tucked inside a big thick hoodie over loose, faded jeans.

Ben looks down at himself, then gives me a once-over. "I do," he says easily. "And I don't know if you're one to talk, party girl. Better zip that jacket up or your hooters are going to freeze."

I glance down at my chest and my cheeks flush hot. My long-sleeved top *is* low cut, but it's not like I have a lot of cleavage to worry about, and I brought a scarf too. I bend to wrestle the skates on, a little ashamed of how bad-mannered I am around Ben.

That's not me.

But I've been doing a lot of things lately that aren't me.

Available at all Major Retailers

About the Author

Kelly Jamieson is a best-selling author of over forty romance novels and novellas. Her writing has been described as "emotionally complex," "sweet and satisfying" and "blisteringly sexy." She likes coffee (black), wine (mostly white), shoes (high) and, of course, watching hockey!

Want more from Kelly Jamieson?

Facebook.com/KellyJamiesonRomanceAuthor
    Twitter.com/KellyJamieson
    Instagram.com/authorkellyjamieson
    Pinterest.com/kellyjamieson/
    Website http://www.kellyjamieson.com/
    Sign-up for my mailing list https://www.kellyjamieson.com/newsletter

Other Books by Kelly Jamieson

Heller Brothers Hockey

Breakaway

Faceoff

One Man Advantage

Hat Trick

Offside

Power Series

Power Struggle

Taming Tara

Power Shift

Rule of Three Series

Rule of Three

Rhythm of Three

Reward of Three

San Amaro Singles

With Strings Attached

How to Love

Slammed

Windy City Kink

Sweet Obsession

All Messed Up

Playing Dirty

Brew Crew

Limited Time Offer

No Obligation Required

Aces Hockey

Major Misconduct

Off Limits

Icing

Top Shelf

Back Check

Slap Shot

Playing Hurt

Big Stick

Game On

Last Shot

Body Shot

Hot Shot

Long Shot

Bayard Hockey

Shut Out

Cross Check

Wynn Hockey

Play to Win

In It To Win It

Win Big

For the Win

Game Changer